ORDINARY
IS PERFECT

Praise for D. Jackson Leigh

Dragon Horse War

"Leigh writes with an emotion that she in turn gives to the characters, allowing us insight into their personalities and their very souls. Filled with fantastic imagery and the down-to-earth flaws that are sometimes the characters' greatest strengths, this first *Dragon Horse War* is a story not to be missed. The writing is flawless, the story, breath-taking—and this is only the beginning."—*Lambda Literary Review*

"The premise is original, the fantasy element is gripping but relevant to our times, the characters come to life, and the writing is phenomenal. It's the author's best work to date and I could not put it down."—*Melina Bickard, Librarian, Waterloo Library (London)*

"Already an accomplished author of many romances, Leigh takes on fantasy and comes up aces…So, even if fantasy isn't quite your thing, you should give this a try. Leigh's backdrop is a world you already recognize with some slight differences, and the characters are marvelous. There's a villain, a love story, and…ah yes, 'thar be dragons.'"—*Out in Print: Queer Book Reviews*

Touch Me Gently

"D. Jackson Leigh understands the value of branding, and delivers more of the familiar and welcome story elements that set her novels apart from other authors in the romance genre."—*The Rainbow Reader*

Swelter

"I don't think there is a single book D. Jackson Leigh has written that I don't like...I recommend this book if you want a nice romance mixed with a little suspense."—*Kris Johnson, Texas Library Association*

"This book is a great mix of romance, action, angst, and emotional drama...The first half of the book focuses on the budding relationship between the two women, and the gradual revealing of secrets. The second half ramps up the action side of things...There were some good sexy scenes, and also an appropriate amount of angst and introspection by both women as feelings more than just the physical started to surface." —*Rainbow Book Reviews*

Call Me Softly

"*Call Me Softly* is a thrilling and enthralling novel of love, lies, intrigue, and Southern charm."—*Bibliophilic Book Blog*

Every Second Counts

"Her prose is clean, lean, and mean—elegantly descriptive..." —*Out in Print*

Riding Passion

"The sex was always hot and the relationships were realistic, each with their difficulties. The technical writing style was impeccable, ranging from poetic to more straightforward and simple. The entire anthology was a demonstration of Leigh's considerable abilities."—*2015 Rainbow Awards*

By the Author

Cherokee Falls Series

Bareback

Long Shot

Every Second Counts

Romances

Call Me Softly

Touch Me Gently

Hold Me Forever

Swelter

Take a Chance

Ordinary Is Perfect

Short Story Collection

Riding Passion

Dragon Horse War Trilogy

The Calling

Tracker and the Spy

Seer and the Shield

Visit us at www.boldstrokesbooks.com

ORDINARY
IS PERFECT

by

D. Jackson Leigh

2019

ORDINARY IS PERFECT

ISBN 13: 978-1-63555-280-5

This Trade Paperback Original Is Published By
Bold Strokes Books, Inc.
P.O. Box 249
Valley Falls, NY 12185

First Edition: January 2019

CREDITS
Editor: Shelley Thrasher
Production Design: Stacia Seaman
Cover Design by Sheri (hindsightgraphics@gmail.com)

Acknowledgments

Elvis inspired this book.

Not the "You Ain't Nothing But a Hound Dog" singer, but a plain brown dog of very mixed heritage—maybe Labrador, maybe German shepherd, possibly Australian shepherd—with a half-length tail and of very average size.

Only, like the singer, Elvis the dog isn't ordinary.

People seem inexplicably drawn to him, as though they are reassured they are not alone because he understands all the things they perceive to be ordinary about themselves.

So, I want to thank Elvis and his exceptional owner, Catherine Woodworth, a loyal reader who became a friend after she offered to drive all the way from Arkansas to Georgia to adopt sweet Elvis upon seeing his photograph and reading his hard-luck story.

Finally, as always, I want to thank my insightful editor, Shelley Thrasher. I value her advice because she always makes my story better.

For Catherine and Elvis.

CHAPTER ONE

A fter a few months, most became numb to everything except the hyper-alert, gut-churning fear that each day, each hour, each patrol, each step onward might be their last. Catherine Daye didn't. Not after a few months, not after many months, not after two and a half tours.

Midway through her third tour, she still felt the sting of the sand against her sun-scorched skin and the beads of sweat that dripped from the sodden strands of her short brown hair. She scanned the buildings ahead, square and bland like the desert surrounding them. Her gut twisted and soured. Something felt very wrong. A few vehicles were parked near structures, and clothes flapped like flags from lines suspended along slanted poles. But she had a clear view of the community well, and the women weren't there. They were always there, waiting for the medical services and food supplies her patrol brought each month.

She and her patrol approached cautiously, sliding their backs along the walls, murmuring reports into wireless com units.

"I don't like this," she said.

"Second that, Sarge." The nasal, edgy voice of Private Tom Michaels sounded in her earbud.

Staff Sergeant Jeff "Hammer" Booker, their patrol leader, issued hand signals for them to advance into the village center and begin clearing houses. They moved in silent pairs, reporting in at each location.

"First on the right is empty. Looks like they left in a hurry. Food's left out, half-eaten." Corporal Bo Ever's soft drawl was calm.

Booker growled an answer. "Chalk it and move to the next." She and Booker had toured together before and were both up for promotion from sergeant to staff sergeant at the same time. But Catherine had asked her colonel to delay her upgrade so they wouldn't be split up and given separate patrols to lead. She'd had a nauseating premonition she wouldn't come back from a third tour if she and Booker weren't able to watch each other's back. So he was leading this patrol, while she took the rear command.

Others in the group checked in with similar reports—Roman, Stormy, Hulk, Bluegrass. They all were christened with nicknames when they arrived. Even Catherine. Sort of. She was the Cat Woman. Clever, stealthy, and deadly when she needed to be.

She ducked in and out between the buildings, checking the village's perimeter. Nothing but empty desert. Appearances could be deceiving, she learned on her first tour. The enemy could rise out of the sand like deadly scorpions before your brain registered why the desert was swarming with them.

She half listened to the check-ins as she crept to the doorway of a one-room adobe house. A chalk mark told her it'd been cleared, but her gut didn't agree.

"Cat? You copy?"

Catherine touched her ear com to key the mike. "I copy."

"Village is clear. How's our backside?"

"Just scratching an itchy spot, Hammer." She tapped her ear com, switching to a private channel. She never used his nickname on the com. It was a signal.

"Yeah. I feel it, too. Where are you?" He'd also switched.

"I'm rechecking building three on the left. I'll be done by the time you guys group up."

"Three minutes. I want to get out of here," Booker said quietly.

"Three minutes," she repeated, switching back to the main channel.

She hesitated in the doorway. *Don't go in there. Don't go in there.* Her chest grew tight, so tight. She sucked in short, rapid breaths. Ignoring her rising panic, she edged inside.

Catherine scanned the floor for trip wires or signs of an IED, then surveyed the twelve-by-twelve room. Sleeping mats were rolled and neatly stacked against one wall. A cooking area took up another wall. Dishes of half-eaten food filled the surface of a low, square table in the middle of the room.

Three minutes. In and out. Chickens pecked at the dirt near a door at the rear of the room, left open to reveal a small awning-shaded yard. The birds wouldn't be that close if the enemy was waiting just outside the door. She glanced over her shoulder and began to back out of the hut when a small noise sounded from some blankets thrown in one corner. *Don't look. Don't look.* Her gaze was drawn to the messy pile that didn't fit with the tidiness of the rest of the room. Sweat dripped from her chin, trickled down her neck. Her breath wheezed in her throat. She extended a telescoping baton, then used it to lift the blankets while she stood off to the side.

The terrified eyes of a frail, elderly woman stared at the automatic rifle Catherine pointed at her, and Catherine immediately swung it away. "I'm not going to hurt you." *That's not right. Tell her to get up and out.* What were the right words? She could speak passable Pashto, but that whining noise was making it hard to think. Her heart began to pound like a bass drum in her ears. Still that whine pierced her brain.

"Incoming!" Booker barked.

A long blade sprouted between the old woman's breasts, and she opened her mouth with a strangled gasp. Catherine dropped to her knees and yanked the woman forward. The aim of the Taliban fighter hiding behind the woman was off, but he pumped an armor-piercing bullet into Catherine's shoulder a split second before she fired two neat shots into his forehead. She cried out against the fire in her flesh, but the sound was lost as a mortar tore through the wall to her left and her ear com exploded with barked commands.

❖

Barking snatched Autumn Swan from a deep, comalike sleep to hyperalert in 0.05. She jumped from her bed and raced out of her bedroom.

Autumn squinted against the sunrise spearing through the mostly glass balcony doors of her airy Decatur, Georgia, apartment, then snatched up dark sunglasses from the sofa table, slapped them on, and danced over to the laptop on the dining-room table that had begun to rap about someone letting dogs out. She paused just long enough to tap the keyboard and confirm what her barking-dog notification indicated.

"Yes, yes, yes." Autumn stretched her arms toward the ceiling and wiggled her fingers in celebration. Her new client's website had hit its business plan's unique-visitors, thirty-day target in only ten days. "Am I good or what?" It wasn't really a question, but she answered it for herself anyway. "I'm good. So good. So good," she chanted, hopping around in a weird, all-her-own dance. Self-affirmation is a good thing, right?

She danced into the kitchen to share the love with her Starbucks espresso machine, then stopped her finger inches from the power button. Nah. She needed to be around people this morning...so she could brag a little. Why brew and froth when someone else could do it for you? She grabbed her phone, snapped a photo of her Starbucks mug, and sent it with a simple meet-me-in-forty-five text. A shower to make herself presentable after only three hours of sleep, then she'd pop in for a triple espresso and an ego boost. She could grab something sweet while she was there, too. When her mind flashed on the new dark-haired barista, a graduate student at Emory, she scolded herself. "To nibble. I meant to eat... ugh. I sound like such a guy," she said. "Cinnamon roll. I'll get one of those delish cinnamon rolls to go with my triple shot."

It wasn't really necessary to explain everything to herself, since she knew what she meant. But she'd grown up an only child and discovered early that she was the best conversationalist she knew. Well, at least when nobody else was around. Okay. That didn't sound right. But her brain worked lightning fast when she was alone or interacting through the screen of the internet. Nobody could hold a candle to her on any social-media platform. She was a blaze of quips, comebacks, and pearls of wisdom. Put her in a group or, heaven forbid, one-on-one with a real person, and she was instantly struck dumb. She'd sought therapy and mostly overcome that tendency when she realized the world would never experience her marketing genius if she couldn't talk to clients. But it worked only in business situations. She still stuttered her way through personal conversations and was most comfortable behind the façade of the internet.

Autumn loved her home. She had lucked into a promotion that offered a five-year lease on this gorgeous second-floor, one-bedroom luxury apartment with an open floor plan, lots of windows, and French doors leading out to a balcony that overlooked a park. Her décor was shades of white and yellow with small splashes of green. Plus, she was only five minutes from downtown Decatur, the business district of the Atlanta metro area gayborhood. It paid to see and be seen in the restaurants and coffee shops there. Especially since it was where the local lesbian population was concentrated. Her mind drifted again to the barista. Hmm. She strutted into the bathroom and flashed a huge smile at the mirror behind the sink. If she hurried, maybe she could ride this wave of confidence long enough to flirt her way to a date.

❖

Catherine curled forward, eyes squinted tight as though that could shut out the pain. She gasped, one breath, two, and opened her eyes to darkness. The pain was subsiding as quickly as it came. Not dark. Dim light. The tendrils of her night terror still pumped her heart double-time, but Booker's sharp commands changed to dog barks. She wasn't in Afghanistan. She was in her farmhouse.

Frantic barking and the loud thump of something against her

front door filtered through her open bedroom door from the living room.

She looked at the clock and scowled. Five fifteen. "What the hell?"

The sound of claws scrabbling against her freshly re-varnished oak door forced her fogged mind and sluggish body into gear.

"Okay, okay." Catherine tossed off the quilt. "Geez. It's supposed to be warming up some by now." She stepped into her jeans and zipped into a thick hoodie. Toenails were clicking a circuitous route on the wood planks of the broad porch, stopping each time they passed the door to jump against it. It had to be Elvis, but why didn't he go around to the pet door at the back of the house? Oh, right. It was still blocked, something she did to keep out varmints when she was away or Elvis was staying next door.

Something felt off. Just like the village. His urgency threatened to throw her back into the desert flashback she'd just escaped. More likely, he'd sensed her flashback and come to rescue her from it. He'd done it before—huddling close, bringing her back, and grounding her in the present. She didn't know how he did it, but he was somehow a magic elixir.

She opened the front door, and Elvis nearly knocked her down. She'd never seen him so frantic, so insistent as he planted his front paws on her hips, only to jump back to the ground and race down the steps, barking. She stared dumbly at him. "What's wrong, Elvis?"

If dogs could roll their eyes, Catherine was sure he would have. Instead, he returned to her, slammed his front feet against her hips again, then whirled and ran back into the yard and barked for her to follow. Only this time, he didn't stop. He ducked under the split-rail fence and raced across a newly plowed field to the line of trees that separated Catherine's farm from the house where her neighbor Becki and her eleven-year-old daughter, Gabe, lived.

Catherine stared after him in disbelief. "Elvis." Her shout frosted in the air, and faint barking drifted over the strange stillness. It could take another thirty to sixty minutes for the sun to crest the mountain to their east, but the night sky was already fading to gray. Another sharp bark drew her attention back to the line of trees where Elvis had disappeared. An ominous chill ran from the back of her neck down her arms, pebbling her flesh.

Catherine turned to step into her short barn boots resting in the muck tray just inside the door, but before she could, her cell phone began to ring, and she ran for the bedroom instead. Nerves still drawn taut from her flashback, she swore. "Damn it. Who in blue blazes is calling this early?" Sliding to a stop in her wool socks, Catherine snatched her phone on the third ring.

"Yeah?"

"Cat. You gotta…something's wrong with Mama. She fell down…I can't get her to talk." Gabriella's words were choked and desperate. "I don't know what to do. You gotta come."

"I'm on my way, Gabe. Did you call 911?" Catherine hurried back to the door, slipped on her boots while she talked, then grabbed her truck keys. Unlike Elvis, she wasn't going to traipse through dark fields and woods.

"They're here. Elvis is barking at 'em."

Catherine climbed into her Ford pickup and slapped the phone onto its magnetic dock to free her hands, changing it to speaker. "Go get Elvis and show them where your mom is so they can help her." The truck bounced and swayed as she raced down the long packed-clay drive without regard to the potholes the cold and snowy winter had left.

"Don't hang up."

Catherine clenched her jaw against the panic in Gabriella's voice, the same fear she'd heard in the boy soldiers' dying pleas for her to stay with them while they took their last breaths. "I won't, Gabe. I'll listen while you talk to them."

She slammed to a stop and jumped out to open the gate exiting her property, drove through it, then jumped out again to close it. Cursing her procrastination about installing an automatic gate wouldn't help now. She stomped on the accelerator. All she could hear was muffled conversation on Gabe's end, but she could see the flash of the ambulance lights reflecting like strobes off the trees across the road from Becki and Gabe's house.

"No, no. I won't." Gabe's frantic shouts rang out over the phone's speaker.

Catherine whipped her truck into Becki's drive and slid to a stop next to the ambulance. The front door stood open, and Elvis ran out to meet her, still barking furiously. Catherine's feet had barely touched the porch when he dashed back inside, and she followed.

Elvis stopped at the mouth of the hallway that led to the bedrooms, loud banging now punctuating his barks. Gabe was trying to kick in the closed door of her mother's bedroom. She put her hand on his head. "Elvis, quiet." A few long strides and she wrapped her arms around Gabe. "It's okay. I'm here."

"They won't let me in there with Mama." Gabriella struggled out of Catherine's embrace, kicked the door again, and yelled. "She's MY mother."

Catherine wrapped her arms around Gabe again, but this time she lifted the girl off her feet to hold her back. "Don't do that. You're going to hurt your foot." She could hear the urgent exchange between two paramedics and the information they were transmitting to the hospital as they went through resuscitation protocol. Her heart sank. *Oh, Becki.* Catherine would rather return to the desert than face what was surely coming. But she'd made a promise.

❖

"You promised." Jay scowled at Autumn over his iced blonde cappuccino. "I already told Evan you'd do it."

His indignation broadcast across the coffee shop, and she shot him a brief, but stern, glare. God. Men could be so loud. "That was before I picked up this new client. Since his online orders have tripled each of the three weeks I've been working his accounts, he's sent me four referrals who want the same package. Evan's *your* boyfriend. I'm sure you can think of a way to make it up to him." Autumn opened an email and smiled. Her thumbnails clicked against the screen of her phone as she confirmed an appointment with this fifth referral and hit Send with a flourish. "I just don't have time to do pro bono marketing for this summer's Pride festival and parade. Paying clients are filling up my calendar. At this rate, I'll have enough work to hire extra help—a finance person or graphic artist. Even a secretary would help. Holy crap. I need to rent real office space." Her eyes never left the screen as she talked because she was busy turning down a sixth request for her services. That guy was notorious for requesting a lot of work but never paying up.

"This is a networking opportunity, Autumn. A lot of connected people are involved in making this series of events happen. People who own businesses. People you should get to know."

"Not really, Jay. Most are college students or other nonprofit people who also need free help." Autumn finally looked up after a long silence met her reply and was surprised by the disappointment in Jay's clear blue eyes. His expression was always easy to read. "What? You know I'm right. The people with influence and deep pockets will be at the annual HRC gala next month. We will definitely be at that event, networking our butts off. Those are the people who'll make us a success."

Jay sighed and dropped his gaze to his cappuccino, swirling the ice around with his straw. The silence between them stretched from one minute to five, then ten. He stirred and looked everywhere but at her while she answered several more emails and texts. Finally, he broke the silence. "You know I love you, Autumn."

She looked up from her phone. He'd better not be warming up to retell his "you sound like my mother explaining why I had to play tennis at the country club instead of at the park with my friends" story.

"I can't even put into words how grateful I'll always be for what you've taught me these past two years. Seeing how you built this company from the beginning has been more valuable than anything I've learned in college."

This conversation was taking a weird turn. Her brain hit rewind. No, no. no. "When I was mumbling about hiring extra help, I didn't mean I was changing our game plan. I meant it when I said I'd make you an associate the minute you graduate. That's only a few months away. I'll still need a full associate who can do everything I do."

He sucked in a breath and straightened his shoulders, then

raised his eyes to meet hers. "That's what I'm trying to say, hon. We're coming up to our proverbial fork in the road. I understand why money is your measure of your success. Really, I do. But I feel a different calling."

What? She blinked at him. Surely she'd heard wrong. "You… you're going into the ministry?"

His hands flew to his mouth, and his eyes widened. They stared at each other for what seemed like…well, the lifespan of a viral tweet. Then Jay let out a cough that rolled into a hysterical cackle and grew in volume until he was gripping his sides. Before Autumn realized it, she was laughing, too, and they were both wiping tears and struggling not to fall from their chairs. People at other tables stared. Finally, they recovered their composure.

"I so wish I'd thought to video your face when you asked that," Jay said, wiping his eyes again. "Evan would piss himself laughing." He took a big swallow of his cappuccino, his expression then turning serious. "I want to work for a nonprofit." He held up his hands to forestall any protest when she opened her mouth to speak. "I know I'll never have a fat bank account working in that field, but there are other ways to measure wealth. And, yes, I did grow up in a house with two parents, a stay-at-home mom, big house in the suburbs, and everything. But when I came out to my parents, I became an outcast in that perfect home. I want to help those kids. I also want to help other kids—ones who age out of foster care and have no idea how to set goals, maintain a household budget, get student loans, and do other things to find their success in life."

Autumn sat back in her chair and crossed her arms over her chest. "Well, that certainly makes me sound like Scrooge counting his money while you go out and save all the Tiny Tims of the world."

Jay half stood to pull her crossed arms apart and take both her hands in his. "You are not a Scrooge." His voice was low, his eyes soft. "You just need to feel financially stable, secure enough that you'll never be that girl who everybody laughed at for wearing a sweater the most popular girl at school had donated to the thrift shop."

Her face heated at the memory.

Although she'd started her business as she was finishing her master's thesis at Emory several years ago, and he was just now finishing the last semester of his undergraduate degree, they were the same age. Autumn was an overachiever, while Jay had lost a year hiding in New York City from his conservative upper-middle-class family until he turned eighteen.

She'd told Jay about the sweater incident—her high school low point—after he'd confessed that he'd tricked a few times in New York when he was desperate for money. They were different but basically the same. They both carried baggage from their childhoods. That bond made this upcoming separation feel like a betrayal.

"So, you're still going to leave me high and dry? Right when I'm swamped with new clients?"

He shook his head but didn't release her hands. "Absolutely not. I'll stay to help you find and train a suitable replacement. In fact, I have a lead on somebody super fantastic, but I don't want to share yet because it's just a tip. She's in an uncomfortable job situation and might be looking to relocate to Atlanta."

Autumn frowned. "That sounds like dyke drama. I don't want to hire someone who's running from a crazy ex-girlfriend."

"I promise that's not it. Evan's family has been friends with hers for generations. He said it's a disagreement on how to run the family business, and Rachel is ready to sell her shares and take her skills elsewhere."

Okay. She'd prepared for this eventuality. She had a budget plan and money tucked away, all waiting for this big moment when she stepped up from a home enterprise to a real office and expansion of her business.

Yes, sir. Autumn always had a plan. Her parents had never planned anything. "Let's just see where the wind blows us," her dad always said. But once her parents had rolled and shared that after-breakfast marijuana joint, the wind had never seemed to blow them much past the front porch. Autumn vowed that would never happen to her. No sir.

She slung her purse over her shoulder and gathered the trash from her breakfast, never taking her eyes from her phone. It vibrated with a call coming in on her business line, but she let it go to voice mail for now. "What classes do you have today?"

He rose and gathered his trash, took hers, and threw it all in the receptacle by the door as they headed down the sidewalk to the Marta station. "This is my short day. I have exercise class, then independent project, which simply means the class credit I'll get for working with you if you ever fill out the paperwork."

"On my to-do list." She dug in her bag for her Marta pass, but Jay reached around her, pulled it from her back pocket, and handed it to her. She frowned. "Exercise class? You can go to the Y another time."

"Okay, so Emory calls it physical education. Doesn't matter what you call it. I hate it. That's why I put it off until my last year. If I don't go, I won't pass, and I won't graduate at the end of the semester."

"Come on, then." Autumn joined the crowd boarding the train that had stopped and spit out a gob of passengers. "You go get physical, then come right back so we can get to work."

Jay turned to her, putting his hands together in a prayerful gesture and furrowing his brow in his version of pleading puppy eyes.

She gave him a dismissive wave, then smiled. "Yes. You can clean up at my place so you don't have to shower with a bunch of straight guys who think it's fun to try to pee on each other's feet."

He pretended to shiver in revulsion.

She grabbed his shoulders and turned serious for a moment. "Don't stop for food, and don't stop for coffee. Come straight to my place. This is AA Swan Inc.'s chance to break out of the pack, Jay. Over the next couple of weeks, nothing will be more important than work."

CHAPTER TWO

Gabe went limp and began to cry as Catherine carried her out to the living room and sat on the worn, comfortable sofa. She cradled the lanky girl in her lap, her head against her shoulder like she was a small child. Elvis hopped up next to them to lay his furry head in Gabe's lap. She needed to distract Gabe while the medics worked. "Can you tell me what happened?" She pulled a soft, worn bandana from her jacket pocket and pressed it into Gabe's hands. It likely had a bit of machinery grease and sweat on it, but she knew Gabe, who was often Catherine's shadow around the farm, wouldn't notice.

"I woke up and had to pee. But when I was walking to the bathroom, Mama's door was open, and I saw her on the floor." Gabe, her hazel eyes red and watery, pulled back to look up at Catherine. "Her eyes were open, but it was like she didn't see me. I called 9-1-1, like she always said to do in an emergency, and then I called you." Gabe clutched at Catherine's jacket. "She's going to be all right, isn't she? She has to, Cat." Her face contorted, and her slender chest heaved in a choked sob. "She can't leave me. I don't have anybody else."

Catherine hugged Gabe to her and held on tight. "You listen to me, kiddo. You've got me and Elvis. We're here with you, aren't we?"

Gabe picked at a healing scrape on her knee, just below the hem of the soft cotton gym shorts she paired with a baggy T-shirt to serve as pajamas. "Yeah, but—" Elvis licked Gabe's hand, then the scrape she was worrying. Gabe's lips pressed into a thin line, and her eyes again filled with tears. Her throat worked as her fingers dug into his unruly fur, and he stopped his ministrations to half crawl into her lap. When Gabe began to comb her fingers through his fur, Catherine had to fight back her own tears. How many nights had Elvis offered her the same comfort when relentless nightmares had nearly driven her to thoughts of suicide?

Catherine pressed her cheek to Gabe's short black curls and stroked her back. "I know, kiddo. You love us, but we're not your mama. I'd be worried if you didn't feel that way."

"I'm scared, Cat." Gabe's voice was small.

"Me, too, Gabe. That's why we have to stick together and stay close to Elvis. He's brave enough for both of us."

Tires sounded on the gravel drive out front at the same time Elvis lifted his head and stared at the hallway entrance. Gabe's head swung around to follow the dog's gaze, but Catherine tightened her grip. She didn't hear a gurney racing down the hall—not a good sign—so she wasn't letting Gabe bolt back there until she knew the lay of the land.

Footsteps shuffled across the porch, and two men let themselves in the front door. Sheriff Ed Cofy took off his hat.

"Down," she said to Elvis, shooing him off the sofa before rising and helping Gabe stand next to her. She acknowledged them with a nod. "Ed. Doc Simmons."

Ted Simmons was an emergency doctor. He was also the county coroner. She figured the two had let themselves in because the guys in the bedroom with Becki had summoned him. Ted nodded but didn't speak before heading down the hallway. Gabe tensed, her head swiveling between the two men. Catherine circled an arm around her shoulders to hug Gabe close against her side. Elvis pressed against Gabe's other side, and she buried her hand in his fur.

"Hey, Cat." Sheriff Ed Cofy's pleasant baritone seemed to soften the tension a small bit. A fellow soldier, Ed had become a friend and mentor to Catherine after she began to report to the nearby U.S. Army Reserve unit to finish out her retirement. His help tonight, however, was for Gabe, not Catherine. "Well, Miss

Gabriella Swan. You're growing up into something, that's for sure. You're what? Ten now?"

Gabe glanced at the hallway, not fooled by his effort at distraction. Regardless, her mother had raised her to be polite to adults. "Eleven. I'll be twelve in June."

He nodded and smiled. "That's right. I should know that since I was the one who drove your mom, lights and sirens blasting, to the hospital to have you."

Gabe didn't return his smile. Catherine knew she'd heard the story many times.

He paused, his expression apologetic as they held Gabe's unreadable one for a few long seconds. "Are you okay, Gabe?"

She lowered her eyes. "I don't know."

Catherine nearly jumped out of her skin, and Gabe flinched at the sound of Doc Simmons clearing his throat. They all looked to the hallway where he paused before walking into the room. "Let's sit down to talk about what's happened tonight," he said.

No, no, no. Catherine was suddenly a woman standing at the door staring at two soldiers in dress uniforms. One soldier was talking. "Ms. Daye, the secretary of the army has asked that I express his deep regret to inform you that your neighbor, Becki Swan, has died of…"

Gentle but firm pressure on her shoulder broke her paralysis, and Ed's steady brown eyes grounded her in the present. She sat on the sofa and pulled Gabe down beside her. Elvis hopped up to join them and pressed shoulder to shoulder with Gabe. They all looked at Doc Simmons expectantly.

"Gabriella, I'm so very sorry to tell you this, but your mother had an…well, her brain started bleeding and was damaged too much to fix. When the brain stops working, other parts do, too."

Gabe frowned and her expression darkened. Although Gabe was a child, she had an unusually high IQ, and underestimating her intelligence was one of her hot buttons. So Catherine stepped in.

"Gabe. You know the headaches and vision problems your mama's been having? She found out they were symptoms caused by a brain tumor. Your mom was going to tell you as soon as her doctor got the final tests back and set a surgery date—tomorrow or the next day. But it sounds like the tumor might have caused an aneurysm that burst and bled into her brain."

Becki had just told her about the diagnosis yesterday, insisting that she had time to make some arrangements before the surgery. Catherine's gut had told her something different…like at the village. It was no wonder she'd been drawn back to the desert, to that last patrol. It'd been nearly two years since she'd had a flashback that detailed, that real.

Gabe glared at Doc Simmons. "Why didn't you say it was an aneurysm? I know what that is."

He cleared his throat. "My apologies. When the paramedics arrived, her left pupil was completely dilated, and her heart wasn't beating. They still ran through the complete protocol for resuscitation but were unable to restart her heart."

Gabe's slender frame went still, then began to tremble against Catherine's side. "No," Gabe whispered.

❖

Autumn snapped her laptop into the docking station.

Prioritize.

Advertise for an administrative assistant Jay can train as soon as possible. Draw up a list of requirements for office space and have Jay line up a Realtor. Put out feelers in the network of social media marketing specialists for an associate since Jay wasn't sticking around.

She emailed a few friends in the business and several professors she knew kept in touch with former students to help circulate word of her openings. Her phone began to ring just as she hit Send for the final time. She glanced at her phone. Her private line, not her business line, was ringing, but she didn't recognize the number calling her.

"Hello?"

"Hello. This is Sheriff Ed Cofy of Elijah County. I'm trying to reach Ms. Autumn Annise Swan."

Autumn's mind shuffled through a million possible reasons a sheriff from Elijah would be calling her. A millisecond produced the only logical explanation—her parents were visiting where her dad grew up and had been busted for carrying drugs. She opened a browser and googled office space available in Decatur. Her mind functioned best when required to multitask.

"Is this Ms. Swan?" Sheriff Coby asked when she didn't immediately respond.

Autumn sighed. "Yes. This is Autumn Swan. Are you calling about my parents?" She couldn't deal with them right now. Her business was exploding with new clients. She clicked on the first of the items her search had brought up. Nope. Those new buildings with residential space above the floors with retail and office space had to be more expensive. She was looking for something cheaper.

"No, ma'am. I'm calling about your cousin, Becki Swan."

"A...Becki?" Autumn's mind raced through memories of her favorite cousin who had lived with Grandma Swan. Where Autumn had spent countless summers until she graduated early and left home for college. "Is Becki in some kind of trouble, Sheriff?" Why else would a sheriff be calling?

"I'm very sorry to have to give you this news, but your cousin Becki passed away last night. She listed you as her next of kin."

Autumn was so stunned, her mind blanked. "Me?" No. This had to be a mistake. Yes. A mistake. Think. Think. "But...wait... yes. Becki had a brother. Gabe. Um, Gabriel Swan."

"Did you know Gabe well, Ms. Swan?"

"Not really. He was older. I think he was two years older than Becki, six years older than me. I met him once. He was about to go off to boot camp. That's when Becki came to live with Grandma Swan. Because he didn't want to leave her with their parents. They're kind of...well, trashy. Becki talked about him a lot, though."

"He was killed during his second tour in Afghanistan."

"Oh." A series of rapping noises in Jay's familiar pattern was a welcome interruption. "Can you hold just a second, Sheriff?" She hurried to the door and let Jay inside, pointed to the phone, pinched her nose to indicate his pungent smell, and pointed toward the bathroom facilities. He dropped his gym bag, then raised his arm and used a handful of mail to fan more odiferous man sweat her way. Finally, he handed her the mail and followed her direction. She slapped at him with the mail, then checked it for any nasty sweat droplets. "Sorry. I had to let my assistant in. We're swamped with work today."

"I understand. I've blindsided you with this news. Becki has known about her condition for several weeks and promised she was going to contact you."

"It sounds like you were friends." She absently set the mail on the table and began to separate personal bills from business mail.

"Yes, ma'am. We were."

She paused, realizing that sorting the mail wouldn't organize what was ahead for her. "I'm sorry. I'm just stunned and at a loss for what I need to do."

"That's why I asked her lawyer to let me call you. He knows the legal aspects of her will, but Becki and I talked a lot over the past few weeks. She asked me to try and help you and Catherine understand some things."

"Catherine?"

"Her neighbor. I can explain everything—well, maybe not everything, but a lot—when you get here. What I can tell you now is that Becki had already made and paid for her own funeral arrangements. You don't have to worry about that. The when and where is up to you as her next of kin."

"I…I need to digest all this and reschedule some appoint-ments." Damn, damn. Would her clients wait until she returned, or would they jump to the next social-media marketer who showed results? God. What kind of person had she become, worrying about business appointments when the cousin who'd been like a big sister to her had died? "Can I let you know when I plan to arrive?"

"Sure. When you call, I'll tell Becki's lawyer so he can hold some time open to discuss her will and distribution of her assets."

She wrote his number on an envelope at the top of the unsorted heap of mail, then picked it up to fan herself. Her brain must be overheating. She ended the call, then realized the sun had inched upward and was glaring through the balcony doors so hot she thought the envelope in her hand would combust. She looked at the number she'd scribbled at the bottom, but her eyes were drawn to her address written in neat cursive, then to the return address in the corner. Becki Swan. She threw the letter down, halfway across the table, and stared at it. The back of her neck tingled as the short hairs there rose and chill bumps raced down her arms. It was like she was speaking to Autumn from beyond.

"Paper cut?"

Autumn screamed and jumped up so fast, her chair slammed back into Jay's crotch, and he doubled over.

He groaned and clutched himself with both hands. "Jesus. I think you just cut John Henry in half."

"For real? I'm having a major crisis here, and you're worried about"—she gestured toward his hips—"about your weenie?" She stomped over to the kitchen area and yanked open the cabinet that held her rarely served hard liquor.

Jay hovered behind her, apparently cured by his curiosity. "What are you doing?"

She began pulling bottles down from the shelf. Okay, the liquor was technically hard, but probably not by some standards. She sorted through peppermint schnapps, cherry vodka, apple Crown Royal, butterscotch schnapps, peach brandy, orange brandy, and, finally, tequila. "José. Just the guy I was looking for."

Jay backed up when she took her tequila to a different cabinet and grabbed a shot glass proclaiming Girls Want to Have Fun in pink. She filled the small glass and knocked back the tequila in one gulp. Autumn closed her eyes and sucked in a breath as the alcohol burned its way down her throat and swelled her sinuses. When she opened her eyes, Jay was staring at her, his hands on his hips.

"Obviously, something has happened while I was at exercise class, or maybe while I was making myself fresh again. And if you don't spill right now what has you hanging with José in the middle of the day, I'm going out to have a mocha latte and tell that cute barista you're crushing on her."

Autumn squinted at him in what she hoped was her meanest

glare, then pulled a second shot glass down for him. She took her bottle of tequila and shot glass back to the dining table. Jay made an impatient noise and grabbed the glass she'd left on the counter. She waited while he went back to the liquor cabinet to retrieve the apple-flavored Crown Royal. He never drank tequila, but he'd also never told her what happened in Key West that turned him against it.

Jay settled across from her, filled his glass, and held it up. Autumn silently refilled hers, then clinked it against his before they both downed their shots in a ritual that had preceded many of their serious talks.

Autumn jerked her head to the side and clenched her teeth at the liquor's bite, then sucked in a breath to enhance its burn. She opened her mouth, but only a wheeze came out, so she coughed to loosen her vocal cords. "I've booked meetings with four potential new clients next week, and I have a fifth who wants to get back with me on a day and time," she said.

Jay nodded. "That's good. Do you want me to start working up backgrounds on them?"

"That would be great, because I'm going to need a lot of help on these."

Jay hunched over the table to clasp her forearm. "Is that what this is about? You're getting cold feet. Autumn, you are the most talented marketer I know. In fact, you're the only one I know who stays up almost twenty-four seven, scheduling tweets and posts, and mining data to get the most page views for your clients."

"Are you kidding? This Superwoman of Social Media does not get cold feet." She tried to muster a smile but was probably failing miserably. "It's just…well…something else has come up."

Jay's expression hardened, and he sat back in his chair, his comforting hand sliding away from her arm. "You're too busy to keep your promise to Evan and the Pride committee, but not too busy for 'something else that's come up'?" He folded his arms over his chest and mimicked her voice. "This is AA Swan Inc.'s chance to break out from the pack. During the next few weeks, nothing is more important than work." His impersonation complete, he poured himself another shot of apple Crown. "Or maybe you really meant to say that nothing is more important than you."

Autumn couldn't look at him. She had let him and Evan down after making a promise, just like she'd let Becki down by never returning her letters or phone calls.

When she didn't reply, Jay slammed back the shot he'd poured and thumped the glass down on the table. "My asshole of a father used to say there were no acceptable excuses in life but death and taxes. Since I open your mail every day, I know you aren't being audited by the IRS. That leaves—"

"Becki died. My cousin. The one who was like a sister to me." Autumn was surprised when her throat tightened and her eyes filled as she looked up.

Jay's hand went to his mouth. "Oh, Autumn. I'm such an ass." He slid from his chair and knelt by hers, taking her hand. "I'm so sorry, sweetie."

When Jay rose and held out his arms, the scared child she hadn't realized still hid inside stepped into his embrace and sobbed into the soft fabric of his T-shirt. Jay didn't offer trite words of comfort. He held her close, stroked her back, and let her cry.

Her cloudburst of emotion seemed to blow over after a few minutes, and Autumn dried her cheeks on Jay's shirt. "Sorry," she said, ridiculously laughing at the horrified expression on his face as she pulled up his shirttail and used it to wipe her nose. "Take it off and I'll throw it in the washer." She held it away from his body as he pulled it over his head. "Go get your stinky gym stuff and throw it in, too." She opened the folding doors that hid the alcove containing her washer and dryer, started the washer, and tossed in the snotty T-shirt. She left the lid up for Jay, switched on the espresso machine, and gathered the liquor to return to the cabinet.

She was washing the glasses they'd used when Jay rested his hand on her shoulder. "Stop. I know this is how you normally cope with problems, but this is not about work. This is about family, and you have to deal with it." He took the shot glasses from Autumn after she rinsed them, placed them on a dish towel to dry, and led her back to the table. They sat, and he waited.

"Elijah County. That's where she lives…lived. The sheriff, who apparently was also Becki's friend, called. She listed me as her next of kin."

"So, you have to make the funeral arrangements? Do you know if she had life insurance? I've heard funerals can be pretty expensive."

"No. The sheriff said she'd made the arrangements and paid for them already. She wanted to be cremated. I just have to set the time and place for the memorial service."

"Then there's no rush, right?"

"Wrong. There are other things that need to be decided… taken care of. I have to be present at the reading of Becki's will and probably have to assume responsibility for some of her assets. She inherited our grandmother's house and property." Autumn shifted and stared at the envelope in the middle of the table. "The sheriff said Becki knew she was ill, and he thought she'd gotten in touch with me before now."

Jay followed her gaze. "That letter. It's from her?"

Autumn nodded.

His eyes darted between her and the letter. "That's so…I don't know…weird." Jay sounded like one of those YouTube ghost hunters speaking in a hushed tone, and he stared at the letter as if it might levitate. "Are you going to read it?" He scanned the room, then dropped his voice to a whisper. "She might be here, waiting to see your reaction." He visibly shuddered. "I think I felt a chill. They say a room gets cold when a ghost is near."

Enough. "You're sitting right under the air-conditioning vent." She stretched over the table to snag the letter. "Of course I'm going to read it." Her bravado, however, wavered once it was in her hands. She ran her fingertip over her name, the letters flowing like brushstrokes. Becki had always wanted to be an artist, and Autumn wondered if she'd fulfilled that dream.

Jay held out her letter opener. She sat again and took it. She slid it into place, then stopped. She chewed her bottom lip. She was about to open a door she'd closed almost ten years ago. What else could she do? She willed her hands to stop trembling. Just rip the Band-Aid off quick. She braced herself for the guilt she feared would pour out and drown her, then slit the envelope open in one quick stroke.

❖

Catherine froze as a sharp pain shot from her shoulder up the right side of her neck. She carefully opened her left eye against the bright sunlight thankfully muted by a coating of winter grime on the window opposite her bed. Her right eyelids seemed to be stuck together and took a half second longer to part. She rubbed with her fingers to remove the tiny crusts of sleep clinging to her lashes and the corner of her eye, then stopped when her mother's voice popped into her head. *Don't rub your eyes, Catherine, or you'll have wrinkles when you get older.*

"Fuck. Everybody gets wrinkles." She tried to suck back the words, though softly muttered, as soon as they left her mouth. She released the breath she was holding when Gabe's lanky five foot body didn't stir. No wonder Catherine's neck was stiff. Gabe's back was pressed against Catherine's left side, her head resting on Catherine's shoulder, and Elvis was snugged against Gabe's front, effectively pinning Catherine's arm between them.

Day was dawning by the time they'd climbed out of the truck at Catherine's house. They put Gabe's duffel in the room where she always slept when she stayed overnight at Catherine's—which was any time Becki needed to be out of town or Catherine and Gabe planned a sunrise fishing expedition. But Gabe's composure had broken, and she had thrown herself into Catherine's arms and sobbed when Catherine had suggested she climb into the bed for a few hours of sleep. Catherine had carried her into the master bedroom, taken both their shoes off, and lay on top of the covers. When Gabe quieted, Elvis followed Catherine's silent signals to drag over the fluffy sherpa blanket folded in her reading chair. She tucked it around them both, and Elvis jumped onto the bed to complete a protective cocoon around Gabe.

Catherine rotated her head and right shoulder to loosen her neck, then slowly, carefully slipped her left arm free while she substituted a pillow for her shoulder. Elvis opened his eyes, and the end of his tail thumped lightly against the bed. She glanced at the clock on the bedside table, surprised to see that she'd slept for three dreamless hours.

She looked down into his intelligent eyes. An old soul gazed back at her. Maybe she was crazy for thinking that, but there'd always been something extraordinary about him. She held her finger to her lips, and he sighed, then closed his eyes as she carefully crawled off the bed. She paused at the door. Even as Gabe slept, her young face was tight with tension. Her mouth curved downward in an uncertain pout, and her brow drew together and twitched every few seconds.

The ever-present ball of self-doubt grew larger in Catherine's stomach. More than five years out of the army, and she still couldn't manage her own trauma. How in the world would she be able to face Gabe's?

❖

Autumn and Jay stared for a few seconds at the neatly folded letter that dropped onto the table before Autumn picked it up and unfolded the pages.

Dear Autumn,

How do I begin?

I guess I should say first that, though we are cousins, I have always loved you like the sister my parents never gave me. I understood, more than you knew, why you withdrew from our summers together. While you thought you needed to harden yourself to go out into the world, Grandma and I wished every day that you'd chosen instead to let us be your safe harbor. We always loved you, and who you would come to love didn't change that fact. Yes. I think we knew before you did that women would be the ones to hold your heart.

I feel that I failed you because you never trusted that I'd keep your deepest secret safe. Now I have to ask that you not fail me in what I'm about to entrust to you—the one thing I treasure most in my life.

I've been diagnosed with a brain tumor and scheduled for surgery in three weeks, but it's risky. If I survive, I might not be competent to make legal decisions. I won't go into detail now, but I need to know someone will protect me and mine from my parents if I'm incapacitated or worse. You are the one person who would understand, the only person I trust to protect my substantial assets and nurture my most significant accomplishment.

My phone number hasn't changed. My email is reswan@gmail.com. If you don't call or email, I'm going to show up on your doorstep and refuse to leave until you talk to me. You know how stubborn I can be. (I'm smiling.)

I love you.
Becki

Autumn laid the letter on the table, gently smoothing the creases.

"Hey, AA, you okay?" Jay's familiar jovial quip was soft and his tone solemn.

She shook her head, sniffing back a sob as she handed the letter to him. Another week, and Becki might have been knocking at her door, pulling her into her arms. God, she regretted every summer, every day, every hour she'd wasted by wallowing in her unfounded fear of rejection.

Jay finished scanning the letter. "Wow."

Autumn stood and began to pace. "God damn me. I never gave Grandma Swan or Becki a chance." She threw up her hands in exasperation and turned to pace in the other direction. "I just assumed they'd be horrified that I was gay. So I walked out of their lives." She stopped, closed her eyes, and wiped tears from her cheeks. "Becki didn't fail me, Jay. I failed her."

Jay stood, his expression stern. "And now?"

Now? Becki was gone. The sheriff had said she'd already made her own funeral arrangements. She could ask him to let the neighbor friend arrange a memorial service for Becki's friends in the community, then contact the lawyer to handle any other legal matters in probating the estate. She could keep her past in the past and focus on making AA Swan Inc. a big dog in the social-media marketing business. She wouldn't have to go back to where she and Becki had played barefoot in the fields, shared Grandma Swan's brownies and glasses of cold milk on the back steps. She wouldn't be tempted to sit in the front-porch rocking chairs to stare at the endless stars winking at her from a midnight-blue sky.

She met Jay's eyes and stared down the challenge they held. "I won't fail her now."

He nodded and retrieved his laptop from his backpack. "Then let's see if we can reschedule some of these appointments or turn some of them into teleconferences."

CHAPTER THREE

Autumn killed the engine of her new Oxford edition Mini-Cooper and stared at the farmhouse. Her ears throbbed with the echoes of Kendrick Lamar's rap in the almost startling quiet. When had she become so conditioned to constant city noise that silence made her uncomfortable? Had she changed that much? She scanned the yard and house. Even though Grandma Swan was gone, some part of her wouldn't have been surprised to see Grandma push open the screen door, wiping her hands on a dish towel while she checked out who had come to visit. Some things were unchanged, but a lot had evolved and updated with the times.

Grandma's dirt drive, which had become a muddy playground after a summer storm, was covered with crushed gravel now. White board fencing had replaced the barbed wire strung between rusting metal posts to separate the house and yard from the surrounding fields and pastures. Instead of the plain, white asbestos-shingle siding she remembered on the house, she saw warm, medium-blue vinyl siding with white trim and blue-black shutters. Flower beds and baskets hung from the frame of the long front porch, a riot of colorful blooms. She smiled and teared at the same time. Becki's warm, inviting personality was everywhere.

Autumn jogged up the steps, but no one responded when she knocked on the door. She tried the doorknob and found it locked. Damn. She really had to pee. Becki and Grandma never locked the house. Back door. Maybe it wasn't locked or someone was in the backyard. She turned and spotted a familiar figure. Could it be? One of his ears was broken off, and she remembered his little vest as red, not purple. But it appeared to be the same ceramic monkey that held Grandma's spare house key. She dashed over and turned him bottom up, extracted a tarnished brass key from his butt, and hurried back to the door.

"An-n-nd, I'm in." Her celebration was short—a millisecond, actually—because her bladder GPS registered the close proximity of relief and issued a fresh, more urgent warning. She dashed down the hall to the bathroom and sighed in relief as her body said good-bye to two Big Gulps of sweet tea and a venti hazelnut mocha coconut-milk macchiato from Starbucks. Well, maybe not all of that. This was the third time she'd made a potty stop in the last three hours of the six-hour drive.

She surveyed the bathroom as she washed her hands—bright-yellow walls and new faux-antique fixtures. The pedestal sink looked new, but the claw-foot tub was the same, except for the showerhead that rose from the tub faucet and anchored a bright daffodil-accented, waterproof curtain that circled the tub. Becki must have done well for herself. These upgrades weren't cheap.

Becki. Even the cheery surroundings didn't stop the suffocating gloom that settled on Autumn's shoulders. Why hadn't she called? Autumn would have come. She would have tried to help. Wouldn't she? Autumn tucked that doubt away. She couldn't deal with her guilt or examine whether her drive for success had evolved into simple self-absorption right now.

She emerged from the bathroom and walked tentatively through the house. "Hello? Anybody home? Hello?" She opened the back door and, instead of the small six-by-six concrete porch, found a wide deck outfitted with patio furniture and both gas and charcoal grills. At the end of the large, neat yard stood the old red barn, its paint fresh, but the structure just as she remembered.

A willowy figure in cut-off overalls and a tank top, face shaded by a wide-brimmed straw hat, stood in the barn's open doorway and waved, then began walking toward her. It couldn't be. Autumn struggled to breathe, suddenly swimming in a whirlpool of nauseating dizziness. She held on to the door with one hand and clutched the door's frame with the other. "Becki?"

"Who are you?"

Autumn startled, then turned toward the challenge that came from a young girl standing behind her. "I, uh…" She pointed to the barn, but the figure was gone. "I thought I saw…maybe—" She couldn't say it. The girl, whose gaze was boring a hole between Autumn's eyes, would think she was crazy. Becki was gone. She shook her head to reset her brain. "You asked me a question?"

"Who are you? How did you get in the house? I locked it up last night."

A dog barked in the distance as Autumn considered her answer. "I'm Autumn. Autumn Swan. Becki is…was my cousin. I got the key out of the monkey's butt to let myself in." It wasn't literally in the monkey's butt, but she and Autumn had liked to say that. It made them giggle. This girl didn't laugh. Didn't even smile. Autumn cleared her throat. "It was an emergency. I had a long drive and had to pee really bad."

The barks were louder and drew closer, and then the scramble of paws and thud of boots on the front porch drew her attention. A broad-shouldered woman of average height wearing jeans, work boots, and a faded red Henley followed a medium-sized brown dog through the front door. The dog went directly to sit next to the girl, his soulful eyes watching Autumn. The woman pulled a battered brown fedora from her head and eyed her, too.

"I'm Catherine Daye, Becki's neighbor. I'm kinda looking after the place until—" She waved her hat in a helpless gesture. "Until things are settled." She cocked her head, her expression turning curious. "I guess I'm not doing a very good job if I left the house open. I thought Gabe locked up last night. I should have checked myself."

"I locked it." The girl, apparently named Gabe, frowned at Autumn. "She got the key out of the monkey's butt."

To her dismay, Autumn was unable to stop the laugh that rolled up from her belly and exploded from her lips. She slapped a hand over her mouth. Gabe glowered as though she wanted to skewer

Autumn. "Sorry. I'm so sorry. It's just that Becki and I always found that so funny. Anytime one of us was upset or gloomy, the other would just say 'monkey butt' and we'd end up holding our sides, laughing."

Gabe's face was stone. "She's not here. She's dead." Her voice was flat, but not emotionless. Each word was edged with sharp anger meant to cut. Gabe flinched when Catherine rested a hand on her slim shoulder.

"Gabe, you and Elvis go feed the chickens and collect the eggs. Miss Franny's getting some of the ladies together to bake cakes and cookies for the memorial, and I promised to take all the eggs we could spare to her house tomorrow. Then, and I know it's early, see if you can get them in the coop so we don't have to come back later."

Gabe shrugged off Catherine's hand and stomped past Autumn to the back door. Elvis looked to Catherine, who flicked her hand toward Gabe, and then he followed. When he passed Autumn, he stopped, gave her a long look, then licked her hand once before continuing and pushing the screened door open to catch up with Gabe.

Catherine cleared her throat again. "I'm sorry. Gabe is normally a well-mannered kid, but this has thrown her hard."

"It's okay." Autumn rubbed her forehead. She felt like she'd fallen off the monster caffeine wave she'd been riding, tossed and tumbled, then spat out onto the beach drained of her last bit of energy. She really needed a nap, but she should check in with Jay first. They had so much to do, so much to reschedule. Her irritation ratcheted up a notch with each task that came to mind, and Catherine's frank appraisal of her was just about the last straw. The last thing she needed was a butch farmer looking to donate some sack time to keep the city girl happy. Everybody knows city girls are sexually fluid and hop from bed to bed like they shop for groceries. Butch on aisle four. Two-for-one on aisle eight. And bi-friendly couple available on aisle twelve.

"You're Becki's cousin, aren't you?" Catherine asked.

Autumn bit back the slap-down she was about to throw out,

realizing her mistake just in time. Catherine hadn't arrived yet when she'd introduced herself to Gabe. "I'm sorry. The trip was long. I did introduce myself to…to Gabe before you got here—" She stuck out her hand. "Yes. I'm Autumn Swan, Becki's younger cousin."

Catherine's hand was large, her knuckles slightly red and chapped. "Nice to finally meet you. Becki talked about you a lot."

"Good things, I hope." Autumn tried to smile to lighten the tension, but she didn't feel very convincing. "I guess that's how you knew not to shoot me for breaking and entering."

Catherine shook her head and pointed to a bookcase against the wall in the front room. "Actually, I recognized you." She walked over to take a framed photograph from the middle shelf and turned it for Autumn to see.

Tears blurred Autumn's vision when she realized the picture was of her and Becki, arms slung over each other's shoulders and grinning at Grandma, who was the photographer. She took it from Catherine and let the memories flow. It was Autumn's last summer at the farm, and in a sudden spurt of growth, she was nearly as tall as Becki. Not that either of them was tall. Five feet six was almost considered short these days.

"Whoa." Catherine's hand that cupped Autumn's elbow was rough with calluses, but her grip was strong.

Autumn realized she'd started to sway, so she let Catherine lead her to the worn sofa draped in a colorful quilt. She was too tired to be embarrassed by the tears that dripped from her chin onto the glass protecting the photograph, but she accepted the tissue Catherine pressed into her hand and wiped the glass clean before dabbing her eyes and nose. She traced Becki's face with her finger. "Grandma was our safe haven every summer. I didn't want to be around while my parents harvested their annual crop of marijuana, and Becki's parents were just redneck trash. The summer she was twelve, she told Grandma she would sleep under her bed when her father's friends came over to party because they scared her when they got drunk. She never went back home after that summer. I don't know how Grandma got custody of her, but she did." She wiped her eyes again to clear her vision. "She was more like a big sister than a cousin. That shirt she's wearing was my favorite. I never considered her clothes hand-me-downs. I wanted to be just like her."

"When was the last time you saw her?"

Autumn swallowed past the lump that seemed stuck in her throat. "At Grandma's funeral, but we didn't get a chance to talk." She huffed. "Both our parents showed up—hers like vultures hoping to pick over Grandma's assets—and got into a loud argument at the graveside. I left without going to the visitation afterward. I'd already received papers about a trust Grandma bequeathed me. She left a similar trust to Becki, as well as the farm. I was fine with that and didn't have any reason to stick around for the 'flower children versus the rednecks' show." Damn it. She was starting to cry again. "I should have stayed and helped Becki run them off."

Catherine shook her head and smiled. "I wasn't living here then, but Becki told me the whole story. She had Sheriff Cofy throw her parents in jail on domestic-violence charges, so they had to stay there overnight. They were furious your parents weren't jailed as well, but more than happy to get the hell out of Dodge the next morning."

Autumn needed to take care of things here and get back to Decatur. She clutched the picture to her chest and straightened to look around. She felt like she was waking from a dream, and everything she needed to do came pouring back like the rude morning sun. "I need to check in with my assistant and let the lawyer know I'm here so he can set up a time to meet about the will."

"Gaylord said he tried to get in touch with you earlier today, but cell signals can be spotty when you drive through the mountains. He wants to read the will at eight tomorrow morning," Catherine said. "He's hoping that'll work for you, because he has to be in court in the next county after lunch. And a few other people are invited, so he had to work around their schedules, too."

Autumn's sinuses were swollen from crying, and her head was starting to pound. "How many people are we talking about?" Had her cousin become a millionaire in the past ten years and nobody told her?

Catherine smiled and shrugged. "Gaylord said it was complicated."

"Okay." She massaged her throbbing temple, then stood and returned the picture to the bookcase, tracing her finger over Becki's image one more time. "I need to head out. The only decent hotel Jay could book for me is thirty minutes away."

"You can stay here."

Autumn turned toward the soft voice. Gabe stood behind the island that separated the kitchen and the living room, studying her sneakers and nervously flicking the tag on Elvis's collar back and forth as he leaned against her leg. A look of bashful regret had mysteriously replaced her defiance. How long had she been standing there?

"It's okay," Autumn said. "I don't want to impose."

"Nobody else here," Gabe said, lifting her eyes to meet and hold Autumn's.

Autumn looked to Catherine, who shrugged. "It's Gabe's call."

"Bacon and eggs in the fridge." Gabe's moment of shyness was gone as quickly as it appeared. Gabe-in-charge strode past them. "Bread should still be fresh enough for toast. I'll put out some clean sheets and towels for you." She disappeared down the hallway, but Elvis stayed, his eyes fixed on Autumn.

"I really appreciate it," Autumn said to Catherine. "But I need high-speed internet to complete some work I had to reschedule to drive up here." She barely had a cell signal here.

"Password to the internet is taped to the bottom of the coffee table." Gabe's voice carried down the hall and into the living room. "It's not exactly Google fiber, but it's the highest speed the cable company offers."

Autumn moved closer to Catherine and lowered her voice. "Are you sure this is okay? I mean, it still feels like Grandma's house to me, but I don't want to upset anyone by staying here."

Gabe reappeared before Catherine could answer. "Really. It's okay. You can use the bedroom on the left," Gabe said.

"Thank you, then. I think I will." The decision to not have to get back in the car seemed to release a wave of fatigue her caffeine high had been holding back. Maybe she'd take something for her stuffy, pounding head and lie down for thirty minutes. She functioned very well on little sleep as long as she could squeeze in a power nap.

Gabe slid her hands into the pockets of her shorts and cast a glance at Catherine before facing Autumn. "I'm sorry for being rude earlier."

"Thank you, but I understand." Autumn waved her hand to dismiss the incident. "We're all a little on edge, I'm sure." She just wanted the air cleared so they would leave, and she could take some aspirin and close her eyes. But who was this girl? She'd assumed that she was Catherine's charge—adopted or fostered because she looked nothing like Catherine. Obviously biracial, Gabe had a smooth, attractive, medium-brown complexion that wasn't a shade you'd get from tanning, and her dark hair was a riot of short, tight, corkscrew curls. It was a startling contrast to her hazel eyes, which were a swirl of green and brown rather than pale and grayish. She'd be very pretty if she would smile. Her high cheekbones, full lips, and the lines of the profile were high model quality despite her boyish mannerisms.

What stumped Autumn, though, was that Gabe was acting like she was in charge of Becki's house. Autumn was Becki's next of kin, and Catherine was her adult neighbor. Gabe was just a child, but Catherine had deferred to her. Autumn stifled a yawn. She was too tired to think about all this now and needed to get her suitcase and laptop from the car. She looked up to find Gabe watching her.

Gabe's expression was thoughtful as their eyes met and held. What was going on inside that girl's head? What more did she have to say or ask of Autumn? Gabe blinked, then looked down to tap Elvis on his head. "Did you forget something?"

Elvis jumped to his feet, his claws scrabbling on the hardwood floors in his race to one of the bedrooms. A few seconds later, he returned triumphant, a twelve-inch rawhide bone in his mouth.

"I guess we're ready, then," Catherine said, as if she saw nothing remarkable about the dog's behavior. She started for the door, then looked back. "Oh, yeah. You can ride with us in the morning, if you like."

Autumn hesitated. "I might need to run other errands afterward. But if you don't mind stopping by, I'd like to follow you in. I'm afraid to trust my phone's GPS since cell service is iffy around here."

"Sure. Not a problem. We'll be by at seven forty." Catherine waved as she walked out.

"Don't be late," Gabe added, turning to follow. "She has this thing about being on time. You'll mess up her whole day if you aren't waiting when we drive up."

Autumn watched through the front windows. Catherine swatted Gabe on the back of her head, then rested her arm across Gabe's shoulders. Gabe didn't seem to mind the playful tap, because she wrapped her arm around Catherine's waist and skipped once to match her stride to Catherine's longer one. Elvis, his bone still in his mouth, looked back over his shoulder at her, then followed them. Catherine lowered the tailgate of the battered truck for Elvis to jump onto, but he seemed to consider it a moment before taking off into the woods. Catherine shrugged, closed the tailgate, and climbed into the truck. They turned onto the highway in the same direction Elvis had gone.

Weird. Becki had strange neighbors.

CHAPTER FOUR

Young lady, you can't bring that dog in here." The stern-faced receptionist with bottle-black hair and penciled-on eyebrows pointed an accusing finger at Elvis. "Dogs carry fleas and ticks and urinate on things. They belong outdoors, not inside homes, and certainly not in places of business."

Gabe had been silent and tense since Elvis's cold, wet nose on Catherine's ear had startled her awake, and he'd led her to the front porch, where Gabe sat huddled in a thin blanket. Catherine had draped her barn jacket over Gabe's shoulders, adding an additional layer of warmth, and retrieved her old army jacket for herself. They'd sat in silence to watch dawn break.

"I guess I'll find out what's going to happen to me when we go to the lawyer's office," Gabe had finally said.

"I suppose." Catherine wasn't sure, so she didn't know what to say.

"I wouldn't be any trouble if I stayed with you. I could help with the farm." Gabe's quiet words failed to hide the undercurrent of pleading.

Catherine pulled her close in a firm, one-armed hug. "I know that, and you know you're always welcome here. But this sort of thing can be complicated by laws and living relatives. Let's just see how everything goes."

"Elvis wants to go, too. He's nervous about everything being weird."

Catherine had allowed Gabe's pretense that it was Elvis's need, not hers. But she'd heard the message loud and clear. Gabe needed Elvis to keep her grounded.

Right now, Gabe needed Catherine to intercede. Her expression resembled a gathering thunderhead, and her glare reminded Catherine of twin lasers aimed to burn through the haughty woman's skull. Elvis and Catherine moved as one—Elvis blocking Gabe's advance toward the enemy and Catherine stepping up to present their credentials.

"The harness Elvis is wearing identifies him as a certified therapy dog. The law allows him to be here to support Gabriella Swan, who has been summoned to witness the reading of her mother's will and learn what the future holds for her as…for her." Catherine mentally slapped herself when she saw the anger in Gabe's eyes falter and reveal for one brief second the uncertainty and fear behind it. Gabe's razor-sharp mind had finished the words Catherine had almost spoken—*as an orphaned minor.*

"If anything has fleas, Edna, it's that possum-fur coat Warren gave you for Christmas." Gaylord Cooper stepped into the small but comfortable reception area.

"It's fox fur, and you know it, Gaylord Cooper." The phone began to ring, and Edna marched back to her desk to answer it.

A woman Catherine had seen visit with Becki several times recently followed Gaylord. A friend or another cousin? Elvis wagged his tail in slow sweeps when this woman walked to him and Gabe.

"Gabriella, it's good to see you again."

Gabe eyed her, ignoring her outstretched hand until Elvis poked her with his nose. She frowned at Elvis but nodded at the woman. "Hi, Ms. Everhart." She wiped her right hand on her jeans and smirked. "Elvis slobbered on my hand. It's kind of sticky." Clearly a lie, not an actual apology.

Enough. "Gabriella Annise Swan." Catherine's growled warning hit home. Gabe ducked her head and her neck flushed. Catherine would allow Gabe some leeway because of the situation, but something told her that Gabe needed familiar boundaries, too, right now.

Autumn froze. She'd stopped by the restroom in the building's lobby and had let herself into the lawyers' suite just in time to hear Catherine growl out Gabe's full name. She stared at Gabe while the puzzle pieces clicked together in her head. Gabriella. Gabriel was Becki's brother. Annise. The same as Autumn's middle name. Swan. This wasn't Catherine's kid. How was she connected to Becki? Maybe Becki's brother, Gabriel, was Gabriella's father. That might make sense. But where was Gabriella's mother? A hard bump to her backside nearly sent her sprawling. She caught herself in time to prevent catastrophic embarrassment. "Oh! Sorry."

"No, I'm sorry." A large man in a sheriff's uniform balanced a cardboard tray holding four cups that smelled deliciously like coffee in one hand and grasped Autumn's elbow with his other hand to steady her. "I was so focused on trying to get through the door without dropping anything, I didn't see you standing so close."

"I shouldn't have been standing in front of the door." Autumn moved around him and held the door while he stepped past it. Damn. Whatever he had in those cups smelled divine. She'd bypassed the eggs and bacon Gabe had advised her were in the fridge. She'd been too nervous and lacked the appetite to cook anything. But her stomach was waking up now.

He walked to the low coffee table surrounded by a sofa and several chairs where clients could wait until Gaylord or his two partners were available to see them. He set the tray and a pink-and-white paper bag on the table, then plucked out one of the cups. Turning back to Autumn, he held out his hand. "I'm Sheriff Ed Cofy. We spoke several times on the phone."

Autumn blinked, realizing that she recognized his voice. "Yes, of course. Autumn Swan." She laughed nervously. "But, obviously, you know that."

He smiled and held up the covered cup in his hand. "Large soy caramel macchiato with extra vanilla for you."

Thank the heavens. She grabbed for the cup. "How did you know?"

"I called your assistant I'd talked to several times to get the arrangements done. He's very informative." He rummaged in the bag, then held up a bulging paper pocket. "Apple fritter. It's not

Starbucks, but we think our local coffee house and bakery, Sweet Anytime, is way better."

"Okay. You've won me over." Autumn sipped her drink, still hot, and hummed with pleasure.

Ed handed a cup and treat to Catherine. "House blend, black, and a multigrain muffin."

Really? Autumn regarded Catherine. She wasn't unattractive, just…well, plain. Her khaki pants were neatly ironed, and the sleeves of her white dress shirt were rolled up to contrast with her tanned forearms. Her eyes were the same unremarkable shade of brown as her hair, which was held back by a tie at her nape. Yep. Plain. Like black coffee and a multigrain muffin.

"Got you hot cocoa and a cinnamon bun," Ed said to Gabe. "Me and Elvis, a couple of peanut butter cookies. Don't tell my wife. I'm not supposed to eat cookies." He flashed the adults an affable smile before turning back to Gabe. "How about you and me sit out here and enjoy our treats while Gaylord goes over some boring legal stuff with Catherine and Autumn. He'll come get us when they're ready to read your mom's will."

Gabe's eyes flicked from the food to each of the adults, apparently weighing the possibility of a ruse to make plans without her input against the lure of the sweets.

"Go ahead," Catherine said softly. "You know I'll tell you whatever we discuss later."

"Okay," Gabe said, already rounding the table to sit and dig her cinnamon roll out of the bag.

Something about the almost tangible trust between Catherine and Gabe made Autumn feel hollow. She'd had that same bond with Becki once, until she turned her back on Becki and Grandma. Jay was her only close friend now, but she'd just ditched her promise to handle the social-media publicity for the annual Pride event. That was hardly trustworthy. Still, she'd had a good excuse both times. Work comes first, right?

"Autumn?" Catherine stood in a doorway down the hall.

"Coming."

She'd expected a conference room where they'd gather around

a table. But Gaylord had led them to another sitting area by the windows at one end of his large office.

Once they all settled, Gaylord began. "Go ahead and enjoy what Ed brought. We just finished donuts and coffee while we were going over some papers before you all arrived. That's why I asked Ed to bring more." He waved around the group. "Some of us know each other, but I'll reintroduce everybody." He started with the woman who sat on his right. "This is Janice Everhart. She's a state social worker assigned to Elijah County." He gestured to Catherine directly across from him. "This is Catherine Daye, longtime neighbor and close friend to Ms. Becki Swan and her daughter, Gabriella." He turned last to Autumn. "This is Autumn Swan, Becki's first cousin and the only living relative she requested to be contacted in the event of her death."

Her daughter, Gabriella. The words rang in Autumn's ears and ricocheted in her brain. Her brain had refused to go there when she'd heard Gabe's full name a few minutes ago, but she couldn't deny it now. The evidence—Becki's cheekbones and eyes—had been staring right at her. Becki had a daughter. Her heart beat wildly and her breath quickened. Becki's daughter was now orphaned. Catherine's eyes caught and held hers. Plain brown eyes, but calm and understanding. The panic squeezing Autumn's chest began to ease.

"You didn't know," Catherine said softly.

Autumn shook her head slowly. "I thought she was your foster or adopted daughter. She and the dog are so comfortable with you. But when you said her full name out there…Annise is my middle name, too…I realized she must be a relative, maybe a child left by Becki's brother. I just didn't imagine she had a…I should have. It's so obvious now. The eyes, her cheekbones. Why didn't I see Becki there before?" God, she was babbling.

Gaylord cleared his throat. "That's why I brought you back here for this meeting. I'm not revealing any part of the will in doing this, but I am allowing Ms. Everhart to prepare you for what Becki told her would be her last wishes." He nodded for Janice to explain.

This was a waking nightmare. Autumn suspected where this

was going, but she couldn't stop it. Couldn't change it. Even worse, she saw Becki everywhere she looked. Janice Everhart could have been Becki's sister. Her long waves of blond hair framed a girl-next-door face. Her eyes were kind and her voice warm. "Becki suspected her symptoms indicated a brain tumor weeks before it was diagnosed. A mutual friend put her in touch with me. She wanted information so she could prepare. When her diagnosis was confirmed, she asked that I help guide and advise her daughter and the two of you until Gabriella reaches legal age."

"Us?" Autumn coughed when the piece of fritter she was swallowing stuck in her throat. A quick swallow of her drink washed it down and revved her stalled brain. This definitely had to be a bizarre dream that she'd wake from any moment. Gaylord and Janice looked at her expectantly, but Catherine had gone still as stone, her face unreadable. Apparently, Autumn wasn't the only surprised person in the room.

Janice picked up a thin laptop computer Autumn hadn't noticed on the glass coffee table between them and flipped it open. A flash drive jutted from one port. "Becki recorded a message for the two of you." She held up a second flash drive. "She also recorded one for Gabriella to listen to later, when she feels ready. Both are about her hopes for her daughter's future." She turned the laptop toward them and hit the key to start the video.

The screen filled with Becki's beautiful smile. "Hi, Autumn. I'm so glad you're here. I've missed you so much and would have loved to watch you get to know my Gabe. I named her after you and Gabriel, the only family I want her to really know. My biggest regret is that we didn't have more time, that I didn't track you down in person and shake some sense into you when you disappeared on us." Becki's smile dimmed, and she dabbed at her eyes with a tissue. "I... well, I feel like I let you down, and I know I don't deserve it, but I'm asking you to become a co-guardian of my sweet Gabe. She needs both you and Catherine. I'm pretty sure she's leaning toward your sexual orientation. Not that it's bad or wrong, but being biracial and an advanced student has already made her an outsider at school." Her smile returned. "She's wicked smart, like you, Autumn. And that's not just her mom talking. I've signed permissions for you and Catherine to access her school records and IQ evaluations. You and Catherine offer different things that Gabe will need. I'm counting on you to nurture this part of her, to find the right opportunities and the right people to help her reach her potential."

Becki looked down for a few seconds, and when her eyes met the camera again, her face had softened. "Hi, Catherine. Weird, but I can actually feel your presence even though I know I'm just talking to a camera and it could be days, weeks, months, or even a few years before you watch this. Your life force is so strong." She made a dismissive gesture. "You'd never admit it, but I know you always thought that was a bunch of psychic manure when I'd tell you that." Her smile widened, her eyes clear of tears now. "You moving in next to us has been a gift. Gabe worships you." She laughed. "And I would have married you if I wasn't so damned heterosexual. You've always been there for both of us—our port in the storm, the mountain of strength I needed when Grandma died, and the touchstone that anchored me when my world felt too overwhelming. I still need you to be that for Gabe. Don't let the world sweep her away when they realize how smart she is. I'm able to leave Gabe more than financially secure because of you. You'll need to explain all of that when she's old enough to handle her own finances."

Autumn struggled to peel her eyes from Becki's image, but she chanced a look at Catherine, whose eyebrows were drawn together and her mouth set in a thin line. Was there some big secret only Catherine knew?

"So, what I'm saying is that Gabe needs both of you. It will all be clear when Gaylord reads the will. I don't want to dwell on details now, but I'm asking the biggest favor of my life. I'm trusting the most important person in my life to the two of you. Please, please don't let her down. I love both of you, but you shouldn't keep Gabe waiting any longer. Go hear what I've got in store for you in my will. I hope the surprises are good."

The screen went black, and nobody spoke for a few seconds. Finally, Gaylord cleared his throat. "Janice, can you show them to the conference room? I'll go get Gabe."

Janice extracted the flash drive from the laptop and fished an identical one from her pocket. "I made a copy so you each could have one."

❖

They gathered around the large conference table. Gaylord, flanked by Janice and Sheriff Cofy, faced Gabe, who sat between Catherine and Autumn. Gaylord shuffled the papers and was about to speak when Gabe stopped him.

"Just a minute." She pushed back from the table and dragged another chair so close it touched hers. Catherine and Autumn had to slide their chairs over to make room. "Elvis, up." Elvis jumped into the added chair and sat primly while Gabe settled beside him. Autumn turned to stare at Elvis. Really? Shouldn't he be sitting at Gabe's feet like a good dog? Elvis whipped his head toward her, and his wet tongue swiped over her lips before she could jerk out of the way.

"Ack."

"Elvis." Gabe scowled at him. "No kissing girls unless they kiss you first." Her voice was stern and serious, but Elvis licked her ear in reply before turning back to Autumn.

Sheriff Cofy chuckled when Autumn leaned as far back out of his tongue's reach as she could without falling out of her chair. Had that dog just winked at her?

Gaylord looked over his half-glasses perched on the end of his nose. "Elvis, behave or I'll send you to sit with Edna."

Elvis laid his ears back and straightened forward. Only then did Autumn realize his antics had changed the tension in the room to an air of anticipation. Gaylord picked up the will and read aloud.

"I, Rebecca Maria Swan, being of sound mind, do hereby bequeath the assets of my estate to the following organizations and individuals as follows—"

Autumn half listened as Gaylord's baritone droned through a list of donations set aside for various charities. The sums Gaylord was reciting weren't millions, but they certainly weren't pocket change either. The Elijah Animal Rescue was to receive a two-hundred-thousand-dollar endowment for a new Shelter to Service program to be administered by Ed Cofy and Catherine Daye. Where did Becki get her money? As far as she could tell, Becki was an artist, woodworker and potter, enjoying moderate success across the state as well as locally. She'd googled Becki and found that she had a website and also sold on a popular internet market. If Becki had asked, Autumn could have done so much to help her market her work. Oh, yeah. Except that she'd shut Becki out. But this wasn't the time to have another wallow in the past. She needed to tune into the present because Gaylord was getting to the good stuff.

"I leave the bulk of my estate to my daughter, Gabriella Annise Swan, in a trust until she reaches the age of twenty-one. Any future income to my estate from my artwork or investments will go directly into that trust. As long as the trust continues, I appoint my neighbor Catherine Daye and my cousin Autumn Annise Swan as co-administrators, each to be compensated ten percent of the trust's annual earnings for their time and labor. Should either become deceased or unable to perform this duty, their portion and responsibility will go to the remaining person.

"My only asset to be held outside the trust is the house, land, and all outbuildings and equipment on the farm. This I bequeath to my cousin, Autumn, with the stipulation that upon her death, she in turn bequeath it back to Gabriella. Autumn and I spent many happy summers there together. It was our safe place. In the event both Autumn and Gabriella become deceased prior to Catherine, the farm and all property on it will transfer to Catherine.

"A word of warning. The land already is bound by a federal conservation agreement so that it can never be used for anything other than agriculture purposes. If Catherine, Autumn, and Gabriella become deceased with no heir to maintain the property, it is to be turned over to the Elijah Wildlife Conservancy.

"At no time, under no circumstances is any part of Gabriella's trust or the farm to be turned over to or shared with my parents or any other children or grandchildren they might have produced."

Gaylord paused and sipped from the glass of water next to him.

His dry throat was a thinly disguised pretense because he used the delay to pin Catherine, then Autumn with a warning stare. Autumn straightened her shoulders and met his gaze without flinching. She was certain she saw a flicker of doubt in his eyes. She had no idea how she would work this out, but no country lawyer was going to look down his nose at her. Yeah, she was young, and maybe her leggings and super-cute, off-the-shoulder top was a little informal, but she was wearing shades of gray. She barely refrained from rolling her eyes when the risqué movie of that title popped into her head. Not like that. Somber. Not black, but her leggings were close to it.

"So, who do I live with?"

Gabe's irritated demand jerked Autumn from her usual internal conversation. Elvis had slumped to rest his head on the table, his only indication of continued interest the twitching of his eyebrows as his eyes shifted from Ed to Janice to Gaylord. Gabe, however, focused a fierce scowl on Gaylord. The kid could be scary. For some reason, that made Autumn want to smile. Catherine did smile but rested her hand on Gabe's forearm. Reassurance or admonishment?

"I'm getting to that, young lady." Gaylord put down the will and took off his glasses. "Becki met with Ms. Everhart and myself to set up a legal arrangement for Catherine Daye and Autumn Swan to assume joint guardianship of Gabriella Annise Swan." He nodded to Janice, who stood and came around the table to place a single sheet of paper and a pen before Catherine, and a second sheet in front of Autumn. "The guardianship is not legally binding until you two sign those papers, attesting that you will share responsibility for Gabe's welfare until she reaches the age of twenty-one. It's also temporary for one year, at which time the relationship and Ms. Gabriella Swan's welfare will be evaluated to make sure everything is working out."

Catherine picked up her paper and extracted a pair of reading glasses from her shirt pocket to begin reading.

"I'm a legal adult at eighteen," Gabe said, crossing her arms over her chest.

Gaylord nodded. "Yes, you are. But you won't inherit your trust until you are twenty-one. And these two ladies will have control of those funds until that time." He squinted at her. "You'd do well not to piss them off while they're still approving your expenses."

Gabe didn't answer, but she reached up to grasp Elvis's therapy-dog harness in a white-knuckled grip. The move was almost imperceptible, but the space between them had closed. Gabe stared down at the table. A minute ticked by, then another.

Catherine put her paper back on the table and removed her glasses. "Could you give Gabe, Autumn, and me a few minutes to talk privately?"

Gaylord hesitated, then stood. "Ms. Everhart?"

Janice also stood. "This joint guardianship is unusual, so I'd be a little worried if you didn't want to talk it over. But we'll need to return before you actually sign the papers. They have to be witnessed by both myself, as a representative for the Department of Children Services, and Mr. Cooper, who will notarize both contracts. You also might have questions for me after you talk."

Autumn had read her paper and already had questions. But the thought of Catherine's private sit-down made her queasy. She wasn't good at one-on-one, and this felt an awful lot like two-on-one since she was the only stranger in the room. Her anxiety built as she watched Gaylord and Janice exit the room, and she realized the annoying noise that was growing louder was her own nervous tapping of her pen against the table. She stopped, and a nanosecond of silence filled the room before the loud click of the conference-room door closing broke it. She looked up to three pairs of eyes staring at her.

Catherine studied Autumn. Damn, but she was cute. That was the problem. Becki had said her cousin was twenty-five, but very mature for her years—a survivor, independent, a self-starter, a successful entrepreneur. But Catherine didn't see the businesswoman she'd expected.

She saw a millennial with multiple ear piercings—she didn't want to know if there were others—and at least three tattoos she could spot peeking out from her clothing. Her light-brown hair was cut short in one of those purposefully messy, spiky styles and tipped with blond highlights. Autumn's fingernails were freshly painted a stylish red to contrast with her tunic that tied at one dark-gray, legging-covered hip, and her black ankle boots looked like something an elf would wear. Was she even wearing a bra? Only the strap of a black racer-back undershirt showed over the bared shoulder.

Altogether, it didn't seem to Catherine like appropriate attire for the reading of a will. Or a business meeting, for that matter. Sure, her face was strikingly pretty, and her eyes were the same mesmerizing hazel as Becki's and Gabe's. But she looked young—translation, cute rather than beautiful. Too young to be in charge of a super-smart preteen on the cusp of the dangerous years of puberty. How good an influence would she be on Gabe? How well did Becki really know the cousin who had been gone since they were teens?

She let her eyes travel over Autumn's slim frame, then drift up to intelligent eyes that challenged hers. Catherine's face heated. She was embarrassed to have been caught looking. Yeah, like embarrassment ever made her sex contract and throb. Damn. How long had it been? Too long, apparently.

Autumn opened her mouth, then closed it.

"What were you going to say?" Catherine's defenses rose. She didn't need some fancy city woman showing up to remind her how lacking she was.

Autumn glanced at Gabe and shook her head, her lips pressed into a thin line. "Nothing."

"It must be something. Go ahead."

Autumn glared at her. "Nothing appropriate in front of Gabe."

Gabe leaned forward, her expression darkening, but Catherine jumped in before the dam broke. "Gabe might not physically be an adult yet, but her IQ is much higher than the majority of the adult population. Anything you would say to me can be said in front of Gabe."

"Fine. I was about to say—" Autumn pushed her chair back and stood close enough that Catherine had to look up from her seated position. "Really? Were you just cruising me?"

"No." Catherine leaned back in her chair to create some space between them. Autumn smelled of chocolate and cinnamon. The shards of forest green shooting through her light-brown irises were igniting sparks in Catherine's belly. "I was conducting advance reconnaissance."

"And what did you deduce? That I'm too young to supervise Gabe, to make sure she doesn't become a self-involved mall rat like so many city teens?"

Gabe had gone quiet, her head turning like a spectator at a tennis match as she watched the exchange between Catherine and Autumn.

Catherine couldn't say what she was actually thinking. That she should absolutely ignore the apparent awakening of her long-slumbering libido because it was stupid to even consider that someone like Autumn would even entertain a one-nighter with someone boring like Catherine. Hell, it wasn't like she would do something like that anyway, even if Autumn was interested. She had too much pride, was too mature for such nonsense. Catherine scowled. Christ. Where did she get so off track? "This isn't about you or me. We're here to talk about Gabe's future."

"That's where you're wrong, Ms. Daye. Apparently, Gabe's future is dependent on who you and I are. Becki and I both had biological parents completely ill-equipped to rear children. I intend to do everything in my power to make sure my niece never finds herself in those same circumstances."

This young, hip millennial had morphed into the fire-breathing, take-no-prisoners CEO of her own company. Maybe she'd misjudged Autumn.

"Then we're in agreement." Catherine pushed her chair back, too, and stood, noting with satisfaction that Autumn had to look up now because Catherine was several inches taller. "You've answered my concern."

Autumn put her hands on her hips. "Which was?"

"How committed you are to Gabe." She moved around Autumn but stopped at the door. "Are you ready to sign some papers?"

Autumn gave a curt nod.

CHAPTER FIVE

I don't know, Jay." Autumn parked next to the battered truck in Catherine's driveway and took a long suck on the straw in her iced latte. The Sweet Everything coffee shop was her first stop after they left Gaylord's office. She'd loaded up on scones, gourmet coffee beans, a grinder, and a French press since she could find only herbal teas in Becki's cabinet. "It's already Thursday. I met with Becki's lawyer this morning, but Catherine and I have to see Becki's banker tomorrow, and I need to take care of several other things immediately. I'm afraid I'll be going back and forth a lot for a while. Shit!"

A bang on the car window next to her head made her almost hop onto the console. Two of Elvis's big front paws were splayed against the glass, and he peered at her from between them, a big, tongue-lolling, doggie smile exposing pearly white canines. "God, Elvis. You nearly scared me to death."

"Elvis? He's not dead?"

"He's reincarnated as a brown mutt."

"Bruh, I think the air must be too thin wherever you are."

Elvis pushed off the window and bounded up the stairs to the porch. Gabe was there, frowning down at her sitting in the car.

"You might be right. Look, Jay. I've got to go. I'll drive back Sunday and fill you in on everything Monday. Go ahead and pack everything you can into the first half of next week, because I'm going to have to turn around and come back here as soon as possible."

He sighed. "I'll see if I can work some magic, but I don't

understand why you have to go right back. The internet is our friend. You can take care of all kinds of things without ever leaving your house."

"Not everything, Jay. Not my cousin's eleven-year-old daughter I'm now co-parenting."

Jay was still sputtering when she disconnected and climbed out of her vehicle.

❖

Catherine took the plate of thick ham slices from the microwave and set it among bowls that held potato salad, summer-squash casserole, creamed corn, and baby lima beans. She checked the apple pie warming in the oven. There'd be a lot more food Saturday, when a lot of the town turned out for the memorial service. Until then, the core group of ladies, who always seemed to coordinate these things, had brought over more than enough so that she and Gabe didn't have to think about cooking.

Gabe slouched into the kitchen with Elvis at her heels.

"Well?"

"She's coming," Gabe said, sounding bored. "She was on the phone again."

Gabe slumped into her usual chair, and Elvis sat politely next to her and raised his muzzle to sample the aromas coming from the table.

"Nothing off the table goes into his mouth until after we eat," Catherine warned Gabe, waving a serving spoon over the table in an unnecessary indication of what "nothing" encompassed before dipping it into the bowl of lima beans. Elvis laid his ears back and sank to the floor, but Gabe played with her fork and didn't look up.

Catherine sighed. She wanted to cut Gabe some slack because she had to feel lost and alone. But if Catherine let this uncharacteristic behavior continue, Becki's sweet, inquisitive kid could become mired in this unattractive attitude of sullen belligerence. "Sit up straight, Gabe. Becki never let you slouch like that at the dinner table."

Gabe still wouldn't look at Catherine. "She's not here, so I reckon I can sit any way I want."

Catherine narrowed her eyes. "And I reckon anyone who slouches at the dinner table can clean out the chicken coop this afternoon. I haven't gotten to it in a while, so it's pretty rank."

Gabe looked up, uncertainty flickering across her face before transforming into defiance. She opened her mouth to speak, but Autumn breezed into the room.

"Oh, man. Grandma used to make us clean the chicken coop when we got into trouble. It was the worst. It used to make me gag, so Becki would dab some of her perfume under my nose so I couldn't smell the chicken shi…uh, chicken poop." She plunked her oversized phone down next to the place setting directly across from Gabe's, leaving the chair at the head of the table for Catherine. She surveyed the selection of food. "Wow. I didn't think I was hungry, but I haven't seen this much homemade food since Grandma cooked for us." She snatched up her napkin and patted the corners of her mouth. "God. I'm drooling on myself."

Gabe sat up and leaned forward to look at the table below Autumn's chin.

"Made you look." Autumn smiled, pointing at Gabe. "Your mom used to pull that trick on me all the time, and I constantly fell for it."

Gabe scowled. "I bet Mom didn't fall for tricks like that."

Catherine forked a couple of slices of ham onto her plate and began passing food around while she listened. This different side of Autumn fascinated her. It was as though the edgy, ambitious, city millennial disappeared when Autumn put her phone down, and a sunny, friendly country girl emerged.

"Nope. Not often." Autumn shook her head, scooping two big spoonfuls of creamed corn onto her plate. "But I remember one time she wished she had." She continued to fill her plate as they passed bowls around the table. "We had our fishing poles and were walking down to the pond. I'd already tried to fool her by claiming to spot a snake. She didn't fall for it, of course. But when we were almost at the pond, I saw a hole on the side of the path and just had to stop and poke a stick down in it. Yellow-jacket wasps, the mean kind that'll chase you, came pouring out. I was stung twice before I could throw down my pole and run. I flew past her, screaming 'yellow jackets!' She just kept strolling along, laughing when I plowed into the water, clothes and all. A few seconds later, she was screaming and running, too, because they'd swarmed her, stinging her eight or ten times before she could dive in after me."

Gabe's eyes were wide, her fork stilled. "Mom's allergic to bees, probably wasps, too."

"She wasn't before, but she was after the wasp fiasco, as Grandma called it. Anyway, we had to sit in the pond for more than an hour before it was safe to go back to the house. Becki's face puffed all up, and she started having trouble breathing, so Grandma rushed her to the hospital. She had to get a couple of shots, and then they made her stay overnight until she could breathe okay again."

"Wow."

"Yeah. It scared all of us—me, Becki, and Grandma. We never joked about serious stuff anymore, like snakes or wasps." Autumn shoved a forkful of ham and potatoes into her mouth and hummed as she chewed. "God, this is so good. If I lived here and ate like this all the time, I'd be as big as a house."

Catherine cleared her throat. "I guess we'd better talk about that. What are your plans now?"

For the first time since she'd accepted her invitation to have lunch at her house, Catherine thought Autumn looked nervous. They waited while she took a long drink of iced tea.

"Well, you and I have an appointment with the banker tomorrow," Autumn said slowly.

Catherine nodded.

"Then the memorial is Saturday."

Before they'd left Gaylord's office, Ed had helped them work out the details for the memorial service. Catherine had made the calls to the ladies who would organize the food, and Ed said he'd take care of lining up music, chairs, and several large canopies in case it rained, as well as volunteers for traffic control and set-up.

Autumn had reluctantly left to run her errands, since she didn't have local resources and contacts to help.

Autumn's shoulders rose and fell before she began. "The day that Sheriff Cofy, uh, Ed called to tell me that Becki had passed away, I'd had a breakthrough with an important client that morning. We blew right past his three-month goal for customer engagement in only ten days. News like that spreads fast in my business, and by noon, I had requests from five new companies for presentations on what I could do for them." She met Catherine's eyes. "This is a giant leap forward for my company, AA Swan, and I had to convince those potential clients to wait so I could take care of family things first. I need to drive back Sunday and meet with them next week. I'll be back, probably by next weekend. If they decide to sign with me, I can set up their accounts and get started from here. I've been working out of my apartment, but we're looking for office space now."

Relief flooded Catherine. Becki's death had been sudden, and she feared another radical change in Gabe's life right now could be devastating. "No rush. Gabe is here. She's got about a month of school left before she's out for the summer." Catherine didn't see any value in changing her school when only a few weeks were left in the term.

Gabe fixed her gaze on Autumn and frowned. "You can come visit as often as you want, but I'm not going to live in the city. I don't even know you."

Autumn smiled. "And I don't know you. But I knew your mom. I loved her, and I'm sure I'm going to love you, too, when I've had a chance to get to know you."

Gabe scowled. "You don't know that. You might not like me at all."

"Maybe you should let me decide that. Besides, you might not like me." Autumn picked up her fork again to resume eating. "Let's both keep an open mind, okay? I'll be coming back...a lot...over the summer—so we can get to know each other before school starts next fall."

Gabe sprang from her chair, knocking it to the floor and causing Elvis to yelp. "I'm not leaving my home." Her words were angry, but her chest heaved with a half sob. She tripped over Elvis, who yelped again, and then stomped to the back door before turning back for a last word. Her lower lip trembled, and tears ran down her cheeks. "This town was good enough for Mama, and it's good enough for me." She flung the screen door open and ran for Catherine's barn.

Autumn looked stunned for only a second. Then Elvis whined and took Catherine's hand in his mouth, tugging in the direction of the door.

"It's okay, Elvis. Let's give her some space on this." She flicked her hand toward the door. "But you go keep an eye on her, and come get me if she gets herself in any trouble."

Elvis didn't hesitate. He shot out the door to catch up with Gabe, who was past the barn now and running for the forested mountain at the back of Catherine's property. She stood and watched until he was at Gabe's heels, then nearly jumped out of her skin when she turned and almost collided with Autumn, who was also watching.

"That went well, huh?" She looked down at the floor and shook her head. "I thought this would be easier. I thought all I needed to do was the exact opposite of what my parents did."

"People seem complicated," Catherine said, more to herself than Autumn, as she stared after Gabe. "But, like animals, we all are driven by the same basic fears and emotions."

"Not really. Animals aren't spiteful."

Catherine frowned at the sadness and uncertainty in Autumn's expressive eyes. *You might not like me when you get to know me.* Damn. What had her parents done to her? Catherine had an overwhelming urge to gather Autumn in her arms and soothe away the dejection she radiated. She wanted to brush her lips against Autumn's pouting mouth and kiss the enticing spot beneath her cute ear.

What was she thinking? She was ten years older. Autumn was beautiful and full of life. She was building a business and looking to grab the brass ring of success. Catherine was thirty-five and little more than a survivor, content to hide away while the world passed by her. She needed the quiet and hard work of the farm to keep her sanity, to save her from drowning in a whirlpool of PTSD.

Catherine had a secret, too—one that kept her more than financially secure and had laid Becki, therefore Gabe, a golden nest egg. A secret she didn't want Autumn to discover. She tried to lighten the dour atmosphere.

"Don't beat yourself up. I actually thought you handled it okay. I'm pretty sure I know where she's going. If she's not back when it gets close to sundown, I'll go get her. In the meantime, how about we put the food away. I'll make some coffee and cut that apple pie so we can have dessert on the front porch and talk about our options without Gabe."

Autumn spied an electric kettle on the counter and imagined Catherine taking a jar of instant coffee from the cabinet. "Actually, I have a million emails to answer, and then I need to run some analytics and monitor the client sites when Jay goes off duty...and...and... great goddess." Her excuses dwindled when Catherine walked around the table and opened the top cabinet doors of a beautiful cherry cabinet, then slid them back into hidden pockets to reveal a coffee bar she had only dreamed about. An array of very high-end machines included a French press, several bean grinders, an espresso-only machine, one that could produce a single serving or a carafe, and one—holy mother of God—amazing does-everything machine that could produce twelve different specialty drinks. "I would kill to have this at my place." She ran her hands over the machines, then surveyed the shelves of small, vacuum-sealed bags of coffee beans.

"Don't do it. I'm pretty sure they won't let you have a coffee bar in prison," Catherine said.

Whoa. Did Catherine just make a joke? Autumn smiled. "You're a coffee connoisseur?"

Catherine's ears turned a cute pink. "More like a coffee snob," she said, tactfully ignoring Autumn's obvious surprise.

Cute? It wasn't a word Autumn would apply to Catherine. She was too serious. Too...too butch. Handsome, in a rugged sort of way. And very sweet with Gabe. But butch wasn't Autumn's type.

She liked cute, flirty girls. Ones who painted their nails and liked to wear dresses and heels to go out dancing. Women whose appearance didn't scream lesbian. But she did love coffee. "Can I make the coffee while you put the food away?"

Catherine hesitated.

"Relax. I might not own machines like these, but I worked my way through college as a barista. I know how to use them."

Catherine glanced nervously at her expensive coffee machines, then back to Autumn. "Okay. If you have any questions, just ask. Milk and half-and-half are in the fridge. And, uh, there's some hazelnut-flavored creamer in there, too."

"Sacrilege."

Catherine smiled. "I know, right? Becki liked it, or I wouldn't have it anywhere near my coffee."

When Catherine smiled, she looked younger than the forty-something Autumn had originally thought. Hmm. Which one first? She wanted to try the really expensive does-everything machine, but she also wanted to impress Catherine with her barista skills by whipping up a work of art. Duh. Maybe she should ask what Catherine would like.

She turned to Catherine. "What's your favorite?"

"The Italian espresso, black."

"Black? No sweetener. Nothing I can froth for you?"

"Just black. I'm a purist. I just keep the fancy stuff for visitors. Not that I get that many. But make yourself whatever you want."

Damn. Maybe she hadn't miscalculated. Catherine was so boring, she had to be old…older. What did Becki say? Catherine anchored her? Yeah. She could see that. Catherine could be a real drag. She needed to open up and join life a little, if for no other reason than for Gabe. The poor kid would think the city was a virtual candy shop after hanging out with Miss Black Coffee Boring.

"Ready?"

Autumn was drawn from her musings. She took the huge slice of apple pie Catherine offered, glad to see that she at least wasn't too boring to add a generous scoop of vanilla-bean ice cream on top, then handed over Catherine's coffee. "Black, no sugar."

"I do add sugar to the dark, strong teas they brew in the Middle East. Not as much as the natives use, but at least a spoonful."

"Wow. Who knew you were such a wild woman?" Autumn picked up her triple-shot Americano and then gestured toward the front of the house. "After you."

❖

Autumn bounced on the balls of her feet, then performed a series of pirouettes and leaps up and down the hallway, through the kitchen, out the back door, across the deck, and onto the vast lawn newly mown for the service and visitation tomorrow afternoon. Pirouette, pirouette, leap, leap. She was overloaded with caffeine and sugar, and her sanity was hanging by a thread since her front-porch chat with Catherine and reality hit.

Screw reality. Pirouette, pirouette, leap, leap. The nearly full moon was her personal spotlight, and a flock of Canada geese, gorging on the fresh grass clippings and the occasional cricket, clapped their wings and honked at her performance as they yielded center stage and settled at the far end of the yard. Pirouette, pirouette, leap. Autumn closed her eyes and breathed the scent of earth and forest. The stars twinkled and spun around her like backup dancers when she opened her eyes mid-pirouette. Her body twirled and soared, her heart pumping fast and strong. But her traitorous mind persisted in drowning her with reality like a dolphin tangled in a commercial fishing net.

When did her life go so off the rails and completely out of control? Five days ago. Five nightmarish days ago. She reviewed the events, searching for the point where karma had grabbed her by the throat.

She was working, chugging along uphill as usual. She closed her laptop and went to bed, then was awakened by dogs barking. Who let the dogs out? That's it! This was all a dream. Pirouette, pirouette, leap. She stared at the moon. Pirouette, pirouette, leap. It was one long, dizzy mind fuck. All she had to do was wake up. Pirouette, leap, splat. Something cold and slimy squished between her toes, and her graceful dance abruptly ended with jerky, one-legged hops. "Gross, gross, gross."

Goose poop. It would have been as funny as saying "monkey's butt" if it wasn't oozing around her piggies. She sighed and gave up the stage. It was only a lawn. Her backup dancers were just stars a trillion miles away, and the geese obviously weren't as impressed as she had imagined since they'd pooped on her ballet.

So it wasn't a dream. The list she'd rattled off to Jay was real. She had a kid to raise. She'd have to give up her wonderful, perfect—except that it had only one bedroom—apartment and hunt for a sedate, much less spectacular, two-bedroom place.

She also needed to find office space and get back to work. Jay had scheduled her to meet with four more potential clients in addition to the ones she'd rescheduled before she left. Oh, and she'd promised to come back in a week to spend some time with Gabe so they could get to know one another. How was she going to keep her business growing while she was six hours away? She needed Jay to go full-time now. Why did he need to finish this last semester anyway? Shit. School. She also needed to start thinking about where to enroll Gabe for school. That wasn't something you could leave until the last minute. The best schools had waiting lists.

Break it down into small tasks, Becki had told her once, then scratch them off the list one by one. She groaned as she hopped over to the water spigot to rinse her contaminated toes enough to hop into the house and begin her list. First, soak in a warm bath to relax. No more caffeine tonight. She gave up hopping and limped awkwardly without letting the tainted toes touch the floor. After a bath, she'd get to work on some of the files Jay had sent. She soaped a washcloth and thoroughly scrubbed her foot, letting the water and soap go down the drain before she plugged the drain in the deep, claw-footed tub and filled it. She wrinkled her nose and tossed the cloth into the hamper, then got a clean one for her bath, continuing her list as she stripped and poured in her favorite bath salts. Make it through the memorial tomorrow. Clean everything up and pack. Sleep and head back to Atlanta first thing Sunday. If she left at dawn, she could work on the files some more Sunday night and hit the ground running on Monday morning. Yes. Plan outlined. Now execute.

Warmth enveloped her, and the faint scent of vanilla and eucalyptus filled her sinuses. She reclined back onto Becki's inflated tub pillow. Mmm. She'd have to get one of these for her bathroom. Well, first she'd have to get a tub, deep like this one. Her apartment only had a shower. A very cool, modern walk-in shower with two heads and eight settings. But no tub. Maybe it wasn't so perfect after all.

CHAPTER SIX

D o I have to go?"
"If I have to, you have to." Catherine didn't want to go to
the memorial either. She closed her eyes and shoved her trembling
hands into the pockets of her "dress" jeans, meaning the only ones
that weren't faded by a hundred washings or spotted with grass or
God-knows-what other stains.

The desert hadn't haunted her night, but a confused swirl of
happy times with Becki who kept morphing into Autumn had. Since
Catherine and Gabe were the only people Autumn would really
know at the memorial, she'd probably Velcro to them like beggar's-
lice seeds did to Elvis's fur every summer.

It wasn't that Catherine found Autumn's company unpleasant.
No, not at all. That was the problem. Becki had been beautiful, and
Catherine had loved her dearly...as a friend. Her heart had warmed
when she dreamed of Becki the night before, but different parts
warmed when Becki turned into Autumn, and that was bad. So bad.
Autumn was in no way Catherine's type...well, if she had a type
and was fifteen years younger. When Catherine was sixteen and sat
through every showing of *Almost Famous* one weekend to drool
over Kate Hudson, Autumn was still wetting her diapers. And there
were so many other differences.

Catherine sucked in a breath and turned to face Gabe, who was
slouching against the sofa like she was too weak to stand and walk
out to the truck, her head down as she studied the floor.

"We both have to go over to the house. Everyone is coming to pay their respects to your mama, Gabe." She knelt down in front of Gabe to see her eyes. "And in an odd way, it's their way of respecting your feelings, too. They'll tell stories about things Becki did for them and funny stories about her to cheer you and everyone up. They're friends—her friends and your friends. Your mama was a burst of sunlight when she walked into a room, and like you, they want to hold on to that a little longer by getting together today and remembering the good times with her."

Gabe let out a resigned sigh. "I'm not going to get up and say anything in front of everybody."

"Nobody expects you to." Catherine grabbed Gabe under the arms and hauled her up to stand tall. "Now buck up, soldier, and stand for final inspection. General Becki ordered this memorial herself, so we're going to give her the best send-off this town has ever witnessed."

It was a familiar game they played behind Becki's back. Gabe's lips turned up in the tiniest of smiles, but she played along, albeit with less enthusiasm than usual. "Ooo-rah, Sergeant."

"Where's Private Elvis?" Catherine extracted a wide hair pick from Gabe's rear pocket and fluffed her curls in the back.

"Don't know. He was AWOL when I woke up."

Catherine shook her head. That dog was something. "Covert op, no doubt. He'll turn up. He always does." She slid the comb back into Gabe's pocket. "You'll meet muster, I suppose. Let's move out."

The crowd was larger, much larger than Catherine had anticipated. She'd expected the local townfolk, but not the volume of out-of-towners that were filling the one-acre front lawn with their cars under the direction of two deputies and several volunteer firemen.

"Good thing we took the path through the woods," Gabe said, frowning.

Gabe headed into the house, but Catherine spotted Ed Cofy supervising the unloading of more folding chairs from two pickup trucks.

"I thought all the chairs were unloaded and set up last night," she said, shading her eyes against the bright sun to survey the situation. Several hundred chairs were arranged in a U-shape, with a small platform at its focal point. On the platform was a beautiful antique table of dark, rich cherrywood. The chairs they'd set out the evening before were filled almost to the seat with ladies in broad-brimmed hats, waving away the gnats and heat with hand fans, and men in khakis and a rainbow of golf shirts, lifting their ball caps, fedoras, or Stetsons to mop their sweaty brows.

"They were, but then the highway patrol radioed two hours ago to say their troopers were setting up to push traffic through several big intersections on the highway because vehicles were stacking up all the way to the interstate. So I called around and wrangled a few hundred more chairs. I don't think the last governor who died drew this many people to his funeral."

Catherine rubbed the back of her neck and pulled her ball cap lower on her forehead. "I hope we have enough food."

Ed laughed. "I sent for more tables, too. The ladies weren't taking a chance that Jesus would show up and feed thousands from five loaves and two fish, so they cooked enough to feed two counties. Keeping the baked stuff warm is no problem, but I called Don to send over a couple of his refrigeration trucks for the rest until it's time to serve."

"Geez. How much is this going to cost?"

Ed glared at her. "I can't believe you asked that. You know Don wouldn't take a penny. Hell, the checks Becki wrote in advance for her cremation, the band, the bakery, and all the rest to make this happen are all in that big bowl in the living room. Nobody cashed 'em. All had stories about how Becki helped this one or that one. I don't think there was a single family or person in this county she hadn't touched in some way."

Catherine shook her head. "If she's the standard for getting into heaven, then I'm surely going to hell."

Ed laughed again, slapping her lightly on the shoulder. His eyes went round in mock surprise. "Maybe Becki's passing was the Rapture, and she was the only one taken."

"Stop it." Catherine almost smiled, then frowned at Ed's shorts and festive shirt sporting large red and green parrots. "This is a funeral, Ed."

His expression turned serious. "Don't, Cat. That isn't what Becki wanted. This is a celebration of her life. There will be tears, for sure. But you and I both know she was certain that an afterlife exists, that the soul doesn't end when it leaves this sphere. She saw dying as her next great adventure."

"I know."

"Hey, what's with the dark jeans and long face?" Ed's chief deputy, Vicki Devine, strode up in blinding white jeans and a hot-pink tank covered by an open shirt made of a breezy weave embroidered with thin gold and pink thread in several patterned stripes down the front.

Catherine did smile at Vicki, another member of their local army-reserve unit. "I wore my only pair of khakis day before yesterday, and Elvis put his muddy feet all over them. I haven't had a chance to wash them." She looked down at her dark jeans and crisp, white shirt. "At least I didn't wear black."

Vicki propped one fist on her hip and gave Catherine the once-over. Her gaze stopped on Catherine's ball cap that sported the local feed-shop logo. "Really, Cat? Bubba's Feed and Seed?"

Ed began to back away. "I think I should check on the…uh, on the band. I need to check on the band." He turned and hurried away.

"Coward," Catherine said. She snugged her hat until it touched the corners of her arched brow. "It's new and, therefore, clean."

"I suspected, so I came equipped." Vicki grabbed the teen pulling chairs off the truck. "I need one of those, Ricky."

"Yes, ma'am. Where do you want it?" He opened the chair and placed it exactly where Vicki pointed.

"Thank you." Vicki pointed to Catherine. "I want you on your knees."

"If I had a dollar for every woman—"

Vicki cut Catherine's grumbling off with a swipe of her hand through the air. "Knees in the chair so I can reach you. I swear, I think you been standing in fertilizer instead of spreading it."

Catherine complied while Vicki plopped her large purse on the grass and extracted a thin gold tie, a hairbrush, and a sky-blue ball cap. "I stopped growing about twenty years ago. Maybe you're getting shorter." She took the ball cap and looked it over while Vicki knotted the tie and arranged it to hang loosely below the open collar of Catherine's shirt. The front of the cap was a bright-yellow sun peeking over the cap's bill with its rays shooting backward like racing stripes. An inscription embroidered on the sun proclaimed Welcome the Dawn. Catherine frowned. "I don't know about this." At least someone had curled the bill properly. She hated those new caps that had flat bills. She thought they looked stupid.

"Hush. Becki picked it out and told me to make you wear it." Vicki whipped off Catherine's choice of headwear, removed the tie that gathered her dark-brown hair at her nape, and brushed upward to gather the ponytail higher.

"What are you doing?" Friend or not, Vicki was moving Catherine out of her comfort zone. "I don't wear my hair in a ponytail."

Vicki took the ball cap from her and threaded Catherine's silky locks through the back as she settled it on Catherine's head. "Not a pony tail. A rooster's tail." She rounded Catherine to face her again. "You are not that old, Cat. I don't know why you insist on dressing like you are."

Catherine disengaged herself from the chair and stepped back. She didn't want to have this conversation. "I'm just practical. Never cared to be frivolous."

"You're hopeless," Vicki said. "Where's Gabriella? I hope you didn't dress her, too."

Catherine put a restraining hand on Vicki's arm. "She dressed herself, and what she's wearing means something to her. So leave her alone." Catherine touched the bill of her new cap. "Now that I think about it, this cap will complement the shirt she's wearing."

"Okay. You know her better than anyone." Vicki hooked her

arm in Catherine's as they walked toward the house. "I won't push, but I'll be hanging close in case you need help with her."

"Thanks." Catherine wasn't one for public displays of affection, but she kissed Vicki's cheek as they neared the front steps.

"Hi, you must be Becki's cousin. It's easy to see the resemblance."

Catherine looked up and into Autumn's eyes—more brown than green today in the shade of a broad-brimmed straw hat Catherine recognized as one of Becki's favorites. She was dressed in a red, deep-V-necked T-shirt, capri jeans, and red running shoes. Catherine liked her country casual look even better than her dressed-up attire.

Autumn held a tall glass of tomato juice—correction, Bloody Mary, judging from the strong smell of vodka—in her left hand and blinked slowly. Her gaze flowed from Catherine to Vicki. "Yes, I am." She came down the steps to Vicki's level and held out her right hand. "Autumn Swan."

Vicki smiled and accepted Autumn's hand. "I'm Vicki. Becki and I've been friends for years."

Autumn cocked her head. "I don't remember you from the summers I spent here."

Vicki smiled. "You wouldn't. My daddy farms on the other side of the county, and I spent my summers helping around the farm from sunup to sundown. The school year was my vacation and the only time I got to spend hanging out with friends."

"Oh, I see." Autumn sipped from her drink. "My parents were farmers, too." Her expression was one of bored disdain. "But their crop was a tad illegal, so I was shipped off to Grandma—my choice—every summer. The last thing I wanted was to end up in foster care if they got arrested."

Catherine stared at her feet, avoiding Vicki's questioning look. No, she hadn't explained to Autumn the source of Becki's fortune. Her financial statements would simply show Becki had a large income from a limited consortium known only as PMM LLC. Autumn drained the last of her drink and stared across the yard, seemingly oblivious to the uncomfortable silence.

"Well, I'd better go see if the ladies need any help out back," Vicki said at last. "Nice to meet you, Autumn."

Autumn nodded but didn't take her eyes from the line of cars still pouring onto the expanse of lawn. "Same here."

"Did you see Gabe inside?" Catherine asked after Vicki disappeared around the side of the house.

"Yes." She still watched the cars, her full lips gathering in an adorable pout. "I don't know any of these people." She snatched the large stalk of celery from her drink and threw it into the yard. Elvis seemed to magically appear and snatch it up. He settled down with it between his paws to munch on the snack, and Autumn turned her glass up to slurp down the last watery bit. She lowered the glass and stared again at the cars. "You would think I'd know some of them from all the summers I spent here. But I don't." She rattled the ice in her glass. "I need another drink."

"Maybe you should eat something," Catherine said.

Autumn stopped with her hand on the screen door's handle. "I did. Then I threw it up." She opened the door and went inside without looking at Catherine.

Catherine caught the door before it closed and slipped in behind Autumn to grab her arm. "Autumn, wait."

Autumn stopped but wouldn't look at Catherine. "Don't. I'm barely holding it together, and if you hug me, I'm going to lose it before the memorial even starts." She tugged her arm free from Catherine's grasp. "I'll be okay, but you should check on Gabe. She was in Becki's room a few minutes ago."

The despair in Autumn's voice made Catherine want to do just that—pull Autumn into her arms and send everybody away. She wanted to protect Autumn. What was she thinking? She hadn't been able to protect her unit or Booker. Not even herself from the night terrors or the panic that seized her anytime she felt surrounded and trapped, like in a city environment. Besides, Autumn was an adult. She needed to take care of the child Becki had entrusted to them.

She expected to find Gabe huddled on her mama's bed, but she was using yellow police evidence tape to secure an official-looking paper sign to the door of Becki's bedroom. The sign read: "Please respect the family's wishes and do not enter for any reason. Sheriff Ed Cofy."

"What is that?" Catherine frowned.

"I don't want people going in there and gawking," Gabe said. "It was Autumn's idea. She said it'd make people know we meant business. I wanted to just put Keep Out and This Means You. She said people would take this more serious and she'd clear it with Sheriff Ed to put his name on it."

A few guitar notes and drum rolls rang out from the backyard, and then the craggy voice of Fire Chief Henry Bradford began a fair rendition of Louie Armstrong's "It's a Wonderful World." The service was beginning.

"Come on. Let's get Autumn and take our seats."

"Nobody's going to preach a sermon, are they?"

"I hope not. I honestly don't know what's planned. Becki hated sermons, but that doesn't mean she hasn't arranged an inspirational speech."

They found Autumn standing at the back door, a fresh drink in hand. Catherine stuffed half a box of tissues in her pocket and held the door for them all to step out onto the deck. Gabe and Autumn stopped, unwilling or unable to go any farther. Elvis poked Catherine's leg with his nose, then slipped under Gabe's dangling hand. When she reflectively latched onto his collar, he led her down the steps and toward the chairs. Catherine took his hint and closed her fingers around Autumn's free hand to bring her along. It vaguely occurred to her to wonder how he knew which seats were reserved for them.

There was no sermon, just people who lined up like it was a high school graduation to take the stage and share some act of kindness or funny situation when Becki had touched their lives. When the story being told brought a song to mind, the band would jump in before the next speaker, and everybody would sing along. It was all very informal, with folks getting up and helping themselves to the long tables of food, then settling back into their seats to listen, sing, and eat.

Some of the oldest left after a few hours, but most stayed. When the storytellers had all said their piece, the chairs were pulled back to the edges of the yard, and they danced to Becki's favorite songs. Then the sun finally dipped behind the tall barn, and Ed took the microphone to call the assembly of friends to order.

"I want to thank you all for coming here to celebrate the life of a truly exceptional woman," he said. "But as you know, Becki always had to have the last word, and today is no different."

He signaled, and Vicki backed her truck up toward the side of the barn where two deputies unfurled a white sheet. Gaylord dragged a power cord over to Vicki, and a moment later, a slide show of Becki's life began—Becki as a child helping Grandma Swan bake cookies, Becki wide-eyed at a baby chick pecking his way into the world, and Becki exploring her artistic talent on the wall of her bedroom. Tears streamed down Autumn's face when several clips showed her summers with Becki, and Gabe slid from her seat to sit on the ground close to Elvis during the clips of Becki holding her right after she was born, then more as Gabe grew from toddler to girl. When the clips ended, Becki was looking out at all of them. She was standing in a field of sunflowers in full bloom, wearing a faded T-shirt with a big sunflower on the front and Here Comes the Sun printed around the flower's edges. Gabe was wearing that very shirt now. Becki waved at the camera.

"Hey, everybody. If you're watching this, then I hope you've all had a good time this afternoon rather than sitting around crying over me. You've all meant so much to me—Ed, Vicki, Gaylord, Janice. Thank you for keeping my confidence and helping me prepare for this. Catherine and Autumn, you don't realize it yet, but you both are old souls that seem to follow me through incarnations. Or maybe I'm following your bright light. This isn't good-bye. We'll meet again before our soul journeys are done. And finally, my sweet, sweet Gabe. My only regret in this life is not being at your side as you go to college, marry, and find your way in this world. I love you, baby. I hope you'll forgive me for not telling you how sick I was. I needed to spend my last days with your smile and enthusiasm for life, not tears and sadness. You have been and will always be the sunshine in my life, in my heart. I know you're sad now, but what do we do when we're sad? Come on. Let's sing it."

Becki's strong, clear voice began. "You are my sunshine, my only sunshine—"

Gabe's lips moved, but no words came out.

"Everybody sing," Becki proclaimed as she began the chorus over.

Voices joined in tentatively, then grew stronger. Many faces were streaked with tears as one, then three, then more rose to their feet as all joined in. Gabe turned and pushed through the crowd in the direction of the house.

"Gabe, wait." Catherine tripped over Elvis. Cursing, she untangled herself from two chairs she'd fallen onto but was knocked down again as Autumn pushed off her shoulders to hop over Catherine and Elvis in her own pursuit of Gabe. "Damn it." Catherine cracked her shin against a third chair in her renewed struggle to stand, then limped toward the house.

She saw Autumn reach the back door and was about to break into a trot when Gaylord stepped into her path.

"Hey. I've been trying to catch up with you to settle some details."

"Not now, Gaylord. I need to see to Gabe."

He followed her gaze to the house. "I know this has to be hard for her."

"Yeah. Autumn, too. More than she wants to show, I think." Catherine glanced around. "Can you and Ed wrap this up and clear everybody out? I'm going to clear the house and lock the doors to give Gabe and Autumn some privacy."

Gaylord nodded and laid his big hand on her shoulder. "Give yourself some time to grieve, too, Catherine. You can't take care of them if you don't take care of yourself."

"I will." But Catherine kept her gaze on the house. She couldn't let Gaylord see the lie in her eyes. She'd never let herself grieve after returning from the desert, afraid it would be an abyss she couldn't escape. She wasn't going to change now.

❖

Autumn's flight into the house was as much to prevent a public demonstration of her grief as it was to catch up with Gabe. Becki's smile and the first line of the song they would sing together almost every day of every summer was too much. She forgot her own feelings, however, the minute she stepped into the kitchen and was assaulted by shouts and what sounded like a Saturday-night bar fight. She snatched up the first weapon she could find and sprinted to the living room at the same time a boy hurdled backward, propelled into the room by Gabe's shoulder in his stomach—a tackle that would make any NFL linebacker proud. The boy, about the same height as Gabe but much heavier, pounded away at her head and torso with his fists.

"Ow, ow. Shit. She's biting me. Get her off me."

Another boy emerged from the hallway and struggled to get a hold on her slender frame while she kicked backward at his legs. He grabbed her shirt, and the thin material ripped almost all the way down her back.

Gabe's shriek sounded more like a battle cry, and she drove the boy in her grip backward again. "Get out of my house," she screamed, pushing him toward the front door.

The boy flung himself to the left, but Gabe held tight. The sofa's arm caught him in back of his thighs, and momentum flipped them partially onto the sofa, rolled them off, bounced them against the coffee table with a crash, and landed them on the floor.

They froze for a split second. They both seemed surprised that he was now on top and had her pinned beneath him. The second boy recovered first.

"Let's get outta here." He whirled toward the door, but Autumn was ready for him.

She raised her left hand, palm out. "Hold on, Skippy. You two have some 'splaining."

Faced with an adult, boy number two skidded to a stop and began to wring his hands. "I wasn't doing nothing. She jumped

Robbie, and I was just trying to get her off him. I didn't mean to tear her shirt."

"Get off me, turd," Gabe said, unsuccessfully bucking her body to dislodge Robbie.

"Who are you?" Robbie eyed Autumn. He still had the baby face of a youth but was big-bodied and obviously didn't have the same respect for adults as his partner in crime did.

"I'm Becki's cousin and, as of Thursday, one of Gabriella's guardians." She swept her hand to indicate their surroundings. "This is our house."

The back door slammed, and Catherine's long stride faltered when she took in the living room standoff. "I heard a crash or something." Her gaze dropped to the upended coffee table and several glasses shattered and strewn across the hardwood floor. "Everything okay?"

"Robbie was about to stand up and help Gabe to her feet," Autumn said. She kept her tone even and, after a quick glance at Catherine, her eyes on the brawlers. "Then he's going to tell me what he and his friend were doing in our house."

"They were in Mama's room," Gabe said. "And Robbie... he—"

Catherine jumped in when Gabe couldn't finish. "Robbie, you and Dustin straighten up this furniture and sweep up this glass, then sit here until I come back. We'll see what Sheriff Cofy has to say about you trespassing in Gabe's house."

"I don't want to go to jail," Dustin whined after Catherine left.

"Shut up. It's that stupid girl's fault," Robbie said, spitting the words at Gabe. "Can't take a joke."

Gabe started for Robbie again, but Autumn caught the back of her sports bra that showed through the tear in her shirt, stopping Gabe mid-launch.

"Sit." Autumn pulled a stool to the end of the granite-topped island that separated the kitchen and living room, pointing Gabe toward it. Then she handed Robbie a broom and dustpan. "Clean up that mess, and then you two sit right there." She indicated two stools in front of the bar.

She set a cutting board on the island's counter, took a lemon and two limes from the refrigerator, and opened the knife drawer. She smiled, probably for the first time that day. Oh, yes, Becki still loved a good set of knives. She picked up several to weigh their fit in her hand, then selected one.

The boys made quick work of righting the coffee table and sweeping up the glass. Too quick. Autumn was sure she'd need to vacuum thoroughly before anyone walked through the room barefoot. Then Robbie started for the front door.

"Sit down, Robbie. Both of you," she said.

The boys stopped but didn't sit. Dustin looked to Robbie for direction.

Autumn smiled at Gabe, who sat in smoldering silence at the end of the bar. "Did Becki ever tell you that I worked as a barista and bartender while I was in college?" She didn't wait for an answer. "Probably not."

"Let's go," Robbie said to Dustin.

Autumn twirled the knife in her fingers and slammed it point first into the cutting board. "I said SIT." The twang of the knife vibrating was the only sound in the shocked quiet after her roar. The boys sat.

She saw Catherine and Ed through the front-door screen, but Gabe and the boys were focused on her knife and didn't appear to hear them slip quietly inside.

"So, as I was saying, I had scholarships that paid my tuition, dorm rent, and meal plan, but I needed some pocket money. You know, for stuff like shampoo, beer, glitter nail polish, beer, clothes, beer…well, you get the idea. So, I worked part-time. It also helped me get out of my shell. I was a bit shy and a lot focused. If I could have my head in a computer twenty-four seven, I was a happy camper. But my jobs made me get out and socialize. That was important."

While she talked, she began to twirl the knife around her fingers, switching it from hand to hand, rolling it around her knuckles, always ending up with it gripped in her right hand, ready for slicing. Then she turned it up a notch, increasing her speed so you could barely follow the knife as it swirled around her fingers before springing upward, flipping, and landing in a perfect stick at the center of the lemon.

"It was important, you see, because it taught me people skills— how to talk to people and, more importantly, how to listen to them. Today's bar customer might be tomorrow's business client. Some of mine are."

She unstuck the knife from the lemon, then sliced a lime with blinding precision and speed. Chop, chop, chop. She paused. "You boys still thinking about leaving?"

"N-n-no ma'am," Dustin said. Robbie's mouth gaped open, but he didn't answer.

She took two highball glasses from the cabinet and set them on the counter about two inches apart. Then she twirled and flipped the knife a little more in the showy pattern she'd used to impress bar patrons. Chop, chop, chop. The second lime was sliced, but this time its center slice popped up into the air, Autumn's knife whipped out, and two neat halves fell, one into each glass.

Autumn looked up at the boys, heaved a big sigh, and smiled. "My cousin Becki was like a big sister to me. Grieving for somebody you love is a private thing, you know? Gabe and I are both pretty private people."

Dustin nodded and looked about to burst into tears. Robbie just stared at her. Gabe's head was bowed so Autumn couldn't see her face. But this was as much for herself as for Gabe.

"Cutting always calms me. I've been on edge all day about all these people coming here today, but I knew I couldn't be selfish. Becki wasn't their cousin, but they all loved her, too. And I expected everybody to respect the sign Gabe and I put up, asking people not to go into that room. You've upset Gabe, and you've upset me. I'm going to have to cut up a lot more stuff to calm down enough to sleep tonight." She put her knife down, got a felt-tipped marker from Becki's catch-all drawer, and plopped the cutting board on the bar in front of Robbie. "Put your hand on the board, Robbie, and spread your fingers."

He hesitated, checking to see that the knife was still on the counter. His hand shook, but he did as she asked. Dustin whimpered. "Don't hurt him. We didn't mean nothing."

Autumn traced the outline of Robbie's hand on the board, then set the board back on the counter where she'd been slicing the fruit. "Gabe's the one you should apologize to, Dustin."

He looked at Gabe, her head still bowed. "I'm sorry, Gabe. I really am. It was Robbie's idea, but I was stupid to go in there with him." His voice shook at first but grew stronger and more sincere. "I know you can't forgive me, but I wish you could. Boys, well, Mama says we just do stupid things sometimes. I don't know why. I'll do anything to make it up to you."

Gabe finally looked up. "I'll talk to Cat about it." But her eyes were fixed on Autumn, rather than Dustin, and the source of the thunk-thunk-thunk.

Autumn held the knife in her fist and was slowly stabbing each area between the fingers drawn on the cutting board. She looked at Robbie without pausing. "What about you, Robbie? Are you sorry?"

Robbie's eyes bounced from hers to the cutting board as the thunk-thunk-thunk of her knife picked up speed. "Huh?"

Her knife was a blur, but she still didn't look down. "Gabe's waiting for your apology."

His face turned a brilliant red, and he glanced at Gabe. "I'm sorry. We shouldn't have gone in there. And...and I'm sorry for what I said when you caught us."

The sound of the knife biting into the wood stopped.

"That piss-poor apology will figure into your sentence, I'm sure, but we'll leave that to Catherine and Gabe to decide later." She looked down at the cutting board. Most of the holes from her knife point were between the fingers, but two fingers bore distinctive marks. "Damn. I still can't get this a hundred percent. Maybe if I used a real hand, it'd up the stakes enough that my brain wouldn't let me miss." She looked at Robbie's hand resting on the bar, and he jerked it back out of sight. She shrugged and placed her own hand on the board. She started slowly, but with less aggression, so it was quieter than before. "I'm trusting there won't be any type of retaliation against Gabe after you complete whatever task Catherine gives you?" Her knife was picking up speed again. Robbie nearly fell as he scrambled off his stool, his eyes fixed on her knife and her hand.

"You're crazy, lady."

She stopped and winked at him. "Don't you forget that, or this—if you bother Gabe again in any way, you'll have to deal with either me or Catherine. And you better hope it's Catherine." She tossed the knife into the sink. "All yours, Sheriff Cofy."

CHAPTER SEVEN

Ed had stopped her with a finger to his lips, then Catherine followed as he quietly slipped past the screen door and they watched Autumn—all five-foot-five, 115 pounds of her—intimidate the two boys like a professional mobster. When she finally summoned him, Ed stepped forward.

"Come on, boys. Your parents are waiting." The boys streaked to freedom, even with the threat of parents waiting outside. "I'll make sure their parents are clear about the restitution for their behavior."

"Thanks, Ed." Catherine sucked in a breath to calm the mix of emotions tangled in her chest, in her belly. Autumn's little display was foolishly reckless, an extremely questionable method of disciplining children, and so incredibly sexy. Gabe, however, didn't seem as impressed.

"I could have beaten him if you hadn't stopped me."

Autumn moved to the sink and began washing her hands without answering Gabe's complaint.

Catherine went to Gabe and began to check her over. "Are you okay? You've got a pretty good lump on your forehead. Did Robbie hit you there?"

Gabe carefully fingered her scalp. "I think I hit it on the coffee table. My back stings a lot. I might have got some glass in it." Catherine gently pushed Gabe away so she could pull back the flaps of the ripped shirt. Gabe's back was scratched up, either from glass or fingernails. Either way, the wounds would need to be thoroughly cleaned. "I saw Jody just a minute ago. She usually has her EMT box in her truck. She can clean up your back, but I mostly want her to check out your head."

Gabe had picked up the knife Autumn left on the cutting board and began stabbing it into the wood. Catherine caught her wrist. "Don't play with—" She stared at the dark stain on the board. "Did you—" Her battle brain speed-read the signs. The blood wasn't Gabe's.

Autumn still stood at the sink with the water running. Her shoulders were shaking, and she swayed a second before her knees buckled.

Catherine sprang forward and caught Autumn in her arms before she hit the floor. When she straightened, she realized the sink was pink with watered blood.

"Her hand's bleeding. It's dripping all over the floor," Gabe said, jumping off her stool.

"Grab a clean dish towel."

Gabe was already pulling one from a cabinet drawer and wrapping it around Autumn's hand before tucking the hand up under Autumn's shirt so it wouldn't continue to dangle.

"At least she's wearing a red shirt."

Catherine stared at Gabe, who shrugged.

"The blood stains won't show up as bad."

Geez. The workings of that kid's brain never ceased to amaze her. "Jody's helping load chairs onto the trucks out by the barn. Tell her to bring her med pack." Catherine's last words were drowned out by the slamming of the backdoor screen and the slap of Gabe's tennis shoes across the deck. Catherine shook her head. She hoped Gabe didn't collapse herself after getting that hard knock on the head.

She rounded the island and laid Autumn on the sofa, then elevated her feet with a cushion. Autumn really was pretty. Not just pretty. Beautiful. She had the same wide mouth and big smile as Becki, but her lashes were darker and longer. When those lashes began to flutter, so did something deep in Catherine's belly. Autumn's full lips began to move, and Catherine withdrew, realizing she had unconsciously bent close, caught in the desire to touch her lips to Autumn's forehead...and maybe her cheek. She shook herself when she realized she'd closed her eyes for a sliver of a second to imagine how her lips tasted.

"Wha-what...oh, God. Tell me I didn't fall out in the middle of the kitchen and cause a scene." Autumn raised her hand to her brow to cover her eyes in dramatic fashion, only to bonk herself with her bandaged hand. She squinted at it. "Why does my arm look like a huge Q-tip?"

Catherine chuckled, relief washing through her. "You didn't make a big scene. Nobody was here but me and Gabe. I noticed you were swaying, then caught you before you hit the floor. The Q-tip is Gabe's handiwork. She's gone to get a friend to take a look at the damage."

"Please don't take me to a hospital. Just thinking about sitting in an ER waiting room half the night makes me nauseous." Autumn seemed to be recovering, refocusing quickly.

"Jody's an old army medic. She's had to stuff guts back into soldiers to transport them. I'm sure she can handle a cut finger."

"You really want to see me puke, don't you?"

"Sorry. Didn't know you fainted at the sight of blood and threw up at the mention of guts. I guess I shouldn't show you the fingertip Gabe found on the floor until Jody's reattached it."

Autumn stared at her. "That's the second one."

Catherine frowned. "Second what?"

"You made a joke. That's the second time you've made a joke."

This remark surprised Catherine. "You think I don't have a sense of humor?"

"You're always so broody. You need to lighten up. Gabe is broody, too, but I imagine Becki balanced her out. If I leave you two together all summer, you'll both just sit around and brood."

"Will not."

"Will, too."

"Do I need to separate you two?" Jody stood by the kitchen island, a medic box in her hand.

Gabe peeked around her. "I hate it when my guardians argue."

Catherine stood from her perch on the edge of the sofa and pushed an ottoman over. Jody sat, then carefully laid Autumn's hand in her lap to unwrap it.

"Ouch. You sliced this thumb pad pretty deep. The good news is that you got the pad, not a joint or a tendon that might affect dexterity. A couple of small stitches will fix you up."

"What's the bad news?"

"It's going to be really sore for a while, and as it heals you'll forget and grab something before you remember how sore it can be. Is that your dominant hand?"

"No. I'm right-handed."

"Good." Jody turned back to Catherine, who held out a shallow bowl and a couple of towels. "Thanks for reading my mind."

Catherine also placed a small trash can on the floor next to Autumn's shoulder. "She gets queasy at the sight of her own blood, so you might want to keep this handy."

Autumn's mouth twisted into a silent mock snarl, but her cheeks had gone from flushed to ghostly white, so Catherine settled on the end of the coffee table while Jody worked. "Who taught you that fancy knife work?"

Jody placed the bowl on Autumn's stomach and moved her hand over it to spray the thumb with a numbing agent. Catherine knew the lidocaine needle would come next, and so did Autumn, judging from the set of her jaw. "Little sting," Jody murmured. Gabe hovered close at Jody's shoulder, holding a flashlight to better illuminate the thumb and watching with fascination.

"Or are you secretly a CIA agent, posing as a social-media marketing entrepreneur?"

"What?" Autumn looked away from Jody bent over her hand to meet Catherine's gaze.

"The knife-twirling act. Pretty fancy."

"Oh. Some guy came into the bar one night when things were slow. He said he came to town for a knife and gun convention that had just ended and, after a few drinks, swiped the knife I was cutting fruit with and started twirling it. I thought it was really sick, so I asked him to show me. I wasn't too good at it, but he turned up the next night with a better, more balanced knife. He came around every night for the rest of the week and coached me."

Catherine's brain had stumbled about midway through the explanation. "You thought it was sick, so you asked him to show you?" Why would she want to learn something she thought was bad?

"Sick means way awesome." Gabe offered the translation without taking her eyes from the stitches Jody was making. "He probably wanted to jump your bones."

"Gabriella." Catherine's growled warning drew a casual shrug from Gabe. "Do you even know what that means?"

In a likely preview of her teen years ahead, Gabe rolled her eyes. "Yes. Mama gave me the sex talk when I was eight and I asked her a bunch of questions about two dogs that were gettin' it on in our yard."

"That'll do it." Autumn smiled, the distraction of conversation returning some color to her face. "But, no, he didn't want to jump my bones. He was a bear and had someone he'd met at the gun show keeping him busy during the day. That someone had to go home to family at night, so he came to the bar to talk to me. At the end of the week, he was off to another gun show in another city. That's how he made a living, selling guns and knives. But he left the practice knife for me."

"He was a Russian?" Gabe, her brow wrinkling, finally looked at Autumn.

"Russian?"

"You said he was a bear. Did you mean that he was from Russia?"

Okay, the kid could wait a few years for the lesson on labels for gay men. Catherine jumped in. "Exactly. Russians make some of the best guns on the market." She turned back to Autumn. "Well, your knife work was impressive until the part where you tried to slice off your thumb. You scared the bejesus out of those two boys. Their parents might sue you if the boys start having nightmares about someone chasing them with a knife."

Autumn grimaced. "I know. I'm already a bad guardian."

"No. It was crazy to watch," Gabe said.

"Twirling that knife got me big tips and jobs at better, more upscale bars, where I made a lot of contacts in Atlanta's business community. That last part with the fingers was just something I saw in a movie. I obviously haven't mastered it."

Jody straightened. "All done."

Autumn blinked. "Oh. Thanks. I didn't feel a thing."

"Well, you will when the lidocaine wears off. You should try to elevate and ice it until you go to sleep."

"I'll make an ice pack," Gabe said.

"I'll get that," Catherine said, stopping Gabe. "And another T-shirt for you. Jody needs to check out your back and that lump on your head."

Autumn studied Jody while she palpated Gabe's lump, checked the reaction of her pupils, and then began cleaning the scratches and cuts on her back. She had seen the silver band on Jody's left ring finger when she peeled off the blue sterile gloves to don clean ones before treating Gabe. "So…if your husband is waiting while you do this, he can come inside. It sounds like everybody else might be gone."

"Around here, Miss Swan, people just ask what they want to know." Jody glanced at her and smiled before returning to her work. "My *wife* is an ER nurse. So many folks had plans to come to Becki's memorial, she couldn't find anyone to work her shift for her. I told her Becki would understand."

"Is there a factory around here that spits out handsome butch women?"

Jody chuckled. "I haven't noticed, but you could ask Susan. That's my wife. She'll probably tell you Cat's the last eligible lesbian in town worth noticing. She let me know after our first date that I was off the market."

Autumn flushed. Probably the lidocaine in her bloodstream. "Oh, I'm not shopping. Not at all. I was making an observation. Butch isn't my type. I'm looking for someone who shares my interests—shopping, getting your nails done, spending a Saturday seeing every movie at a multiplex theater. That kind of thing."

Jody shook her head. "Well, Cat's safe then. That woman would rather be whipped than to spend all day in a dark movie theater. Even if it was pouring rain, she'd prefer curling up with a book and a good cup of coffee."

"Safe from what?" Catherine emerged from the hallway with a T-shirt for Gabe in one hand and a cold pack in the other.

"Nothing," Autumn said quickly. "Jody was telling me about Susan."

Jody repacked her medical kit and handed off the small bin holding the trash from her work rather than Autumn's regurgitated stomach contents. "Speaking of Susan, I better head that way. She gets off work in about twenty minutes, and I have a plate of food for her." She stood. "Ed said to tell you everything is cleaned up. Anything that needed to stay here is in the barn. He put the chickens up for the night, too."

❖

"Thanks, Jody. Any instructions for the walking wounded?" Catherine asked as she walked her out to the front yard where her truck was waiting.

"You need to keep an eye on both of them. Gabe seems okay, but you probably should wake her up a few times during the night to check on her. And Autumn should keep that hand elevated and iced off and on for the next twenty-four hours. It's going to throb like a son of a bitch, but a few Tylenol should make it bearable."

Catherine lowered her voice to a whisper. "Don't say *bear* around Gabe. I don't want to start that discussion again." She cleared her throat and spoke in a normal tone. "I'll take care of them."

Jody paused at the bottom of the porch stairs and turned to smile at Catherine. "I don't expect that will be much of a hardship where Becki's cousin is concerned. She's a hottie."

"Aren't you going to be late picking up Susan?"

Jody laughed and climbed into her truck, waving before turning down the long drive.

❖

Autumn was alone in the living room when Catherine went back inside. She was sitting up, her bandaged left hand resting on a pillow and holding the cold pack. In her right hand, she clutched Gabe's torn T-shirt to her chest. Tears ran down her cheeks. Catherine didn't know what to do. She looked around the room.

"Gabe's gone to look in the barn for Elvis," Autumn said, her voice low and choked. She seemed like she was going to say more but couldn't force out the words. Instead, she tucked her chin against the shirt she held as if it were a lifeline.

Catherine approached cautiously and sat on the ottoman next to the sofa. "Are you okay?"

Autumn shook her head slowly, her tears coming faster and dripping from her cheeks. When her shoulders heaved with a huge, suppressed sob, Catherine didn't stop to think. She slid from the ottoman onto the sofa and wrapped Autumn in a hug. Autumn didn't resist. She fit perfectly against her chest, and Catherine rested her cheek against Autumn's head. She smelled of soft lavender, and Catherine closed her eyes against the emotion that gripped her chest and leaked from her own eyes.

Gabe's fight with the boys had held their grief at bay, but the memorial service and Becki's image and the finality of their loss came flooding back as they sat in the quiet, surrounded by everything that was Becki.

Autumn pressed deeper into Catherine's embrace and found her voice after a few ragged sobs. "When I came for Grandma's funeral, she wanted to talk, but people kept interrupting with hugs and condolences or questions about the arrangements. So she asked me to stay afterward. Then my parents and her parents showed up and caused a scene, and I did what I do best." She began to cry again. "I left. I walked out when I should have stepped in and helped her." She rubbed the T-shirt against her cheek as if she needed the connection to walk through this memory. "I gave her this shirt the last summer I spent here. When I saw Gabe wearing it, I couldn't believe it had lasted all these years. I was shocked…she kept it even though I never came back."

"It was her favorite." Gabe, water droplets glinting among her dark curls, stood by the kitchen island. "She said the big sunflower on the front made her feel like the sun was radiating out of her chest and shining on everything around her."

Catherine sat back but kept her right arm around Autumn as she extended her left in invitation for Gabe to join them. Gabe hesitated, then snugged herself against Catherine's other side. The day had been an emotional roller coaster. Their dread of sharing their grief with so many other people, Autumn's ill-advised liquid breakfast—thank the heavens she didn't throw all that up—plus the strain of Becki so alive and flashing that big Julia Roberts smile on the video. Catherine recognized that the confrontation with the two boys, Autumn's controlled anger and scary show, then their banter to distract Autumn from the stitches going in her thumb were a bit of weird hysteria.

The day was over, though, and that reality settled over them. Becki wouldn't walk into the room and light it up with her smile. She'd never again tuck Gabe in at night, or kiss Catherine's cheek and send her home with a bag of fresh-baked goodies, or hug Autumn and softly sing their favorite song in her ear when Autumn was sad.

A huge clap of thunder made them all jump, and Catherine pulled them even tighter together. The sky seemed to open and pour rain onto the metal roof of their snug cottage, but a mournful howl sounded over the storm's drumming.

"Elvis was in the barn, curled up in his bed where he liked to nap while Mama painted," Gabe said. "I tried to get him to come inside, but he wouldn't budge."

"Did you close the doors? Maybe he's scared of the storm and wants to be inside with us now," Autumn said, sitting forward to snag the box of tissues on the coffee table, taking a few before offering it as an alternative to Gabe's use of her shirttail to wipe her nose. Gabe took the hint, and Catherine was surprised when Autumn tugged Catherine's arm across her shoulders to snuggle against her side again.

"He has a doggie door. He'll be here when he wants," Catherine explained.

They sat quietly for several long moments, listening to the rain and Elvis howl two more times. Like a twenty-one-gun salute, seven rifles fired three times. Catherine almost expected a lone trumpet to begin playing "Taps."

"Sometimes, the coyotes answer him," Gabe said.

But they heard no answering howls tonight. Not another clap of thunder. Even Autumn's constantly pinging and vibrating cell phone was silent. The room had darkened with the sky, and they simply sat and listened to the rain.

❖

Autumn jerked awake. The sun was boring through her eyelids and spiked into her eyes when she opened them. Her mouth tasted and felt like she'd been licking a glue stick. She rolled away from the window and struggled to figure out where she was. The pillow under her head smelled distinctly like sandalwood. It felt familiar. Was it a scent Becki had worn? Her eyes settled on familiar photos of Gabe. It must be Becki's scent because she was in Becki's bed. She sat up, alarm flooding her. She was in Becki's bedroom, in her bed. How'd she ended up here? Gabe would freak. She needed to get up and get out before Gabe saw her. Besides, she'd planned to be on the road to Atlanta at daybreak, and she'd obviously slept well past that. She put her hand out to push up to a sitting position and hissed when pain shot up her left forearm.

"Fuck." She stared at her bandaged thumb, and glimpses of the previous evening trickled into the conscious—make that barely conscious—part of her brain. She'd stupidly cut her thumb. Tall, butch, and married had sewed her up. Becki's, no, Gabe's torn shirt. The last she could recall was her, Gabe, and Catherine huddled on the sofa, listening to the rain. Catherine warm and solid, her arm around Autumn's shoulders strong and sheltering. Yes. She could understand why Becki had called Catherine her anchor.

But the memory of snuggling against Catherine's side was stirring more than feelings of security. Nope. Not going there. It was too ridiculous to consider. Just a weak moment of vulnerability caused by, you know, her cousin dying and the pressure of a daunting to-do list. Because she couldn't possibly be interested—

The smell of bacon penetrated her semi-panic, and her stomach growled loudly at this new information. She dangled her feet off the bed and took stock. Jeans, check. V-neck shirt, check. Shoes gone, but that was understandable. She narrowed her eyes and put her hands to her breasts. Bra, gone. Hmm.

She made the bed and found her bra neatly folded on top of her shoes in the ladder-back chair by the door. Someone obviously knew she'd slept there, so erasing evidence of her trespassing was stupid. Wait. She might be emotionally trespassing, but not illegally. She owned the house now until she died or signed it over to either Gabe or Catherine. She shook her head. She had to stop holding conversations with herself. She needed therapy. Better yet, she needed to follow the delicious scent wafting from the kitchen.

Autumn dropped her things in Gabe's room, where she'd been staying, and shuffled through the living room to see who was cooking. To her surprise, Gabe stood at the stove, flipping French toast and keeping an eye on a pan of sizzling bacon. Catherine sat at the table, sipping coffee and reading the morning paper.

"French toast and bacon?" Gabe asked.

Autumn eyed her. There was no broad smile she'd expect if Becki had been the one offering, only a raised eyebrow that perfectly mimicked Catherine. She tried to speak, but her tongue was still stuck to the roof of her mouth. She cleared her throat and dislodged her tongue. "That smells awesome, but I have to shower and hit the road."

"You've got time for breakfast," Catherine said, lowering her paper. "Dish her up a plate when it's ready, Gabe."

Autumn's jaw clenched at Catherine's assumption. Nobody told her what to do. Her parents hadn't since she was about ten years old. And some bossy butch wasn't going to now. She opened her mouth to tell Catherine that, but stopped when the bossy...uh, oh my god, wonderful, thoughtful woman held up a huge thermos, unscrewed the top, and filled the coffee mug at the place setting closest to where Autumn stood. She nearly swooned at the aroma. Her mouth watered and her stomach growled.

"When I went back to my place this morning to collect eggs and take care of the morning feeding, I brewed some Americano for you from my special blend. I see you've already added a French press to the kitchen, though, so feel free if you prefer to brew your own."

Autumn was already sliding into the chair, her eyes fixed on the steaming mug. "No, this is fine." She took her first sip, closed her eyes, and hummed. "If you tell me that you secretly love to dress up in a sexy cocktail dress and go dancing on Saturday nights, I'll have to get down on my knees right now and propose."

Gabe's laughter rang through the kitchen, and Catherine even smiled a little.

"Now that's something I'll never live long enough to see," Gabe said, nearly dropping the plate she handed over to Autumn.

"Me on my knees?"

Another burst of laughter. "No. Cat in a cocktail dress and heels. I'd have to wash my eyes out." Gabe turned off the stove and brought a plate for Catherine and herself to the table, sitting across from Autumn.

"You're really funny, kid. Keep it up. I was just thinking that the chicken coop still hasn't been cleaned."

"Aw, Cat. You said you'd take me fishing today."

"I did. But I looked in my closet this morning, and all I have to wear is the same T-shirt I wore fishing last time. I might need to go shopping at the mall first. I mean, what if we see somebody else at the lake. It'll be all over town that I wore the same shirt fishing twice in a row."

Gabe barely managed to swallow the orange juice in her mouth, then pealed off another loud round of laughter while Catherine smiled and shot glances at Autumn.

"Go ahead and make fun of the femme," Autumn said with haughty affectation, chuckling along with them while she delivered a gentle slap to Catherine's forearm.

After their laughter died down, an uncomfortable silence fell, and they all stared at their plates. Autumn looked up when a wind chime tinkled outside the window behind Gabe. A cloud beyond moved against the vibrant-blue spring sky, and the emerging sun was caught by a single pane of stained-glass at the window's center, flooding the kitchen with its rainbow-colored message. Here Comes the Sun.

Autumn nodded. Message received. She picked up the bottle of maple syrup and drowned her French toast. "It's okay, you guys. Becki wouldn't want us to mope around. If she was here, she'd laugh, too. She'd be really happy that we're becoming friends." She hesitated, tripped up by a nudge of uncertainty. "We are, aren't we?"

Catherine smiled and picked up her fork. "You're okay for a city girl."

"Woman," Autumn said, pointing her own fork at Catherine. "I stopped being a girl when I turned eighteen and was old enough to drive, vote, and sign a contract." She frowned when she tried to pick up her knife to cut up her toast. "Shit. I mean, ow." This sore thumb was a nuisance.

Gabe gave Catherine an exaggerated guess-she-told-you look, then came around the table and quickly cut Autumn's food for her. Autumn was a bit startled by the act. Maybe they both were. They exchanged tentative smiles, and then Gabe went back to her seat.

"So," Gabe said around a mouthful of syrup and toast. "What shirt are you going to wear to the fishing hole? Because, you know, I don't want to wear the same thing either. People might talk."

CHAPTER EIGHT

Autumn rubbed her eyes. Six hours on the road, then four hours answering email and reviewing her presentation for her first new potential client had kept her up until three in the morning. Then her alarm began barking at five thirty. She usually thrived on catnaps amid the fast pace of her city life. This morning, she felt jet-lagged, like she'd just flown back from the other side of the world and crossed twenty time zones. That was ridiculous, of course. But even a semi-cold shower—because nobody really turns on only the cold water and stands under it, do they?—hadn't perked her up. So she'd texted Jay at six o'clock. *Bring juice.* Only Jay would know that she was referring to energy, not fruit juice.

"Thank the goddess," she groaned when his trademark knock sounded at her apartment door. She almost resented his bright eyes, perfectly shaved face, and big smile. Damn, he looked as fresh as a tomato just picked from the garden. She groaned again. One week in the country and she was thinking like a farm wife. Wife? Her subconscious must be operating in an alternate universe today. "You look like a perfect Ken doll. I hate you."

Jay air-kissed both sides of her face, then held up a large cup and a pastry bag. "You look horribly worn out, girlfriend. But you can't hate your main man, because he brought you a triple-shot Red Eye and orange juice and a fresh-out-of-the-oven huge cinnamon roll." He looked around the apartment. "Where's the kid? I brought an orange juice and another cinnamon roll for her."

"She's with Catherine, probably until school starts. I guess I'll have to eat two." She did a brief happy dance. "All by myself."

"Who's Catherine?"

"Her other guardian. I'm co-parenting. It's complicated, but I don't have time to explain right now. I need energy and for you to catch me up on business." She set the goodies on the dining table next to her laptop and dug the treats out of the bag. "This isn't Starbucks."

Jay stood over her, his hands on his hips. "Of course not. They're from the Sweet Bean."

She peeled away a piece of the fluffy roll, studded with raisins and dripping with sugary glaze, and popped it into her mouth. She raised both eyebrows at him and hummed her approval. It seemed to melt in her mouth. "Sweet Bean?"

"It just opened last week. You know that storefront we were wondering about because the windows were covered so we couldn't see in? Well, the paper came off the windows Tuesday, and they opened Wednesday. It's a coffee house slash bakery, owned by Sasha Steele. She's the coffee expert, and her wife is a pastry chef."

She was only half listening because she was savoring another huge bite. "Should I know who Sasha Steele is?"

"You are an epic failure as a lesbian. She's like a soccer legend, retired after the last World Cup because she's like thirty-something, and that's old in soccer years."

She shrugged and tested the heat of the coffee before taking a big sip. Jay knew just how she liked it. "I don't know anything about soccer."

"They want to talk to you about handling their social-media marketing."

"But I can learn. Alexa, add 'research Sasha Steele' to my work list."

The Amazon tower lit up and recited, "Adding 'research Sasha Steele' to your work list."

The cinnamon roll was huge, so she decided to save the second one for later, when her sugar rush began to wear off. She closed the bag and set it next to the Keurig. Sighing, she thought of Catherine's wonderful coffee bar. Someday, she'd have one just like it. But only if she worked hard. She refused to think of the money from Becki that would have transferred to her account on Friday. She washed the sticky residue from her hands in the kitchen sink before returning to her laptop. "It's six thirty. Tell me what I'm doing the rest of today."

❖

"You're very quiet today. You okay?" Catherine cast her line in an efficient arc that plopped her bait and bobber about ten yards into the pond. She glanced at Gabe, who had been staring blankly at her own red-and-white one.

"Yeah. I'm good."

"You'd tell me if you weren't?" She worried again that Gabe was holding her grief inside, rather than working through it. Should she make an appointment with a child psychiatrist? Not for Gabe, but for herself so she could get some coaching on what to say or do to help Gabe. What signs would tell her that Gabe's sadness was turning into dangerous depression? She knew too well the suicide rate of soldiers returning from war. And she was aware of the high rate of suicide among teens. Gabe would be twelve in a few weeks, but it was obvious from the changes in her body that she was one of those girls who hit puberty early. To complicate things, she had the intellect of an adult. So Catherine wasn't sure how to treat her. Like a kid, like a teen, or more adult? She so needed help.

"Yeah."

They watched their bobbers ride the ripples of the water's surface. Catherine was thinking she should take Gabe higher in the mountains and teach her to fly-fish, when Gabe spoke up.

"I miss her most at night, I guess." She glanced over at Catherine. "After I climbed into bed each night, she would come in and always ask me questions."

"Questions?" This type of parenting was foreign to Catherine. She'd always put herself to bed every night with a book for company.

"Yeah. What did you learn today? What are your plans for tomorrow?"

Catherine nodded. Good questions, the second ending Gabe's day by looking ahead.

"Then she'd ask what she called a wild-card question."

"A wild card?"

"Yeah. If you could be anybody in the world for a day, who would it be? Or if you had the power to change one thing in this world, what would it be?"

"Hmm. That's a lot to think about."

"Sometimes we'd talk for a whole hour."

Catherine's days weren't that interesting—cleaning the chicken coop, adding peppers to her huge garden, Skyping with Peter on business matters. He'd saved her when she was at her darkest, when she was drowning in an abyss of night terrors, daytime flashbacks, and the remnants of physical damage that'd allowed her to opt for a military discharge rather than transfer to army financial services. She'd pretty much reached her potential there because the PTSD in her medical record would make promotions hard to come by.

It wasn't difficult to achieve her usual level of average. She'd accepted long ago that she was average in every way. She wasn't ugly, but not beautiful either. She was athletic, but never the star of any sport she played. She scored well on tests, but not exceptional. She'd given up trying to be exceptional at anything long ago, accepting that she was pretty ordinary and so were her days.

"But that's not what I've been thinking about." Gabe's voice jerked Catherine back to their conversation.

"No?"

Gabe shook her head. "You've got a bite." She pointed to Catherine's bobber bouncing in the water. It stopped without going fully under, and Catherine reeled it in. Turtle probably nibbled her bait off. Gabe watched her rebait her hook and cast out again.

"So, what have you been thinking about?" Catherine asked, settling back into her low lawn chair.

"About Mom's cousin."

"Autumn." Catherine worried that Gabe rarely spoke Autumn's name when referring to her—like a mechanism to keep her at arm's length.

"Yeah. Autumn. What kind of name is that?"

"I think it's a very pretty name."

Gabe gave her a sidelong glance, her mouth quirking into a small smile. "You think *she's* pretty."

"You don't?"

Gabe seemed to contemplate this question for a few seconds. "Yeah. She's pretty, but she's smart, too. She started her own business. I heard her talking on the phone, setting up appointments and talking about business stuff."

"Is that what you might want to do? Start your own business?"

"I don't know." She smirked at Catherine. "I'm still a kid, ya know. It's not like I have to decide tomorrow." Gabe shrugged. "I might want to be a firefighter or a doctor. Or maybe both...a medic like Jody. I like farming with you, too, but I might want to design video games. I probably could farm and design video games."

Catherine laughed. Yeah. Gabe was still a kid. "You can do anything you want. Everything you want, probably."

Something big hit Catherine's line, and they spent the next ten minutes hauling in and netting a bass Gabe declared would weigh in at nearly four pounds. She rarely fished for more than she could eat right away, so they packed their equipment and headed back to Catherine's house. The chicken coop was waiting to be cleaned, along with a checklist of other necessary chores. Catherine was ticking off that list in her head as they walked, when Gabe's question caught her off guard.

"So, are you going to ask her out?"

"What? Ask who?"

"Autumn."

Catherine sputtered. "What in the world made you ask that?"

Gabe laughed. "You should see your face."

"Punk." Catherine swung her foot out in a pretended tripping move, but Gabe hopped out of the way—just like Catherine knew she would, just like Gabe always did. "No. I'm not going to ask her out."

"Why not? She's pretty, and you don't have a girlfriend. Besides, I think she likes you. You know, likes-likes you."

"First of all, I'm fine without a girlfriend. Secondly, I'm too old for her. And third, she likes cities and shopping. I like wide-open spaces and fishing."

Gabe was quiet for a while. "You still have trouble being around a lot of people?"

Catherine sighed. "Who told you that?"

"I heard you and Mama talking one day. I was lying on her bed, reading, and the window was open. You guys were on the back deck talking. I didn't mean to listen, but I couldn't stop. I thought y'all were talking about me all those times you'd go quiet when I walked into the room. But you weren't, were you?"

"We were talking about adult stuff, Gabe. Private stuff."

"I know what PTSD is, Cat. I googled it. I know about the medicine you take when the nightmares are bad."

They'd reached the barn, so she stowed their fishing equipment and turned to grasp Gabe's shoulders.

"I want you to listen to me, Gabe. This is important."

Gabe's earnest brown eyes met hers. "Sure, Cat. I'm listening."

"You can't talk about my nightmares or the *medicine* with anyone but Sheriff Ed. He knows and understands. But if other people knew, they might say I wasn't stable enough to be your guardian. Do you understand? They might make you go live with Autumn in the city all the time. Or something worse." She stopped her panic short of threatening foster care. She didn't want to scare Gabe.

But Gabe wasn't stupid. "You mean they'd put me in a foster home." She scowled at Catherine. "You know I wouldn't tell anyone, Cat. I thought you trusted me."

Catherine pulled Gabe's slender frame into a tight hug. She didn't usually hug much, but she'd done a lot of it in the past few weeks. Becki's passing had changed everything. No. That wasn't completely truthful. Becki's passing had brought Autumn into their lives. And Autumn was changing things, with her hugs and quick wit and youthful energy.

Catherine didn't manage change easily. Changes in her

routine and crowds were triggers for her sometime fragile psyche. And cities. The press of buildings, the dark alleys and shadowed doorways screamed ambush. You'd never see the enemy coming… like the desert rats that blended with the sand. "I do trust you, kiddo. I just don't want to lose you."

Gabe wrapped her arms tight round Catherine in return. "I don't want to lose you either, Cat."

Catherine patted Gabe's back, and they let go to continue their trek to the house.

"I don't want to go to the city," Gabe said. "I want to stay with you and Elvis."

"I know. But you're growing up, Gabe. You need to spread your wings and see what else is out there in the big world. Home, me, and Elvis will always be here waiting for you."

❖

By one thirty, Autumn had given two presentations and signed both clients to contracts, including Sasha Steele and wife at the Sweet Bean. Now she was settling into a back booth at the Sweet Bean with a triple espresso and death-by-chocolate-dessert lunch to interview the woman Jay was recommending she hire as an associate.

Rachel Avery was a tall woman with a quick smile, and Autumn liked her from the moment they shook hands. She'd been cautious when Jay had admitted Rachel was gay.

"She's not obvious, is she?" Autumn asked.

Jay scowled. "Are you saying you'd discriminate against her if she is?"

"That's not fair. I just don't want AA Swan to get a reputation as being 'that gay company.'"

"What's unfair is you judging her by her outward appearance. It's the same as you taking her weight, gender, age, religion, or hair color to be a job qualification."

"Hair color?"

"Some people have preconceived opinions drawn from stereotypes of blondes and redheads."

"Okay, okay. Point taken."

Still, she was relieved that Rachel turned out to be one of those ambiguous, classically beautiful types who wore a business suit like battle dress. And she was way overqualified for Autumn's little start-up.

Rachel seemed unfazed that she was being interviewed in a back booth of the Sweet Bean, as prearranged by Jay. Or that she had to wait while Autumn finished a text to Catherine before introducing herself.

Will need G's med recs for skool app—A

"Sorry. I just got back into town and am trying to set a record for multitasking to catch up with everything. Thanks for coming on such short notice."

"I understand." Rachel smiled as she slid into the opposite side of their booth. "Jay and Evan explained the situation. Please accept my sincere condolences for your loss. I have two brothers and one sister, and I'd be crushed if I lost any of them."

"Thanks." Autumn hadn't expected Rachel to be so open, so personal.

"I have to confess that I'm very interested in your company. I flew down yesterday on the off chance Jay could fit me in your schedule this week."

She also hadn't expected such honesty.

"Your resume has a lot of job titles, but why don't you just sum up your experience and why you're interested in AA Swan."

Rachel had explained that she'd basically saved her conservative family's advertising firm by leading them into the digital-marketing field, only to have her father hire a man from outside to head the fledgling department when it took hold and began to thrive. He'd explained that his clients were more comfortable with a male, hashing out contracts over drinks or on the golf course.

"That is so...so...I don't have words for it." If she ever met the man, Autumn thought she'd want to kick him in the ass. But the injustice done to Rachel wasn't Autumn's to avenge. She needed to make this hire based on ability, not to right a wrong.

Rachel shrugged. "Actually, my father's company was too monochrome—white male Christian—for me. Not that I have anything against Christianity. I just see religion as a personal, not a public or government, matter. To be honest—"

When Rachel paused, Autumn looked up from her laptop where she was taking notes. Their gazes locked, and Autumn thought she saw a decision register in Rachel's eyes.

"To be honest, I'm not looking for a job."

"You're not?"

Rachel shook her head. "I'm looking for a partnership. I have significant capital to invest and contacts to bring to the table. I understand the technology of staying on top of changing browser algorithms and the mastering and measuring aggregation. But I'm so impressed with your innovative use of video and your instinct for picking the right format, right time, and most advantageous digital vehicle for your clients. That's what has you riding this crest of success."

Autumn closed her laptop and tried to ignore that her phone pinged with a text twice while Rachel was talking.

"I'm not looking for a partner."

"Hear me out."

Autumn shrugged. "Okay."

"From what Jay has told me, your business is going viral, and you've got potential clients clamoring for your services." She held up her index finger in a gesture to forestall any reply. "You might have set aside resources but weren't likely prepared for how fast you'd need to gear up. And you certainly didn't expect a family crisis in the middle of all this."

"I can manage." Although she might not sleep for the next year. She itched to pick up her phone when it pinged again.

Rachel rested her forearms on the table, her gaze direct but not challenging. "I'm sure you can. But without the right help, you will have casualties. Some clients will go to another company because your waiting list is too long. Others might not even consider you because they've heard your client list is too big for your staffing. There are also friends and family who are neglected because you're spending all your time at work."

Autumn drummed her fingers on the table, but she couldn't deny these were real possibilities. But if Rachel was going to be honest, then so should she. "If you have the money, the technical and business experience, and good contacts, why aren't you starting your own business? You could hire creative people to work the accounts."

Rachel sat back and nodded. "I could, but I need balance in life. You should know up front that I have a fiancée, and in a few years, we expect to adopt a child or several children. I don't want to miss special moments with them because I'm working all the time."

Autumn's phone pinged a fourth time, and Rachel pointed to it. "You better check that. It might be an emergency."

Autumn frowned but grabbed her phone and tapped in the unlock code. It pinged a fifth time and she read the string of messages.

Who is this?
Hi, Aut. I told Cat it B U.
I don't have texting on my phone. Call me. Catherine.
Lame. R texting now. Medical records. FdX or Em?
Call so I'll know this is really you. Catherine.

Ah. The farmer and the kid. Autumn frowned, then typed.

Busy. Will call later

She looked up at Rachel. "Sorry."

"If there's a fire you need to put out, go ahead."

"No, it's not work. It's, um, family." It felt odd but strangely… nice to say that. Family.

Rachel's smile was quick and wide. "This is exactly what I'm talking about. I want a partner at work so I can be a good partner at home. I don't want to be my parents and let my kids raise themselves."

Autumn turned this statement over in her mind. AA Swan was her baby. She'd never for one second considered sharing control of her company with anyone else. A week ago, however, work had been her only responsibility in life. "I don't know. I've never considered taking on a partner."

"Fair enough." It was Rachel's turn to drum her fingers on the table. "How many other candidates are you interviewing for the associate's job?"

Autumn snorted. "You mean Jay hasn't already told you that you're the only one so far?"

That quick smile again. "Actually, no. I didn't ask, and he hasn't volunteered." Rachel leaned forward again. "Suppose we negotiate."

"Negotiate?" Autumn flashed back to the evening spent enjoying coffee and pie while on Catherine's front porch and hammered out the beginnings of a plan for Gabe's future. That few seconds slowed so that she could almost feel the pleasantly warm air, smell the freshly turned soil, and hear the soothing alto of Catherine's voice accented by the woody squeaks of their rocking chairs.

"If I've managed to convince you of my qualifications today, I'll sign a contract to work as a senior associate for one year, at which time we evaluate whether to extend the contract a second year or terminate it or negotiate a partnership. If we extend the contract for a second year, then we'll either negotiate a partnership at the end of that second year or I'll seek my fortune elsewhere."

Autumn finished her third espresso while she considered this suggestion. She had done her homework on Rachel Avery, and she was everything she advertised in her resume. "That's a win-win for me. Are you sure?"

"My gut tells me this is my brass ring. I like your work, and I like this town. My fiancée is a forensic scientist and already has an offer on the table from the Georgia Bureau of Investigation to work in downtown Atlanta."

Autumn reached across the table and smiled when Rachel took her hand. "You've got a deal, Ms. Avery. I'll tell Jay to have my attorney get in touch with your attorney, and we'll hammer out a contract."

Chapter Nine

Autumn tapped the call icon on the text message while she walked the ten blocks to her apartment building.

"Hello. Who is this? Identify yourself." Catherine's voice was smooth and full...and a bit teasing.

"This is Donald Trump, and I'm going to make America great again."

"I'll have to say, Mr. Trump, that you don't sound much like yourself. You sound more like Autumn Swan doing a really bad impersonation of you."

Autumn laughed. "Why did I need to call if you knew this was my number?"

"I don't mind emails, but I hate typing on those tiny phone keyboards. If you have more than a few words to convey, then just call, for God's sake. People today don't know how to communicate face-to-face."

Autumn smiled. "Then get Gabe to show you how to FaceTime and Skype."

"I don't know about all that. Where are you? It sounds like you're walking down an interstate highway."

Only two more blocks to go. "I'm on my way back to my apartment from my meeting with a woman I hired to handle some of my workload. I'm almost home." Autumn checked the traffic and crossed another street. "Why am I calling you?"

"Do you need all of Gabe's medical records or just her vaccinations?"

"I don't know. The application isn't specific, but I'd think any school should have full records in case of an accident. They should know of any allergies to medications, or food, or things like bees. Also, her blood type, whether she has any history of heart or other problems. So, everything, I think. I'll send you an email so you can add me to your contacts."

"Okay. I'll check on getting those records first thing in the morning."

"Good." Autumn stopped by the door of her apartment building, reluctant to end their call and go inside. "Hey, Catherine?"

"Yeah?"

"Maybe I'll phone again in the next couple of days if I can find a quiet moment. You know, so you can let me know how Gabe's doing."

"Okay. Good idea."

"I'll text first to make sure you're free to talk."

Catherine laughed. "Okay. You can text me."

"Later."

"Bye, Autumn."

She ended the call, pressed her security fob against the panel to let herself into the building, then eschewed the elevator to run up the stairs with an energy that belied her few hours of sleep. Must be the espressos kicking in.

Her worries that a week away at such a crucial time would fizzle the flame of AA Swan when it'd just begun to blaze were unfounded. And she knew who'd made this happen for her. Autumn waited while Jay ended the call he was taking and made a few notes on his iPad, then wrapped him in a big hug from behind and pressed her cheek against his.

"Hey," he said, smiling. "I'm guessing that all went well?"

"It's like I only stepped away for a few minutes, not a whole week. You are amazing."

His ears reddened in an uncharacteristic flush. "I was worried about you. And I didn't want you anxious about things here."

She sat in the chair next to his and held her hand up, palm out.

"I have a proposal to make, and I want you to hear me out before you say no."

Merriment shone in his eyes as he made his sad clown face. "I love you, sweetie, but I can't marry you. I'm already betrothed to Evan."

She slapped his arm. "This is a business proposal."

He was instantly serious. "Autumn, I already told——"

She put her hand up again. "Just listen."

He nodded and sat back in his chair.

"I know you want to work for a nonprofit, but I'd like to make you a full associate retroactive to last Monday."

"You didn't hire Rachel?"

"Yes, I did. But that's another story, and I still need you. I talked with my attorney, and he'll have a one-year contract for you to review by Wednesday. The salary and commission package I want to offer is negotiable, but I think you'll find it generous. After a year, you'll have the option to go out on your own or renegotiate your financial package. It will have the normal noncompete clause, of course, if you should decide to strike out on your own in the private sector."

He was already shaking his head. "Money isn't the issue, Autumn. I thought you understood that."

"I do. But I also want to put you in charge of finding and coordinating two or three pro bono projects each year for AA Swan." She leaned toward him and clasped his hand. "We're on our way up, Jay, and I want you with me. If you stay only a year or a few years, you'll raise your profile in the business community working with me. That could land you the nonprofit job of your dreams or give you the cred to start your own. What do you say? Are you with me?" She could almost hear the wheels turning in his head.

Despite his seeming reluctance, she could see he was very interested. "I'll need to talk it over with Evan."

"Fair enough." She released his hand and scrubbed her face. The sugar and caffeine she'd been running on was fading. "I'm going to have other demands on my time besides work."

"You still haven't told me about your week in the country, the kid who's coming to live with you, and this Catherine woman you plan to raise a child with."

The memory of Catherine's smile, of her hug when Autumn left warmed her. When had she stopped seeing a tall, too-butch woman with ordinary features and started remembering her as a handsome, athletic gentlewoman with a smooth, sexy voice? Sexy? Yeah. Okay. Catherine wasn't her type, but that didn't mean she wasn't sexy…especially that tight ass in the dark jeans she wore at the memorial. Oh, yeah.

"It's a long story, and I'm not sure where to begin, but I'll try. Tonight. I'll tell all tonight." She grabbed her purse and fished out her wallet to hand him a credit card. "Call Evan and tell him we need a Thai-and-tell night. Then go online, order everything we like, and put it on my card. Do you mind going to pick it up? Around seven? I really need a power nap."

"I love Thai-and-tell nights." Jay punched a speed-dial number on his phone. "You go nap. I'll call Evan, and he can pick up the food on his way over. Should I invite Rachel? I don't know if she told you, but she's staying with us."

"Absolutely. She's going to be part of the family now." Autumn stood and hugged him again. "I don't know what I'd do without you."

❖

"You're like a mom now?" Evan and Jay stared at Autumn as if she were growing a second head.

"You sound like that's the most ridiculous thing in the world." She scowled at them. "I'm very responsible, more than financially stable with the tidy sum my cousin left me. So is Catherine. Besides, Gabriella comes with her own trust to cover her expenses."

Evan waved off her indignation. "You are well situated financially, and you've been taking care of yourself since you were a kid. But that's just it."

Jay nodded his agreement to what Evan had left unspoken.

"What's just it?" Her defenses were rising. They were supposed to be her two best friends. They were supposed to support her, not drag her down.

"Autumn, hon, you're good at taking care of yourself, but not someone else. Kids demand a lot of time—teacher conferences, soccer practice, music recitals, and shopping for clothes. Well, on second thought, you'll be a natural at shopping."

"That's true," Jay said. "But kids need a regular schedule so they get enough sleep, do their homework, and make it to school on time." He waved his arm over the cardboard and Styrofoam containers that were the remnants of their Thai dinner. "They can't live on takeout. It's not healthy. You'll have to learn to shop for groceries and cook like normal people."

"I grocery shop."

"For real food," Jay said. "Not just coffee, soda, snacks, and a few frozen lean dinners."

"I grew up on hot dogs, ramen noodles, and cheap boxes of mac and cheese. It didn't hurt me. Besides, she'll get lots of healthy food when she's with Catherine."

"Hold on there, guys." Rachel waved her chopsticks between them and Autumn to interrupt their back-and-forth "Nobody has a track record as a parent until they are one."

But Autumn knew Jay was right about some points. Warming things in the microwave was the extent of her cooking abilities. "I'll take cooking lessons. I bet Catherine can cook. I'll ask her to teach me when I go back. Or she can probably tell me who I can hire there to give me a crash course. I bet I can be a great cook."

Jay and Evan shared a "when pigs fly" look that deflated her defense, and she wanted to shake her head. They were perfect together, almost finishing each other's thoughts. Would she ever meet someone like that? The yang to her yin?

"Don't listen to them, Autumn. Kids are easy. Didn't you say this one is almost twelve years old? They're nearly self-sufficient at that point. They have their own friends and busy schedules with school and after-school activities." Rachel gave Autumn a thumbs-up. "Jay and Evan are projecting their own parenting insecurities onto you. I had two younger brothers that I practically raised because my parents worked all the time. You've got this."

Evan shook his head. "I love you, Rachel, but you don't know Autumn as well as we do. Routine isn't even in her vocabulary. She eats and sleeps only when her body demands food and rest. She's a workaholic. She never stops, even when she's supposed to be relaxing."

"I do not."

"Tell her, Jay."

Jay nodded. "Remember last month when Evan hooked you up with his friend's sister, and we even made it a double date so you'd feel more comfortable?"

"Yeah, but—"

"We ended up taking her to the theater with us because you turned dinner into a sales meeting when the restaurant's owner visited our table to say hello."

"Stop it." Rachel, who was more Catherine's age than theirs, used her big-sister voice, which was really close to a mommy voice. "Why don't you tell us about your new charge?"

Autumn nodded, taking note of how Rachel's tone shut the guys up. Catherine had a similar commanding tone, but hers sounded more like a drill sergeant's, and she rarely used it. Clearly, she needed to develop a voice like theirs for her arsenal. She'd practice later. What was Rachel's question? Gabe. Right.

"Okay." How should she describe Gabe? Damn. She wished she'd taken a photo. "Gabriella—she prefers to be called Gabe— isn't what I'd have expected. Becki, my cousin, was beautiful, blond and feminine in a girl-next-door kind of way. She was artistic and creative, open and gregarious." She shook her head. "Gabe is so different."

"How do you mean?" Jay picked up another spring roll and took a big bite. "I love these things."

"She might be artistic like Becki, but she leans more toward brainy. She's…she's…I don't know how to explain this, but she feels like an old soul one minute and an eleven-year-old kid the next. She's curious about everything, mostly how things work—technology, science, that sort of stuff. I met with her counselor at school." She paused, because she could hardly believe it herself. "Gabe's IQ has tested to be about one-forty."

"Wow." Evan's eyes were big. "That's really smart."

Autumn nodded. "I need to find a school here that can challenge her. Her trust can pay for private school, but she's not going to any boarding-school situation. Catherine and I agree on that. Kids need family. They're not animals you send off to be trained."

Rachel cocked her head. "Who's Catherine? You've mentioned her a lot."

Autumn flashed on Catherine in jeans and a crisp white shirt. Jay nudged Evan, who nodded. What was that about? She frowned at them. "Um, Catherine is the neighbor, the farmer next door to Becki, who arranged before her death for the two of us to be co-guardians. Gabe worships Catherine and tags along after her all the time. In fact, Gabe is more like Catherine than Becki in a lot of ways."

"In what way?" Jay had been fishing at every chance for more about Catherine, and she couldn't imagine why.

"Gabe's tall and...outdoorsy." She didn't want to use "tomboyish" because she believed physically strong girls shouldn't be described as boyish. They're girls. Strong girls. "She's in that skinny stage where her muscles are trying to catch up with her bones' growth spurt, but she moves like an athlete. She'd rather go fishing with Catherine than shopping. I know that alone doesn't mean anything, but she has a strong budding-lesbian vibe. I'm not sure she has a lot of friends at school."

"Why not?" Jay's expressive face had empathy written all over it. He'd been bullied at school once he came out as gay.

"Well, for starters, she's extra smart and isn't interested in what the other girls care about, like boys and clothes. And, well, she's obviously biracial in a small, rural town."

"Where's her father? Is he deceased?" Rachel asked.

"I don't think so. Becki's lawyer said he wasn't a US citizen and had signed over his parental rights and left the country when Gabe was still an infant. So he's not really a factor in Gabe's makeup, other than his DNA."

"She sounds interesting."

"She really is." Autumn wondered what Gabe and Catherine might be doing right now. "Oh, and she has a dog, Elvis."

Evan laughed. "Elvis really isn't dead?"

Jay high-fived Evan for responding exactly like he had the first time Autumn had mentioned Elvis.

"Nope. Not dead." She shook her head and grinned. "But he ain't nothing but a hound dog."

Evan and Jay howled. Literally.

Autumn grew serious again once they quieted. "Actually, I don't know if Elvis belongs to Catherine or Gabe." She paused. "I'm not sure if that matters since they live in the same house now."

"What about your cousin's house?" Jay asked.

"See? That's one of the things I haven't figured out. The house is technically mine now. Gabe can't live there alone, so she's staying at Catherine's. I guess I'll sleep there when I visit, which I don't think will be that often. So, should I rent it out? It seems weird to do that with her right next door." She threw up her hands. "I just don't know. I can't think about all this because I need to focus on my business right now."

"You haven't told us much about Catherine," Rachel said.

Jay glared at Autumn. "She's right. No dodging. Spill."

"I told you that she owns the farm next door and takes Gabe fishing."

Evan shook his head. "We want details. What does she look like? Is she married, divorced, single? Gay, straight?"

Autumn thought back. Did she know for sure? "She's tall."

Jay snorted. "Everybody seems tall to you, short stuff."

Autumn stuck her tongue out at him. Mature, right? She gathered her thoughts. "She has straight brown hair, about shoulder length, that she pulls back in a ponytail. But not a cheerleader ponytail. More of a metro-man type—several inches above her nape." She pointed to her own head to indicate what she meant.

"She's not stocky, but really strong. When I cut my thumb, I sort of passed out in the kitchen. It bled a lot."

Jay grimaced in empathy when she held up her bandaged digit.

"But Catherine apparently caught me and carried me into the living room. I don't remember, because I was passed out, but Gabe told me later that Catherine just scooped me up and carried me to the sofa."

"Swoon," Evan declared, his hand pressed against his chest. "All you needed was a grand staircase for her to climb with you in her arms. That was the best scene in *Gone with the Wind*. I fell in love with Clark Gable the first time I saw that movie."

"Does she have a girlfriend?" Jay asked.

"Didn't meet one." Autumn gave Jay a pointed glare. "Farmer isn't my style, so don't get any ideas about matchmaking."

"What color are her eyes?" Evan asked.

"Brown." Autumn answered without thinking, then narrowed her eyes at Evan. "Why does that matter?"

Evan grinned. "Just checking to see if you'd noticed."

Autumn's face heated. "I notice a lot about everything. That's what makes me a good businesswoman."

"You're blushing," Jay said.

"Hot flash from the curry." She had to put a halt to this before Jay started plotting. He was always scheming to match her up with an eligible woman. "Catherine is very nice but too serious, too butch, hates city living, and sort of…beat up."

Jay and Evan leaned forward, their eyebrows raised. "Beat up?" they asked in unison.

Damn it. She'd drawn more interest, rather than cooled it. "She's…I don't know…sort of weathered. I don't mean her face really. She's not unattractive, but she isn't what you'd call beautiful. She just acts older than I think she really is. Everybody seems to know her, but it's clear she'd rather go unnoticed."

"Maybe she's hiding out." Jay had an active imagination. "Like in the witness protection plan. Or she's someone famous who's dropped out of sight because they couldn't stand the constant spotlight. Wait. I know. She had an affair with somebody famous or the wife of somebody famous and was bought off. Now she's keeping a low profile and pining for her lost love."

Autumn laughed. "Or maybe she's just an ordinary person content to live an ordinary life. Some people have no ambition. Trust me. I was raised by two of them." She chewed on her lip, uneasy with that depiction of Catherine. "I don't want to give a bad impression of her. She seems very steady. In a video Becki made before her death, she called Catherine her anchor."

Rachel gathered the empty food containers and carried them to the trash disposal in the kitchen. "So don't stress. There's no harm in letting the house stay empty for a while. It's touchy. Gabe could see selling or renting it as you trying to erase memories of her mother. On the other hand, keeping it like it is could hinder her from moving forward with her life. But it sounds like you have an able co-guardian. Talk to Catherine about it. Since she's around Gabe more right now and knows her better, she should be able to advise you about what to do."

Autumn brightened. "I will. Thanks, Rachel."

Jay came around to wrap her in a tight hug. "You have a village here, and it sounds like you do there, too. Let us help. Let your farmer woman help. You don't have to do this by yourself."

That was just it. She'd always done everything herself. She didn't know how to live in a village.

❖

"You haven't told her?"

Catherine rubbed her forehead, holding the phone to her ear with her other hand. "No. Apparently, her business made a breakthrough almost right at the time Becki passed away, so she was dealing with a lot and didn't ask to go over the financials very thoroughly."

"You dodged a big bullet, Cat."

"I know, Pete. One you should have taken care of a long time ago."

"Hell, she hasn't spoken to me or her mother in years. Becki and I planned to sit her down after Mom's funeral and explain everything, but my asshole brother and his trashy wife showed up and started yelling that Daddy meant the farm to be his, but his own daughter and her black brat were stealing it out from under him."

"I'm afraid she had a skewed memory of that, too," Catherine said. "She's really smart. At some point, she's going to have time to track down where Becki got all that money and the investment that's still pouring money into Gabe's trust each month."

"I need to visit. It'll go better if we bring it up rather than wait for her to find it. I just don't know how to justify hiding it from her all these years."

"She might be an adult now, but she's still your child. You need to remember who's the parent. You did keep a secret, but you had good reasons to when she was a kid. You left plenty of clues once she got older, but she didn't want to let go of her childhood resentment and see the truth."

"You are an extraordinary person, Catherine Daye."

"No. I'm just an ordinary person who was in the right place at the right time."

"So when do you think is the right time for me to come talk to my daughter? I want to clear this up. I've missed too much of her life, and now I'm missing out on Gabe's life. She's effectively my granddaughter now, you know."

Catherine chuckled. "I hadn't thought about it that way, but Gabe will be surprised to have a grandfather other than the one Becki's warned her to stay away from. I wouldn't advise that you come yet. Gabe needs some time to bond with Autumn, I think. And I don't want to mess that up."

"You like her? Has she turned out okay despite mine and Mari's shortcomings as parents?"

"She's pretty awesome, Pete. You won't be anything but proud when you see the woman she's become."

❖

Catherine was tediously typing into a spreadsheet when her phone pinged. She pounced on it so quick, it slipped from her hand,

and she juggled it for a few tense seconds before she got a solid grip on it and read the incoming text. It'd been nearly five days since Autumn had said she'd call when she got a quiet minute, and Catherine had kept her phone charged and in reach the entire time. She hated texting until Gabe showed her how to speak her message and let the phone type her reply.

What are you doing? Busy?

I'm charting fertilizer applications and rainfall into a spreadsheet.

What are you wearing?

Nothing. You? She shook her head as her brain filtered that reply before her fingers began typing. Ah. Let's see I'm-too-hip-for-the-hicks top this.

My bunny pajamas.

Seriously?

When I pull the ears down and stroke them, it helps me fall asleep.

Open the email I just sent you and click on the Hangouts invite.

And I don't have to look for slippers if I get up at night because they already have feet in them.

Open the email and click on the invite.

Just have to remember to lock Elvis out or he tries to bite me in the cottontail.

CLICK ON THE INVITE

Catherine grinned and clicked on the invite in her email. Gabe had set it up for her a couple of nights before and taught her how to use the software that let them video-chat together.

"You brat."

Catherine laughed at Autumn's crossed arms and pouting lips when she saw what Catherine was really wearing, her usual T-shirt. The webcam was too close to show the skin-hugging navy boxers that completed her sleepwear.

"When you least expect it, I'll get you back for that little trick," Autumn said, unfolding her arms and wagging her finger at Catherine's image on her screen. "I just wanted to know if you were decent so we could chat."

Catherine stopped mid-chuckle and nearly choked on her own saliva when Autumn dropped her arms to reveal her sleepwear—a thin, ribbed tank that nearly outlined her erect nipples. Then a camera adjustment on Autumn's end raised the view to cut off right above her breasts. Catherine had no idea where her bold move came from, but she sat back and answered Autumn's raised eyebrow with a nonchalant lift of her shoulder.

"So, how has your week been?" she asked.

Autumn seemed to accept the move back to safer ground. She cocked her head as if tallying the day in her head. "Extremely hectic. My part-time assistant and longtime friend, Jay, graduated Emory, and I hired him as an associate. I also hired a very experienced senior associate with an option to consider a partnership in a year or two."

"Wow. Were you looking for a partner?"

"No. And honestly, I'm not sure I can share control of my company with anyone else." Autumn looked away, as if that admission embarrassed her.

"I can understand that." Catherine wanted to choose her words carefully. "Sharing the workload, though, can sometimes increase your yield exponentially."

"Did you grow up in a commune?"

"No. Not at all." Catherine shook her head, but she didn't want to go into the details of how she grew up. Peter had told her about the very lean years he, Mari, and Autumn had suffered through, so she didn't think Autumn could feel much sympathy for her poor-little-rich-girl childhood. "Working together for at least a year sounds like a great way for you guys to find out how you do together."

"Unlike us. Becki just threw us together." Autumn looked pensive. "Except she knew both of us and sort of decided for us, didn't she?"

Did Becki do that simply for Gabe's sake? Or did she have a dual motive? That seemed to be the elephant in the room as they stared through cyberspace at each other. Nah. They were too different. Becki had to see that. Autumn was glitz and glam, a mover and shaker. Catherine was a flower on the wallpaper of life. She built the stages, held the spotlight, ushered the audience for people like Autumn who became the stars.

"What will you do tomorrow?" Catherine asked.

"Jay and I plan to review analytics on a couple of new clients. We'll look at their page-view numbers, unique visitors, audience-engagement numbers, chart what they've been doing and how well it's been working. And we'll compare them to their competitors. Most companies are setting goals to beat their competition, which are often too low. We want to set and meet goals that reflect their potential."

"That sounds—"

Autumn laughed. "Boring. I know. But it's not. Analyzing data is like a treasure hunt. You mine for the gems your client has been ignoring, turn them into profit, and voilà. They think you're a genius. The truth is that digital is so new, most companies are just learning how to make it work for them. The market will get much tougher once more people figure it out. But enough about me. What will you do tomorrow?"

"If the forecast holds up, I'll turn under the fields on either side of my front yard and the one next to Becki...I mean your house. I'm working with the state organic farmers' association to test different natural fertilizers. We'll plant corn over at your place and vegetables in my fields." Catherine hesitated. "We haven't talked about it, but I lease Becki's fields. I hadn't really thought about it until just now, but we can discuss the agreement when you come back."

Catherine was suddenly staring at the top of Autumn's head because Autumn was staring at her lap.

"Yeah. About that. I've still got so much to do. I'm not going to make it back this weekend like I planned. I need at least another week here."

"It's fine. Gabe's fine. She's still up and down emotionally, and she really doesn't want to go back to school. She says everybody will be weird because her mother died, and they already see her as an oddity."

"She said oddity?"

"No. That's my word, and you know it." God. Did she just flip Autumn the finger? Well, so what. The little tease deserved it. "She said something like 'spaz-o-matic.' I don't think that's a real word, but it gets the meaning across."

Autumn laughed. "How many weeks left?"

Catherine checked the calendar on her phone. "Three. Four, if you count the end-of-grade testing week."

"I'm taking for granted she had perfect grades, considering her IQ."

"Yeah. But she still has to go to school a certain number of days to pass."

"Most school systems have home-school programs and special exceptions allowed for children who can't keep regular school schedules…like a child actor or one who has a serious illness. I'll do some research on your state. Maybe she won't have to go back this year. Especially since she'll be enrolling here in the fall."

"How about I call Janice, and maybe Gabe's school counselor, to see if they think schooling at home or going back with the other kids will be best for her emotionally."

"You're right." Autumn looked down and frowned. "I should have thought of that."

"Autumn." Without thinking, when Autumn looked up,

Catherine touched the cheek of her screen image. "That's why Becki wanted Gabe to have a team, co-guardians. We have each other's back."

"Yeah, okay." Autumn's mouth slowly curled into a smile. "Does that mean I'm the mommy and you're the daddy?"

"Brat. I'm hanging up now." But Catherine was laughing as she said it.

"Okay."

"Good night, then."

"Cat?"

"Yeah?"

"You could call me, too. Anytime. Tomorrow night or whenever."

Catherine's breath caught. "Sure. I'd like that."

"Good night, then."

The screen reverted to the app sign-in, but all Catherine could see was Autumn's parting smile. It seemed…shy?

CHAPTER TEN

Autumn climbed out of her car and groaned as she stretched. She was too young to be feeling so old and tired. She'd intended to return to Elijah within a week, but that had stretched into two, then three, and now four had passed since she'd stood in front of Becki's house. Her house. No, not hers. She was only holding on to it until Gabe came of age.

She was mentally and physically tired.

They'd signed ten more clients, doubling her stable of accounts. Jay and Evan had finally set a wedding date, likely inspired by Rachel and Samantha, who had finally admitted to each other that neither wanted a big wedding. They promptly eloped and were settling into their new home as a married couple. The honeymoon was postponed until ski season, their favorite pastime.

With Jay and Rachel's help, she'd leased office space large enough for the three of them, along with an admin to handle the work Jay used to do since he was working accounts now. Jay and Evan had sublet Autumn's sunny little apartment, and she'd moved into a much larger, though more traditional space about six blocks from the exclusive private school where she thought she'd have to promise her firstborn to enroll Gabe. Turned out that when they saw Gabe's test scores, all she had to promise was to maintain their social-media presence and policies pro bono and write a check for an exorbitant amount of money. Good thing that was all they wanted, though, because she was never going to do that birthing-a-baby thing. No, ma'am. She'd seen that on television once, and it had scarred her for life. No firstborn in her future. That's why there were orphans. So traumatized people like her could adopt.

Considering all that, she should be standing in Elijah County feeling proud of all she'd accomplished. Instead, she was scared to death.

Even though she and Catherine had been chatting often…like about every other night, the next month would be the really hard part. She had to earn her right to be included in the Catherine-and-Gabe Club.

It wasn't fair that Gabe already worshipped Catherine, or that they shared a common interest in everything outdoorsy. But it really wasn't about Catherine's already established relationship with Gabe. Her dread was something she'd walled off years ago: that sick, helpless feeling of being outside the circle, excluded on the playground, in the school lunchroom, from parties and everything else. The fact that she was an adult now, the owner of her own company, and had a few really good friends never seemed to kill the lonely little girl inside.

Before she could wallow any deeper in her pity party, Elvis rounded the house and began barking his head off. She started to jump on the hood of the car, then realized his half-length tail was sweeping back and forth as he literally hopped toward her, his mouth wide in a panting happy dog grin. His barks were not aggressive, but happy yips. Well, someone was glad to see her. He grasped her hand, gently but firmly, in his mouth and tugged her toward the side of the house.

"Okay, okay. I'm coming."

He released her hand once she was moving in the right direction, then ran ahead. She stopped cold when she rounded the house. About thirty yards away, Catherine turned to see who Elvis had found. The weathered brown fedora was the same, as was the short ponytail sticking out a few inches above Catherine's nape. Even the faded blue T-shirt was familiar. But the long, tanned legs left bare from the mid-thigh fringe of her cut-off jeans to the top of her running shoes were a new, very pleasant addition. The late afternoon seemed to grow hot, and the air thickened. Autumn fanned her face, then stopped when she realized how revealing her gesture might be. Crap. Maybe Catherine would think she was fanning away gnats.

"Hey," she called out, then tried to stroll casually to where Catherine stood next to an ancient tractor. Only the lower half of Gabe was showing since she was kneeling on the other side of the tractor.

Catherine's smile transformed her face into the woman of her late-night talks...but ten times better. Some things didn't show up well on a computer screen, no matter how good the resolution. Catherine actually had a faint dimple when she smiled, and the eyes Autumn had remembered as dark were actually the color of very rich chocolate.

"Hey, you did make it."

"Yeah," Autumn said, biting back the defensive retort that dropped from her brain and onto her tongue. She had promised twice before that she was coming, then canceled the morning she was supposed to get on the road. "I finally got everything lined up, and I'll be able to work from here for a while unless there's a crisis of some kind."

Catherine's smile grew. Yep. That was definitely a dimple. Autumn's traitorous libido warmed again, and she realized she was smiling back. No. They weren't smiling and staring at each other. They were just saying hello. Because Autumn wasn't attracted to butch women. Or women who liked country living. She eyed the old tractor they were repairing. Rural and poor. Wait. Becki wasn't poor. Neither was Catherine, considering the financial windfall Autumn knew she'd received from Becki's estate.

"Found it," Gabe sang out. She ducked under the tractor to emerge on their side and triumphantly held up a short, frayed wire. "Look here." She held it out to Catherine. "The insulation is worn away, and the wire was touching the frame of the tractor, shorting out the electrical system."

"Good job," Catherine said. "My hands are too big to get into that small space. I would have had to take half the engine apart to reach it."

Gabe grimaced at her skinned knuckles. "Mine are almost too

big." She looked at Autumn's hands. "Maybe Aut can put the new wire in. Her hands are smaller." Gabe's eyes held a hint of challenge, but it was difficult to be intimidated when she had grass sticking out of the adorable black corkscrew curls that fell onto her forehead and a cute smudge of grease on her left cheek.

"Only after I see with my own eyes that the battery is fully disconnected." Autumn didn't comment on the shortening of her name somewhere other than in a text. She wasn't sure if she liked it. Nobody had given her a nickname before. That is, if you didn't count the nasty one uttered by stupid boys and mean girls in high school. Gabe routinely shortened Catherine's name to Cat, so this nickname felt like her acceptance letter or a tattoo that indicates you're officially a member of the gang. Yeah. She smiled at them both. "And only after I go visit the ladies' room." She walked backward a few steps, realizing that the pressure low in her belly might be her bladder, not her libido, talking. "Two large lattes and only one pit stop means I'm going to be doing the pee-pee dance if I don't hurry."

Gabe's laughter followed Autumn's sprint into the house.

❖

Catherine was relieved to have another adult on hand to share the parenting load and, at the same time, worried Autumn wouldn't have the patience to deal with Gabe, who had been on an emotional roller coaster during the past month.

The relaxed, happy Gabe had worked on the tractor with Catherine that afternoon and seemed genuinely glad when Autumn arrived. But the moody, depressed Gabe was pushing her food around her dinner plate now, and Catherine had no clue what had flipped her switch. She never did.

"My burger is great," Autumn said. "Aren't you hungry, Gabe?"

Gabe shrugged. Yep. She was in one of her silent moods.

Autumn put her burger down. "I was surprised to see an Xbox 360 in Becki's room. Was she a gamer?"

"Not really. We played some games together." Gabe didn't

look up at Autumn as she answered but shot a sideways glance at Catherine.

"Becki moved it into her room after she found that Gabe was gaming most of the night after Becki went to bed." Catherine aimed a pointed stare at Gabe as she ratted her out.

Autumn laughed. "I've done that before. It's hard to stop sometimes."

Gabe perked up. "You have an Xbox?"

"Xbox, PlayStation. I actually have one of those old Space Invaders arcade games in the corner of my living room. Sometimes the retro games are really fun."

"Shut up!"

"Gabe." Catherine frowned at her. "You don't tell people to shut up."

Autumn laughed again. "It's an expression of exclamation. Like you might say 'get out' but you're not telling me to leave."

Catherine's face heated. "I knew that." She felt foolish because she did know it. She was so deep into parent mode, she'd forgotten herself. Damn. Autumn must think her an old, out-of-touch idiot. And that bothered her. A lot more than it should have.

"So, what type of games do you like?" Gabe asked.

"Mostly games that involve mysteries you have to solve or fantasy worlds. I really haven't had time lately, but the last I played was the *Star Wars* one."

Catherine began to clear the dishes while Gabe and Autumn launched into a lively discussion about gaming. She had nothing to contribute to the conversation. Was she really expecting to co-parent with somebody who seemed at times to be as much a kid as Gabe?

"Don't tell anyone, but I also really like fighting and battle games."

"Yeah? My friend Henry has *Call of Duty Black Ops*. It's awesome," Gabe said.

"No kidding. I love that one."

Catherine gripped the sink. Her vision darkened, and the sounds of automatic gunfire, shouts, and explosions filled her ears. Images of soldiers, her soldiers, bleeding, dying flashed through her mind in sync with the pop-pop-pop of single shots. She whirled to face Gabe and Autumn. "Battle is NOT a game."

They stared at her, Autumn's mouth agape and Gabe's face screwing up.

"Not everything is about you," Gabe spat out as she shoved her chair back and ran from the kitchen. Autumn flinched when Gabe's departure was followed seconds later by the loud slamming of a door in the adjacent hallway.

Catherine's head spun with the effort to stay in the present. Anxiety squeezed her chest. She needed air. She focused on the screen door, but her feet were lead, every step a struggle. She finally stumbled onto the back deck. But days were long this time of year and the sun still too bright, the air too warm and heavy. She made it to the steps before her legs gave out, and she grabbed the railing as she sank down to sit. Closing her eyes, she fought to slow her rapid gasps. Something warm and solid pressed against her side. Elvis. She dug her fingers into his fur when he licked at the sweat trickling down her neck. She was so dizzy she felt sick. No, she couldn't pass out.

Then something very cold pressed against her nape, and a cool, damp cloth wiped along her face. Soft murmuring replaced the sounds of battle, and her chest began to loosen. She concentrated on taking long, slow breaths.

Her heart still pounded, but her vision cleared, and she grabbed the hand holding the cool cloth. "Sorry. I'm sorry. I'm okay now." Her hands still shook, and Elvis moved in front of her while Autumn took his place next to Catherine.

Autumn, eyes bright with concern, gently flipped their hands so that the cloth was in Catherine's but didn't let go.

Catherine turned her head, unable to hold Autumn's gaze. She was deeply embarrassed, but Autumn needed an explanation…for Gabe's sake. She just didn't think she could do that right now. "You should check on Gabe."

Autumn released Catherine's hand, leaving the cloth, and laid down the cold compress she'd been holding to Catherine's nape.

"I will in a bit. Let's give her some space, so she can calm down. I always needed it when I was her age and ran to hide in my room. I was probably a little high-strung, and I think Gabe might be the same." Autumn's smile was soft when Catherine looked back at her, and she couldn't remember why less than an hour before she'd been questioning Autumn's maturity and ability to parent. She knew better from the long conversations they'd had so many nights. Elvis seemed to agree. He was looking at Autumn like she was his queen.

Catherine shook her head. "I don't know if I'm handling things right with her. She treats me like I'm her shelter. Then the next minute, she goes silent and shuts me out." She pulled the tie from her hair to free it, then combed it back with her fingers. The fine strands were damp with sweat. She needed a shower. "I'm afraid she's bottling everything up and not properly grieving."

"Sometimes your anger and your sadness get all mixed up, and it's hard to separate them." Autumn's chin dropped to her chest, and they were quiet for a long time before Autumn spoke again. "Anxiety attack?"

"Not really. But something like that." Shame heated her ears and face again.

A cow lowed in the distance, and Canada geese honked as they flew overhead in formation, then disappeared behind the treetops near one of the farm's ponds.

"It was a flashback, wasn't it? From your time in the army?" Maybe they did need to talk about this, even if Catherine wasn't ready.

"They've been rare in the past couple of years, but more frequent in the past month. I'm not sure why. Probably the stress of Becki being sick, then dying, and then wondering if I'm totally screwing up with Gabe."

"Does Gabe know about the flashbacks?"

"Yes. Becki taught her..." Catherine closed her eyes and felt Elvis rest his head on her knee. "Taught her what to do if I freak out."

"Is there any danger you'd hurt her when one happens?"

"She knows not to touch me and to let Elvis handle it."

Autumn paused and looked down at Elvis's head resting on Catherine's knee. "Oh. I guess I thought he belonged to Gabe and Becki." She brushed his head with her fingertips and scratched lightly behind his ears. "But I'd heard dogs are being trained to help people who suffer from PTSD."

"Actually, Elvis hasn't been trained and doesn't really belong to either of us."

"But he had that harness on at the lawyer's office."

"It's pretty easy to buy one on the internet."

"Then how does he know what to do, if he's never been trained?"

How did she explain Elvis? He was a plain, brown, forty-five-pound mutt with bloodlines as tangled as a child's fishing line. His ears half stood, half flopped, and his tail appeared to have stopped growing when it reached half the length it should be. As ordinary as he seemed on the outside, there'd always been something extraordinary about Elvis. His brown eyes held an eerie intelligence, and his compact frame radiated something intangible that called to the vulnerable near him.

Sensitive to Catherine's anxiety around crowds, Becki had reserved a table at the edge of the outdoor seating at a marina on the nearby lake. She knew that being near water soothed Catherine, and Elvis settled next to Catherine's chair. While they waited for their food, a boy approached. Catherine judged him to be between thirteen and fifteen years old, arms and legs too long and thin, waiting for his body to catch up. Braces on his teeth and red splotches of acne added to his awkwardness.

"Can I pet your dog?" he asked, averting his eyes as he spoke.

Becki smiled warmly at the boy. "You sure can." The boy laughed when Elvis offered his paw to shake, then gently stroked Elvis's head until he was called to return to the table he shared with an older couple.

"I need a dog just like this," he said as he stood to leave. "Thanks for letting me pet him."

"Catherine?" Autumn's voice shook her from the memory. "Are you okay?"

Autumn's shoulder was inches away but no longer pressed against hers. She shook herself mentally. Autumn probably thought she was losing her grip on reality again. "I'm good. Just remembering a time when Becki and Elvis took me to the marina for dinner once. What was the question?"

"Who takes care of Elvis?"

"Sometimes me. Sometimes Becki would. He just showed up one day and never left. He decides where he stays each night." She paused. "He always seems to stay with whoever needs him most."

Autumn touched Elvis's head. "When I was Gabe's age, I needed a dog just like him."

Elvis's ears went up when something buzzed, and Catherine could feel the vibration in the wooden step she was sitting on. Autumn reached into her back pocket and pulled out her phone. She tapped the screen, read a text, then typed a quick reply.

Still wound tight from her flashback, Catherine wanted to snatch the phone from her hand and throw it into the woods. What if Autumn's phone addiction transferred to Gabe? Not if she could help it. She wiped the cloth she still held over her face, but she couldn't wash away her irritation, so she stood. "You're probably tired from driving all day. I'll go collect Gabe. Morning comes early on the farm."

"I'm almost done here." Autumn's thumbnails tap-danced on the phone's screen. "I'll be right in. Don't leave just yet."

Catherine didn't reply as she headed inside and found Gabe in Becki's room, glaring at the television screen as she manipulated the Xbox controls.

"I'm staying here tonight...at my house." Gabe hadn't waited for Catherine to speak and didn't look away from the game. "Autumn will be here."

"Okay." Catherine's irritation dissolved into deep, sad fatigue. Dusk had begun to fall, and the living room had darkened Becki's cheerful décor to monochrome. Autumn stepped out from the shadows. "She wants to stay with you."

"Will you be okay? Maybe we should all stay together." Autumn stepped close and touched Catherine's arm. "We're a team, remember?"

Catherine closed her eyes. Autumn smelled like freshly washed sheets warming on the clothesline. Like honeysuckle in full bloom. The odor of blood and guns and ruptured innards on scorching sand was gone. She opened her eyes and bent to kiss Autumn's cheek. Catherine touched her fingers to Autumn's opposite cheek and struggled against the urge to kiss her lips. "Thank you. I'll be fine. You've chased it away, but I could use a little solitude."

Autumn covered Catherine's hand, trapping it against her cheek a little longer. "I forgot that you've gone from living alone to having someone else with you constantly. I'll watch over Gabe. It'll give us a chance to get to know each other a little. Go take care of yourself."

Catherine nodded and brushed her lips against Autumn's cheek again. "Good night." She gently slid her hand from under Autumn's and slipped out the front door.

CHAPTER ELEVEN

H oly crap." Autumn's brain stuttered.

She and Gabe had been running down a city street, shooting zombies that popped out from alleys, doorways, and overturned cars. Catherine stood at the end of the street by a sign that read Safe Zone, beckoning for them to hurry. A crowd of zombies was gaining on them, arms reaching for them. She heard barking that grew louder and louder until a pack of zombie dogs was nipping at their heels. Her phaser was empty, so she activated her light sword and was turning to keep the dogs at bay so Gabe could escape when a deafening bark threw her into a new scene.

Sun flooded the room. Where was she? Oz? Heaven? Wait. The deep-pink and medium-green décor was familiar. Becki's room. She was sitting up in Becki's bed, eyes wide open.

"Are you going to answer that?" Gabe was lying next to her. Something wet nudged at her hand, and she looked down into deep-brown eyes. Elvis pushed his nose against her hand again when a chorus of barks sounded, then backed up and looked down at something on the floor. Her phone.

Autumn groaned but half dangled over the edge of the bed to grab and swipe it. "Hel…hello?"

"I'm sorry. Did I wake you? It's Rachel. I only called because Jay said you were an early riser."

"No. it's fine. I usually am, but I was up most of the night shooting zombies." Well, that should make a great impression.

Rachel chuckled, apparently unfazed by her explanation. "You'll have to explain that later. I won't keep you on the phone since you obviously haven't had your first cup of coffee, but I've got news. Which do you want first—the good news or the good news?"

"Well, I guess I want the good news first." Autumn smiled, her zombie hangover vaporized by Rachel's enthusiasm.

"I've got three more new clients interested in what we can do for them. I'm emailing their portfolios to see if you want to work up proposals for them."

"Awesome. I should have something for them next week. And the other good news?"

"I have a friend who can get you the same office furniture you ordered, but for twenty-five percent less. And he can have it delivered in ten days, rather than the three weeks promised by the other company. Are you interested? Should I tell Jay to cancel the first order?"

"Yes! Of course."

"Consider it done."

"Wow. Thanks, Rachel. I felt bad about leaving town and dumping everything on you so soon, but you obviously have everything in hand. I can't tell you how much this means to me."

"Not a problem. Samantha is working some long hours, trying to get settled and learn the ropes of her new job, so I'm happy to stay busy. There's no rush on those portfolios. I told them it would be the end of next week when I got back in touch, so don't let it take away too much of your time with Gabriella."

"I won't. I'll let you know what I think after I've had a chance to look them over and check the analytics. Thanks again." Autumn ended the call and tapped her phone against her chin. This was working out so well.

Jay was great at social-media work for the accounts they already had, but he wasn't much of a salesman and hated schmoozing at parties and events to raise their company profile. So she was the creative person, he was operations, and Rachel was the salesperson. Yea!

She jumped onto the bed. "Get up, get up! We can't sleep away the day." She bounced around Gabe's curled form while Elvis barked at her display of exuberance. A horn sounded outside the house, and Elvis rocketed to the living room with Autumn right behind him. "It's Catherine," she yelled to Gabe. Then she flung the front door open to step onto the sun-drenched porch.

"Hey, Cat. We just woke up." The porch's wood floor was warm under her bare feet, and purple morning glories that covered a wire terrace at one end were in full bloom. She flung her arms out. "It's a beautiful day. Come inside and we'll make breakfast."

Catherine looked tired, but her answering smile was broad. She was leaning on the truck's fender, dressed in cargo shorts, a sleeveless T-shirt, and ratty running shoes. She jogged to the porch and up the steps in the smooth stride of someone accustomed to running. "I'll make you both a quick to-go breakfast while you get dressed."

Autumn looked down at her silky boxers and spaghetti-strap tank top. "What? You don't like my outfit?" She instantly regretted the tease when Catherine's gaze ran over her body like a hot breath. Catherine's neck and ears reddened, and Autumn's nipples hardened in response. Though she knew they were clearly visible under the thin cloth, she fought down her impulse to cross her arms because it would draw even more attention.

Catherine held the screen door open for Autumn. "We're going to be working in the garden, so shorts and tennis shoes or sandals are okay, but I'd recommend a T-shirt to protect your shoulders, maybe one of Becki's straw hats, and sunscreen." Catherine headed into the kitchen, calling back over her shoulder. "Hurry, because we have people waiting for us."

Gabe was out of bed, dressed, and brushing her teeth while Autumn stared down at her suitcase.

"Come on," Gabe said. "They'll all be waiting."

Autumn frowned at her, taking in Gabe's shorts, T-shirt, and flip-flops. "I didn't exactly pack for farmwork."

Gabe slapped her hands to her cheeks, her mouth a perfect O as she feigned disbelief. Then she smiled. "Wear those cut-offs." She went to Becki's chest of drawers and took out a red T-shirt. "This was kind of tight on Mom, so it shouldn't be too baggy on you. Do you want one of Mom's straw hats?"

"Sure. Or a ball cap if that's easier."

Gabe picked up a ball cap that proclaimed Best Mom Ever, then hung it back on the wall rack and selected one that stated No. 1 Elvis Fan.

"Thank you. Thank you very much," Autumn said in the worst-ever imitation of the legendary singer's voice.

Gabe groaned dramatically. "That was so bad," she said, putting the ball cap back and reverting to the original straw-hat plan. "I think this one."

"Are you guys going to take all day?" Catherine's voice rang out from the kitchen, but they could hear her footsteps heading for the front door.

"Come *on*," Gabe said. "Cat will leave us if she gets in the truck before we do."

"Maybe she'll leave you, but not me," Autumn said, pulling on her shorts and T-shirt.

"I'm headed out to the truck," Catherine called out. "You know what happens if you aren't there, Gabe."

"She better not leave me," Autumn muttered, checking the set of her hat in the mirror.

Gabe swiped Autumn's shoes and ran for the door. "You can put these on in the truck."

Autumn raced after her. Catherine was starting the truck when Gabe grabbed the passenger door and yanked it open. She jumped into the truck and reached back to pull Autumn in after her as the truck began to move. "Damn. You were going to leave me, weren't you?"

Catherine grinned. "You bet. A rule's a rule."

"Ha. And I've never met a rule that didn't need—"

Catherine's raised eyebrow stopped her mid-sentence. Autumn's eyes followed the very slight tip of Catherine's head. Gabe's eyebrow raised in a perfect imitation of Catherine, and her smirk challenged Autumn to finish her sentence.

"Never met a rule that didn't need to be honored." Damn, this parenting thing was hard. "Yep. Rule keeper. That's my middle name. Always keep the rules."

Catherine flashed that smile again—the one that made Autumn feel light and happy. She wouldn't say Catherine was striking, or even beautiful. More like handsome. Sort of sexy when she smiled… in a butch, outdoorsy sort of way. It was really, really too bad butch wasn't Autumn's type.

❖

"So, we're picking up day laborers?" Autumn eyed the group of people congregating under a huge shade tree that seemed to be the focal point of the village of neat single-wide trailers. A few men mingled there, but mostly women and children—lots of children running among the adults, laughing when one of the men would swing a child up onto his shoulders, or tugging on one of the women's skirts for attention. The people called out greetings in English and Spanish as Catherine stopped the truck.

Autumn's exuberant mood deflated. They were spending the day with all these people? Her stomach roiled with the familiar dread she'd always felt as she approached the high school each day. She could see, could feel their sense of community. She again would be an outsider.

"Looks like Angelique is coming along today, Gabe." Catherine pointed to a willowy girl with long, dark hair and a beautiful face. "That should make your day. You guys haven't seen each other in weeks."

Gabe looked like she wanted to crawl under the dash of the truck as much as Autumn did. This Gabe wasn't the competitive kid she'd played video games with the previous night, or the sweet kid who'd helped her dress for the day.

"I'll just wait in the truck," Gabe said.

"You'll get hot in here," Catherine said. "It's going to take about thirty minutes to get organized and on our way back to the farm."

"I'll keep the windows down."

Catherine frowned. "You guys have a fight or something?"

Gabe shook her head. "I just don't want to get out, okay?"

Autumn had an idea what was troubling Gabe, but Catherine didn't seem to be catching on. Time to throw herself in front of the bus and save Gabe from the same fear of public humiliation that had haunted Autumn's childhood. She wasn't the poor kid going to school in a thrift-shop sweater. She wasn't a powerless child any longer. And her designer shorts weren't hand-me-downs.

She patted Gabe's leg. "It's probably that egg sandwich. You wolfed it down so fast, I thought you were going to accidently eat your fingers too." She handed Gabe the bottle of water she'd left unopened because the iced latte Catherine had brought in a thermos was so much more her style. "Why don't you just sit here and sip on this. Roll your window down, Catherine, and I'll put mine down too so maybe she'll catch a breeze while she lets her stomach settle."

Gabe took the bottle. "Thanks."

Catherine shot both of them an irritated look but followed when Autumn got out of the truck. "Do you know what's going on with her? Angelique is her best friend at school, but she's acting like she doesn't want to see her."

Autumn stopped and faced Catherine. "Didn't you tell me that Gabe didn't go back to school after Becki died?"

Catherine shrugged. "She was so far ahead of the other kids, and with only four or five weeks remaining in the school year, her counselor just brought her schoolwork over each week so she could finish her lessons, then proctored her end-of-grade test at home. Gabe didn't want to go to school and face all that sympathy over losing her mom."

"So, she hasn't seen her best friend since Becki died?"

"No. She's pretty much stayed on the farm with me." Catherine's tone made it clear she still didn't understand.

"She's scared, Catherine. Afraid that when Angelique looks into her eyes and recognizes the pain Gabe's bottled up, it'll all come spilling out. And she doesn't want to be humiliated by crying in front of everybody."

"Damn. I didn't even think of that." Catherine's shoulders slumped. "You're good at this, and I suck so bad."

Autumn looped her arm in Catherine's and turned her toward the people they came to see. "Don't even. That kid worships you. I'm new and shiny. The cool guardian. But when she scrapes her knee—I'm speaking figuratively, of course—you're the one she'll run to."

Catherine's frown relaxed into a small smile. "Maybe."

"It takes a village," Autumn said. "Now let's get this show on the road."

❖

"Hello, my friends. Mother Luna tells me it's time. I've got three acres ready for corn, and two more ready for beans, tomatoes, peppers, squash, and potatoes." As Catherine expected, they cheered her announcement, even though they already knew this. She'd sent word several days ago and told them to be ready to work today.

A middle-aged woman wearing a straw cowboy hat pushed through the crowd and walked toward them, her arms outstretched.

Catherine's face heated, but she submitted to Maria's hug and kisses on each cheek.

Maria held her hand out to Autumn. "Hello. I'm Maria."

Autumn smiled and accepted the handshake. "Autumn."

"Yes. I saw you at the memorial. You're Becki's cousin and now Gabriella's guardian."

Autumn nodded. "Yes. Well, co-guardian with Catherine."

Maria turned to Catherine. "Angel has been very worried about Gabe."

"Gabe hasn't really felt like having company around. I'm a little surprised she wanted to come today." Catherine glanced back at the truck. "She didn't want to get out once we got here, though."

They paused to watch Angelique open the passenger door and crawl in beside Gabe. Catherine shifted uneasily, then stilled when Autumn's hand closed around hers.

"They'll be fine," Autumn said. "Let's just leave them alone while we get the rest organized."

Autumn seemed as at ease as Catherine felt agitated, still raw from the flashback and tired from a sleepless night. But she realized Autumn was just better at hiding her feelings. The hand that had grasped Catherine's was damp with nervous sweat. So, when Autumn released Catherine's hand, she caught it again and didn't let go, tugging Autumn toward the waiting workers.

The men respectfully removed their hats, holding them to their chests as they nodded and greeted Autumn, some responding in English and some in Spanish when Catherine introduced them. They were Hispanic laborers and had learned to be wary of touching white women, even for a handshake. The women had no such reservations, most extending their hands to her even if they had to put down a child or shift a baby to a different hip to do it. Only a few eyed her and were polite, but not warm.

"Everybody on the bus. We are wasting daylight." Maria issued her orders in Spanish, then English. While some adults hurried to load tools and coolers full of food and drinks, others herded the children onto a bus.

Catherine was glad she'd bought that old school bus last year and given it to the residents of Shady Grove Trailer Park. She helped by paying for parts and paint, but the residents pitched in the skills and labor to refurbish the lumbering vehicle so children could be loaded up and driven directly to their schools, workers could be driven into town or to a work site, or the women could gather and go shopping together. Fans were installed to circulate air, and several rows of seats were removed in the back to create a play area for babies and toddlers. Today, it would serve as transport, nursery, and siesta lounge while they worked.

❖

Autumn dug into the black soil with her hand spade, but dirt fell into the hole she'd made before she could fill it with the young tomato plant set out to be planted. Her back ached, and sweat dripped from her chin. She dropped the spade to dig out the hole again with her fingers and cursed for the hundredth time that morning. Her fingernails were never going to be clean again. She slammed the plant into the hole before it could fill a second time, then pounded the dirt around it.

"You have to be careful and not pack the soil so tightly. The roots are tender at this stage."

Autumn looked up into a pair of dark wraparound sunglasses. Catherine's words were soft and her tone held no admonishment, but she was focused on rescuing the abused plants.

"I…I guess I'm not cut out to be a farmer." Autumn sat back and watched Catherine as she carefully loosened the soil Autumn had jammed around the last three plants. If she hadn't been working near her all morning, she'd swear that Catherine had gone to the house and napped for a few hours. Her movements were smooth and relaxed, and the tightness in her voice and the signs of tension and fatigue had disappeared from her face. "But you seem to be. This work relaxes you, doesn't it?"

Catherine didn't look up. "I suppose it does. It's easy to lose yourself in the repetition of planting. And I love the smell of a freshly turned field, knowing that what I'm growing will feed hungry people. I like the self-sufficiency of farming. If I wanted, I could produce everything I needed right here on this farm." She finished her task, then picked up the next plant set out along that row. "Watch how I do this."

She drove the eight-inch spade into dirt and, with a flick of her wrist, twisted it to open a hole. She simultaneously dropped the plant alongside the tool, then nudged soil to fill around it as she withdrew the tool. She lightly patted the soil around the plant to secure it and moved to the next. Autumn was mesmerized by Catherine's efficient movements and concentration. In less than the time it had taken Autumn to place one plant, Catherine had put three in the ground.

"Now come on. You try it."

Autumn shuffled forward on her knees. She raised her spade but was stopped by Catherine's hand on her wrist.

"Pick up the plant with your other hand and think of this as one movement, not two separate ones."

Autumn nodded, then made a clumsy, unsuccessful attempt to imitate what Catherine had done.

Catherine carefully dug the small plant out and took Autumn's spade from her.

"I can do it. That was just my first try." She didn't like failure. Ever. No matter if it was just being able to plant a damn tomato seedling.

"I know. But this should help." Catherine smiled and took out her pocket knife, scratching a line near the top of the tool's blade. "Stab the spade into the dirt all the way to this line. You want the hole deep enough to bury two-thirds of the stem." She stood to move behind Autumn, rather than facing her. "Let's try that again, shall we?"

Without waiting for Autumn to reply, Catherine dropped to her knees behind Autumn and laid the plant in her hand. Catherine shuffled close, leaned over Autumn's back, and put her hands over Autumn's.

"You just need to get the feel of the movements. Place the plant instead of dropping it. You do that by sliding your plant-hand in as you twist to push back the dirt. Ready?"

Autumn nodded and tried to focus on the task rather than Catherine's breath on her ear and Catherine's enticing scent—sweat mixed with the coconut oil of her sunscreen. Her hands were gentle but firm as she guided Autumn through the motion. Stab, twist-place, cover, gently pat.

"Good. Let's do it again."

Catherine leaned back, and they knee-walked the two feet to the next plant. Autumn picked up the plant, readied her spade, and closed her eyes to savor the feel of Catherine against her back again, the perfect fit of Catherine's long arms around her, Catherine's strong hands cupping hers.

"Ready?"

She nodded, opened her eyes, and they placed a second plant perfectly.

"Got the hang of it now?" Catherine asked, her breath washing over Autumn's neck.

"One more time?"

"Once more." Catherine withdrew, and they shuffled to the next plant.

Autumn picked up the next plant, lifted her tool, and was struggling to focus when Catherine's arms slid around her a third time. This time, Catherine's hand cupped but didn't guide Autumn's hands. Then she sat back while Autumn administered the finishing pats.

"I think you've got it down," Catherine said, her voice husky.

Autumn's phone began the R2D2 beeps that signaled a text, and Catherine stood. She shoved her hands into her pockets, appearing a little uncertain. "Everybody breaks for lunch and a short siesta when they reach the end of their row. They'll have food and drinks for everyone over at the bus."

"Okay," Autumn said, feeling…something. She watched Catherine's long strides to where she knelt six or eight rows away from Autumn. What did she feel? She peered down her row. The rest of the workers were way ahead of both her and Catherine, but Catherine was working fast and gaining on most of them. Damn. She was even farther behind than Catherine. And these rows seemed to go on forever. At this rate she might get her lunch break around three that afternoon. Her phone sounded a text notification again, but she ignored it, shuffled forward and picked up the next plant.

❖

Stab, twist-place, cover, pat, next.

Catherine repeated the words in her head to push out any other thoughts. She'd let Autumn drive her truck to the fields so Angelique could ride with Gabe. Maria had offered for her to ride in the bus but nodded her understanding when Catherine indicated she would be riding with Miguel.

"Go," Maria said. "I can see your demons are back. Miguel can help."

She didn't like smoking the cannabis that a lot of soldiers found gave them gentle relief from the flashbacks and nightmares without the debilitating side effects of standard psychiatric drugs. It didn't help the worst cases, but it'd helped her and many others. She normally had some pure cannabis extract on hand, now a recognized medical product legal in many states. But it'd been a long time since she'd suffered much from the flashbacks, so she'd never replenished her supply when the last of what she had was gone. And it wasn't legal in this state where she'd settled…yet.

So, she and Miguel hung back until the others had left, and then they went to his trailer, where he filled a small pipe and waited for her to smoke it. He didn't expect her to share it because Miguel didn't keep the cannabis for recreational use. The residents of Shady Grove were poor, and because few had health insurance, they made use of the natural medicines their parents, grandparents, and great-grandparents had used. Cannabis was useful for many ailments.

The cannabis had quieted her agitation and settled her mind. But it also heightened her senses and lowered her inhibitions. Otherwise, she would have never pressed against Autumn's back, breathed in the remnants of her perfume, and cupped her hands as they worked the earth. It had taken every bit of her concentration to refrain from tasting her lovely neck.

Spade, twist-place, cover, pat, next.

She'd regret it when the cannabis wore off. At the moment, she would focus on the task at hand.

Spade, twist-place, cover, pat, next.

She'd shut down the images that were a flashing tease in her head.

Spade, twist-place, cover, pat, next.

Images of Autumn naked, maybe standing at the window while dawn caressed the curves of her body. Or writhing under her, beautiful against the soft sherpa blanket on Catherine's bed.

Spade, twist-place, cover, pat, next.

Distraction. She needed distraction. Catherine paused and scanned for Gabe. But Gabe was fine. She and Angelique were bent over the same row, planting two seedlings at a time. They should have completed a full row and at least a third of a second. But they talked as they worked, and Catherine saw Maria and her sister making fast work of the second row assigned to the girls. Maria looked up, checking on Gabe and Angelique, then finding Catherine to share a smile. Catherine mouthed a silent "thank you" and stood. She'd finished her row. Autumn still had a third left, so Catherine blamed the cannabis in her system and knelt at the end of Autumn's furrow, working her way back toward the too-young, too-city, too-beautiful woman who was way out of Catherine's league.

❖

"So, what is it that you do in the city?" Maria and several other women had brought their plates of food and sat with Autumn.

Her hasty breakfast was a distant memory, but she just wanted to fill her belly and lie back on the blanket spread under the shade trees that lined the field where they were working. She flashed back to a day when a group of mean girls had brought their plates over to the cafeteria table where she sat alone and began to ask questions meant to humiliate. "Where'd you get that sweater? It looks like my old one my mother donated to the thrift shop. Look. It even has ink on the sleeve like mine did. I wouldn't be seen wearing it after I got ink on it." The questions had continued about her parents, where she lived, why she brought her lunch when she surely qualified for the poor kids' free lunch plan.

She put her plate down. "I own a digital marketing company."

They stared at her. Then Maria broke into a huge smile and pushed the shoulder of the woman sitting next to her.

"See, Helena? What did I tell you? Autumn is young, but she owns her own company. You should stop telling Serena that she should quit making her jewelry and marry a husband with a good job."

"I have no idea what this digital thing means," Helena said. "Is it legal?"

"Explain this to us," Maria said to Autumn.

Autumn looked around for Catherine, but she was some

distance away, in deep discussion with two of the men who were pointing toward another field. Since no rescue seemed likely, she gathered her thoughts. She explained her work and how it would raise a company's image at every presentation she gave to new clients. She held her finger up while she took a big drink from her water bottle. Then she wiped her mouth.

"Okay. Let's say that Maria sells used cars. She has many parked in a lot by the highway and big signs to get the attention of anyone who drives past. But most of the people who drive past are the same every day, and she's already sold cars to them. She needs to tell people who don't drive down her road about her great car deals."

"She needs to sell vegetables instead of cars," Helena said. "People need tomatoes every day. They can drive a car for years before they need a new one."

Maria swatted Helena again. "Don't interrupt. I want to hear this."

"It's okay," Autumn said. "I can explain it to you later. I don't want to bore everybody else."

"No, no." The other women reached for her when she started to stand. "We want to hear this," one of the women said.

"When you say digital marketing, are you talking about markets on the internet, like eBay and Etsy?" a younger woman asked.

"Not exactly." Autumn sat again. "Ten years ago, if Maria wanted to sell more cars, she would pay for an advertisement in the newspaper or a commercial to air on a local television station. But people don't read newspapers so much anymore, and they record shows on television so they can fast-forward past the commercials."

Maria nodded. "I do that all the time."

Autumn looked at one of young women. "How do you get your news?"

Helena snorted. "She spends all her time on Facebook and twits."

The younger woman laughed. "Tweets, Mama."

Autumn smiled. "Exactly. If Maria came to my company, we could make a plan to have her advertisement pop up in the Facebook feeds of anyone who has been looking at cars on the internet. We'd make a Facebook page for her car lot and post on it every time she gets a new car to sell or offers a special deal or makes a sale to a happy customer. We'd set up her social media so that every post would also show up on Twitter and Instagram. And our account representative would track how many people were looking at your ads, what area they live in, and which posts are drawing the most interest. Then they'd advise you on what to post and when to get the best results."

The young woman brightened with excitement. "Serena's jewelry is beautiful. I know she could sell a lot more if people knew about it. She sells on Etsy, but so do lots of others. She just needs to do something to get noticed."

"Thirty minutes," Catherine called.

The women jumped up and began collecting the trash from their lunch.

"What are we doing?" Autumn asked, confused by the sudden scramble.

"Back to work in thirty minutes, so we have that long for siesta," Maria said. "You don't have to do this work, you know. But if you want to last the afternoon, your back will thank you later for lying flat on this blanket now."

"You don't have to tell me twice." Autumn closed her eyes and groaned when her back straightened after being hunched between the dirt furrows for hours. "This is hard work. I hope Catherine pays you guys a living wage."

"I don't pay them anything."

Autumn squinted up at Catherine, who was lowering herself to stretch out on the other side of the blanket. "What?"

"They actually pay me to work in my field—corn for the freezer, jars of vegetables and pickles, and dried beans. Enough to last me through the winter and then some."

Maria laughed at Autumn's frown. "We don't work for Cat. We work for ourselves. We are planting the vegetables for our families. Catherine is very generous to let us use her fields, but she also prepares the ground for our planting and starts the seedlings in her greenhouses." Maria's expression grew serious. "Sometimes, it's hard to find work, and our men have to follow the harvest or take a construction job a long way from our home. It's not good to drag children around from town to town, so the food we grow here for ourselves allows most of the women to stay here and keep the children in school."

"The produce I get in exchange means I don't have to shop much for groceries," Catherine said, her sunglasses still hiding her eyes. Her words were a bit slow and her tone sleepy. "And I hate grocery stores."

❖

Catherine settled into her usual front-porch rocking chair. Gabe had gone with Angelique for a sleepover, so she'd thrown a couple of hamburgers on her grill for her and Autumn. They ate in the kitchen, and then Catherine took their desserts to the front porch to watch the sun set. It was her daily ritual.

She held out one of the two small plates loaded with warm apple pie and big dollops of vanilla-bean ice cream to Autumn, who in turn handed Catherine a mug of rich, dark coffee. Catherine took a cautious sip to gauge its heat, then took a larger swallow in her mouth and swished it over her tongue like she was judging fine wine. "God, this is good."

Autumn smiled. "My own blend of beans. I thought you'd like it. I'll give you the recipe so you can grind your own fresh all winter." She took a big bite of pie and hummed her approval. "What did you drizzle on the ice cream?"

"Orange brandy. It's from Napa."

"It's delicious."

"Hold on." Catherine put her plate and mug on the porch railing, then ducked back into the house and brought out a double shot glass of the brandy for Autumn. "You can sip that or pour more on your ice cream."

Autumn immediately sipped from the tall shot glass. "Oh my god, that's yummy."

"The pie is a special recipe of mine, too."

Autumn looked up from her plate in surprise. "You baked this pie?"

Catherine laughed. She loved how expressive Autumn's face could be. "My recipe is really simple. I get into my truck and drive to Sweet Anytime, where I buy the pie and ice cream—they churn their own—and cinnamon rolls, fresh baked bread, and assorted bagels. All the staples of life."

Autumn swatted Catherine's arm. "And I used to think you didn't have a sense of humor."

"You seem to bring it out." The instant the words were out of her mouth, she wished she could take them back. After her chummy lesson in how to plant tomatoes, Autumn would probably read unintended innuendo into them. She sighed and set her empty plate beside her rocking chair. She had to explain. "Becki did, too. She shone light into my dark corners and kept me from being so serious and morose."

Autumn's expression changed like a switch had toggled from relaxed and happy to dark and wary. "I'm not sunny like Becki," she said. "I grew up dark and angry." She put her empty plate down and stared grimly at the horizon. "But I turned that anger into the resourcefulness and determination that got me through school early and laid the groundwork to start my own business."

The setting sun bathed Autumn's face in its soft light, but Catherine's desire to burn it into her memory cowered in the glare of their differences. Autumn had used her life circumstances like a warrior picks up a weapon. Catherine had run from her childhood—joining the army after college to escape her parents' expectations—and then from active duty to hide out on this farm. Only exceptional people like Autumn had the courage to fight their demons and win.

Catherine ducked her head in shame. She excelled in one thing—being absolutely ordinary. And most ordinary people never conquered their demons. "I wish I had your strength, Becki's strength. I've spent the past five years hiding here and licking my wounds."

Autumn opened her mouth to reply, but her phone signaled an

incoming call. She growled and swiped it to answer. "I'll call you back in fifteen minutes, Jay." She punched the screen to end the call and stood. "I've put him off as long as I can. I need to go take care of some work issues."

Sunset had given way to dusk that was darkening into the twilight that preceded moonrise. Catherine stood. "Leave the dishes here. I'll get the truck keys and drive you home."

Autumn cocked her head. "Gabe says there's a path from your house to ours. Can we walk instead?"

"Sure. We'll have to skirt the cornfield now that it's planted, so we should go through the house." She gathered the dishes. "I'll drop these in the sink and grab a flashlight on our way out the back."

They walked in silence through the warm night. When they reached the span of trees that separated the two farms, Catherine clicked on the flashlight to illuminate any roots that might trip them or limbs that might swat them as they pass. When they emerged on the other side, a small group of geese settling in that corner of the yard for the night startled, flapping their wings and honking noisily as they waddled away.

Autumn's hand on Catherine's arm stopped her at the woods' edge. "I think I'm fine from here. Thanks for walking me through the woods."

The moon was rising, and Catherine switched off the flashlight, needing the cloak of half-light as she turned to Autumn. "Are you going to tell Janice about my flashbacks?"

Autumn blinked up at her. "What? No. Why would I?"

Catherine averted her eyes, afraid she'd see indecision or, worse, pity in Autumn's gaze. "Because she might decide I was too unstable to be Gabe's co-guardian." Catherine swallowed hard. If that happened, she might lose Gabe and Autumn from her life. She'd already lost Becki. The Swans were her sunlight. If they were gone from her, she'd have nothing to hold her back from the dark abyss that had once almost swallowed her.

"Cat, look at me."

Catherine never cared one way or the other when people shortened her name, but she reveled in the way Autumn's voice lowered and seemed to purr it. She felt strong and feline—like a dark panther standing protectively at Autumn's side. That cat wanted to rub her face along Autumn's thighs, marking Autumn with her scent. Mine. She wished with every cell of her body that she could be that Cat. She'd always been content to hide quietly. But Autumn made her want again. Want to be worthy. Want to trust. Want to reach for a full life again. Yet she was a prisoner of her mediocrity, and the wanting was her torture.

Autumn's hand slid into hers, and their fingers entwined as naturally as a seed pushes up through the dark soil in search of sunlight.

"You are stronger than you believe." Autumn's fingers tightened around hers while her other hand cupped Catherine's nape and tugged her down until their lips met. Autumn's lips tasted of orange brandy. Catherine closed her eyes and lost herself when Autumn's mouth parted and her tongue traced a teasing invitation along Catherine's lips. If she'd stopped to think, she would have withdrawn. So many things were wrong with this. But she'd temporarily lost her ability to reason. Catherine wrapped her arms around Autumn, drawing Autumn against her, and plunged her tongue into the velvet depths of Autumn's mouth. She might have died from lack of oxygen if Autumn hadn't, finally, gently disengaged and stepped back.

Elvis appeared out of the darkness and licked at their joined hands before turning toward Becki's...no, Autumn's house...to indicate that was where he'd stay that night.

"Good night, Cat," Autumn said, her words soft.

Catherine held out the flashlight. "Take this."

"You'll need it to go back through the woods."

Catherine smiled and touched her lips to see if they felt different. "I'll be fine. I've walked that path many times in the dark." *And I feel like I'm radiating sunlight after that kiss.* "You need the light to watch for goose poop." She gave a tiny wave, and Autumn's "Ec-ew, yuck" then laughter followed as Catherine turned back to the dark woods.

CHAPTER TWELVE

I can't believe you've been ignoring my texts." Jay crossed his arms, and Autumn didn't even need three-dimensional imaging to see the jut of his pouting lips.

"I've been out all day, planting. You know cell service is spotty here." It wasn't a lie, but the next words were...a small, white falsehood...because she couldn't and didn't want to try to explain why she hadn't wanted work to intrude on her time with Catherine. Gabe and Catherine. She meant Gabe and Catherine. "When we came in for dinner, I guess I was so tired I forgot to check until your call rang through."

"Planting? Do I need to buy a pair of designer overalls and ship it to you?"

"Tomatoes, cucumbers, potatoes, squash, onions, peppers, and beans. The men pulled some kind of machine around with a tractor to plant the corn." She swiped at her burning eyes, regretting that she'd forgotten to take sunglasses with her that morning. She needed eye drops, a hot bath, and clean sheets. "Just tell me what's so urgent that I can't take a day off to spend with Gabe."

Jay relented. "Rachel's a machine. She signed up two more clients."

"Since I talked to her this morning?"

"Yes. That's five accounts that need data analyzed and strategy plans mapped."

"Okay. Have you gathered the data on them?"

"Hon, I've been working twelve hours a day just to keep up the more than twenty accounts you already have active. I've scheduled so many Facebook posts I'm dreaming about Twitter and Facebook when I try to sleep at night. We need more help."

"What? I just hired you and Rachel a few weeks ago. Have you advertised the admin position yet?"

"I sent three resumes to you last week. You haven't even opened the folders, have you?"

She massaged her temples. Her head was starting to pound. Too much sun and not enough sleep. "I'm sorry, Jay. Ask Rachel to look over the folders and pick one if they meet our requirements. Tell her to figure a competitive wage for the job, then add a little if she feels the candidate is worth it."

"Okay." He was quiet a few seconds before he spoke again. "You look sunburnt and tired, Snow White."

She smiled at his tender tone. They'd been two struggling souls when they met and had weathered many storms to get where they were today. He was the brother she always felt she should have had, like Becki had had Gabriel. "I need a few hours of sleep right now, but let's do a conference call in the morning when it's convenient for you and Rachel to discuss getting a few more dwarfs to help you out, Grumpy."

"Sure thing, sweetie. Talk to you tomorrow."

"Bye. Oh, and give Evan a hug for me. Tell him we're going to see what we can do about cutting your hours back to only ten a day."

"He'll be thrilled. Ta-ta."

Catherine washed the dishes, cleaned the coffee machine, and caught up the paperwork on the farm and her financial investments. She'd be in good shape for filing second-quarter taxes. Still, she was too restless to sleep. Autumn's kiss had stirred her up inside and awakened a need, a desire so strong it scared her. She went into her bedroom and retrieved Miguel's pouch she'd secreted there earlier. She loaded the bowl of her small pipe and returned to the porch. It was full dark now, the moon only a sliver in the sky. She lit the pipe and took a long pull from it, closing her eyes against the reflex to cough when it burned in her lungs. The rocking chair was making her dizzy, so she relocated to the center of the porch, in front of the screened door, and sat cross-legged on the worn boards like Pete had shown her. After a few more tokes on the pipe emptied the bowl, she sat with back erect and hands resting on her knees to close her eyes and begin clearing her mind. Only it wouldn't clear.

Shutting her eyes opened a collage of mental videos. Autumn naked under a waterfall. Autumn naked under her. Autumn writhing over her as she rode Catherine's fingers. Autumn bent over her bed begging as Catherine thrust into her. *Harder, yes, like that.* Catherine sprang to her feet, swaying and putting an arm out to steady herself. Her head was spinning and her gut clenching in near orgasm. She leaned against the house, panting. Holy fuck. She'd nearly orgasmed just from thinking about…her.

Catherine stumbled inside, slamming the door behind her and stripping and discarding clothes on her way to the bathroom. She twisted the cold-water handle and stepped under the icy spray, gasping when it hit her overheated flesh. But the cold water did nothing to quell the ache between her thighs. She slid her hand down her belly and fingered her very swollen clit. She put her other hand out to brace against the tiled wall and ducked under the spray.

The water didn't seem so cold now. God, she was slick with lubrication. It'd been so long, she'd forgotten how her fingers felt gliding over that spot that felt too sensitive to touch, yet begged for it again and again. Two strokes, five, and her legs began to tremble. She wanted to stop, to prolong the pleasure, but the picture of Autumn bent over her bed was too much. The shower echoed with her yell when her clit exploded and pleasure grabbed and twisted low in her belly. She milked the aftershocks as long as she could, then washed her body with shaking hands.

She climbed into bed naked and pulled up the sheet to cover herself. She felt drained and ready for sleep, but her desire still burned, and when she closed her eyes, naked Autumn was squatting over her thighs. She stared into Catherine's eyes as she lubed one end of a double-headed dildo while licking the bulbous head of the other. *Open for me, Cat.*

Catherine groaned out loud, even though she was aware the image was a waking dream. Or was she still awake? Didn't matter. She was wet again. She opened her thighs and pushed two fingers into herself, feeling for that rough spot, as the Autumn in her head plunged the lubed end of the dildo into her. She groaned again when Autumn rose on her knees to impale herself on the larger opposite end that jutted up from Catherine's crotch. Then Autumn began to ride her—up and down, back and forth, up and down, back and forth. Catherine pressed harder and moved her fingers in time with Autumn's image. The build-up was slower the second time, and Catherine had never come from penetration, but a telltale pressure began to gather. "Oh yeah, babe. Like that. Ride me," she whispered to her bedroom walls. Then the explosion hit and Catherine cried out, thrusting into herself over and over.

Autumn sipped the coffee she'd made with the French press and logged in to join the video call. Rachel and Jay were already waiting. "Good morning, people. How's Hotlanta today?"

"It's hot," Rachel said. "It got plenty hot in Arizona, but the humidity in the South changes everything. I feel wilted before I get to work. It might be a while before my body adjusts."

Autumn smiled and shook her head. "Even we natives have a hard time with the humidity. We just run from air-conditioned building to air-conditioned car to air-conditioned store. Or embrace it with short skirts or sleeveless dresses and cute sandals. Pantyhose are yesterday, and business suits are reserved for corporate board meetings or arguing a case before the Georgia State Supreme Court."

"That's great for you girls, but they don't make sleeveless dress shirts for men."

"You can wear khakis and a golf shirt or one of those V-neck Ralph Lauren Ts you like so much. But no sandals. Big hairy toes have to stay inside loafers or Top-Siders. You don't have to wear socks, as long as your feet don't start to stink us out."

"That's harsh," Jay whined. "I don't complain when you have a 'no-appointments' day and refuse to wear a bra. What does human resources say about that double standard, Rachel?"

Rachel laughed. "We don't have a human-resources department, but if you want to call a vote, I'm afraid I have to side with Autumn. Keep your hairy toes in shoes, please."

"I should be working in an office with straight women. They have a better appreciation for manly attributes."

"How about we cover the business at hand, shall we?" Autumn said. She had so much work to catch up on.

After a warm bath and a couple of aspirin, she'd climbed into bed. She fell asleep so quickly she didn't even remember pulling up the sheet, only to wake up an hour later in the throes of orgasm and wisps of a wet dream lingering in her head. She vaguely recalled noting the time on her phone, which was propped up in its charger on the bedside table, then waking up at seven the next morning. Eight hours. She never slept that long. And she'd had wet dreams before, but never one so real that it actually made her come. Wow. She obviously needed to date more, if a mere kiss could work her up that much.

"...and of the three, I think Kim Albertson is the most qualified," Rachel was saying when Autumn tuned back in to the meeting.

"I'm sorry. What's her experience?" She had to focus.

"She's been personal assistant for the past five years to one of the top lawyers in one of Atlanta's largest firms but says she's tired of his condescending attitude and his habit of invading her personal space and making remarks full of innuendo but not blatant enough to prove sexual harassment in court."

"Why hasn't she asked the firm to assign her to someone different?"

"She has, but he's the managing partner and refuses to approve her request. I know somebody who dates one of the other lawyers in the firm. She confirmed that everybody knows about the guy, but nobody will stand up to him."

"I liked her, but that's a big change from a huge firm to our little group," Jay said. "You think she'll be happy here?"

Rachel began to answer Jay, but tires on the gravel drive out front drew Autumn's attention. She turned back to her laptop and jumped in before Jay could ask another question. "She sounds good to me, Rachel. Go ahead and hire her. Someone just pulled up out front, so I'm going to have to cut this short. One quick thing, though. Can you look at our financial projections and give me an estimate on how soon we would be in the position to hire another associate to help Jay work the accounts we already have?"

"Don't have to look. Autumn, you've more than doubled your client list in the past two months. You're at a point that you'll lose customers if you don't have enough staff to monitor and work their accounts properly. Your monthly revenue is more than enough to hire two more people."

"God. We don't have that much space in the office."

"They can Tweet and post on Facebook and modify websites from home. That's the new trend in employment now. Or you can exercise the option on the rooms adjacent to our office that's in your current lease."

"I don't remember asking for that option."

Rachel shrugged. "I might have added it. It cost nothing extra, but the option allows us to expand without the landlord trying to gouge us because he knows we need the space."

"I should have thought of that."

Rachel shook her head. "You've had a lot of other stuff to deal with. Like I promised when you hired me, I've got your back."

"And I'm so grateful. I'll be working on the new-client accounts the rest of today, so just email if you need anything."

"Will do," Jay said.

Autumn ended the call and turned to Catherine, who stood just inside the front door. She wore khaki cargo shorts and a loose T-shirt with the sleeves cut out so that a dark-blue sports bra showed in the oversized armholes. She'd pulled her hair through the back of her ball cap and hadn't removed her wraparound sunglasses. Autumn swallowed hard. She'd hoped Catherine would show up looking like the farmer Autumn had seen when they first met, so she could blame the kiss last night on the brandy or a sugar overload from the pie. Instead, Catherine looked tough and dangerously sexy. Catherine had changed in the short two months they'd known each other. Or maybe Autumn was seeing her differently. Autumn realized they were staring at each other. At least she thought Catherine was staring back. It was impossible to tell with those dark sunglasses. "Hi."

"Good morning." Catherine sounded hoarse and cleared her throat. "I didn't mean to eavesdrop, but it sounds like you're not going to play gardener with us today." She pointed to the laptop, indicating the call Autumn had just concluded.

Autumn stepped closer. "No. I'm afraid not." She gestured to the laptop, acknowledging that it, indeed, was the culprit conspiring to imprison Autumn in the house. "As much as I was hoping for a second day of sweaty, back-torturing fun, I still have a business to run."

"Okay. Sure. I understand." Catherine pushed the screen door open, then hesitated. "Is being here for a month going to hurt your business? I mean, can you really run it from here?"

"Yes, I can. I've hired a few extra people, one who seems to be doing a better job of managing the business end than I did. Rachel is turning out to be a real gem." She shrugged. "I'm more of the creative mind behind the company, which is what I'll be doing today. Analyzing data and creating social-media marketing plans for a bunch of new clients."

Catherine shoved her hands into her pockets, letting the door bump against her back. "But you'll need to go back before too long."

"Of course. Even if I could work remotely most of the time, I'd still be going back so Gabe can enroll in a school that can challenge her."

Catherine cleared her throat again. "Speaking of Gabe, she and the others are probably waiting for us to get started. We're planting squash and cucumbers today." She shuffled her feet a few seconds, then stepped out onto the porch, releasing the screen door.

Autumn caught the door with her hand and followed Catherine out onto the porch. "Why don't you and Gabe come here for dinner tonight? I brought a couple of pounds of barbecued ribs from my favorite take-out place."

Catherine nodded. "Sounds good." She tapped her fingers against her thigh, making no move to leave.

Autumn could almost feel her indecision. The elephant in the room was trumpeting and waving his trunk for attention. "So…the kiss."

Catherine turned her head away. "I'm sorry. I don't usually do that sort of thing."

Autumn cocked her head. "Kiss women."

"No. I mean I do…I have kissed women." Catherine raised her hand as if she was about to make a proclamation, then shook her head and dropped it back to her side. "I don't jump women in the dark. But last night, I apparently lost my good sense, and I was out of line. I'm sorry. It won't happen again."

Autumn didn't know if she was relieved or disappointed. "Actually, I think I was the one who did the jumping. You weren't exactly resisting, but now I feel like I should apologize."

"No apology necessary." Catherine crossed her arms over her chest. "We'll write it off as too much sun during the day and too much moonlight and stars last night."

"Temporary moon madness?"

Catherine nodded, smiling a little. "Yeah."

"Because?"

"Because it'd be a very bad idea. We have to think about Gabe. She just lost her mother and is about to go to a new school in a new place. We need to focus on her."

Autumn couldn't deny that they'd be playing with dynamite. She did need to concentrate on AA Swan and Gabe. She didn't need to have an affair with her co-guardian to split her energy in a third direction. Still, the memory of Catherine's kiss lingered.

"Autumn?" Catherine finally took her sunglasses off, and Autumn stared up into her dark, liquid eyes.

"You're right, of course. It must have been that double shot of brandy. Then the walk under the stars…I plead temporary insanity."

Catherine held out her hand. "Friends?"

Autumn slipped her hand into Catherine's, shaking it twice to confirm their new pact. "Right. Friends." But instead of releasing Catherine's hand, Autumn held on and stepped into Catherine's personal space. "And friends can hug." Not that she hugged everyone...okay, anyone. Except Jay. Because he had taught her to, hugged her until she got used to it.

Catherine was stiff at first, then relaxed, her arms closing around Autumn. Her cheek rested on Autumn's head, and Autumn wanted to sigh when she felt Catherine's nipple harden against her own cheek.

"Cat?"

"Yeah?"

"I just want to say...for the record...that kiss was wow."

Catherine folded her napkin and watched Gabe lick the barbecue sauce from her fingers. After spending the night with Angelique, the tense set of Gabe's shoulders had relaxed for the first time since her mother's death. She'd gnawed her way through a half rack of barbecued ribs before her eyes began to droop.

"Uh, can I be excused? I need to take a shower," Gabe said, rubbing her eyes with the back of her hands.

Catherine looked to Autumn, who smiled and nodded. "Sure. We'll clean up here," Catherine said.

Gabe muttered her thanks and was a few steps from the table when she hesitated and turned back to them. "Those ribs were really good, Aut. Thanks for dinner."

Autumn smiled. "You're welcome."

Catherine helped clean away the remains of their meal, and then they shared coffee and little bits of their day. Autumn had worked on her new accounts and videoconferenced. Catherine had planted beans and corn with the Shady Grove folks. This was how Catherine pictured a real family, a real couple would have dinner. When she realized night had fallen and the chickens were still loose, she went in search of Gabe.

Gabe lay sprawled across the twin bed in her room, mouth open and sound asleep. Elvis was curled next to her side, his head resting protectively on her thigh. Catherine stood in the doorway, trying to decide if she should wake Gabe or leave her there for the night when she felt Autumn's hand on her back. She moved over a half step so Autumn could see Gabe, too.

They stood together in the bedroom's doorway like two parents watching their kid drool on her pillow.

"Is she okay?" Autumn's hand dropped to Catherine's hip. Catherine wasn't a person who touched easily, but Autumn's arm resting against the small of Catherine's back felt natural and easy. So easy that Catherine realized she'd dropped her own arm to rest across Autumn's shoulders while she considered the whispered question. Was this what it would feel like if they were a real family? If she and Autumn were a couple?

"Probably just exhausted." Catherine drew the door almost closed and guided Autumn back to the living room so they wouldn't have to whisper. "Maria said Gabe and Angelique were up talking very late, and they had their heads together all day while they helped in the fields. I think Angelique is good for Gabe. She lost her brother to gang violence before her parents moved their family to the United States, so she can relate to Gabe's loss in a way that we can't as adults."

Autumn glanced down the hallway. "She can stay here tonight, if that's okay with you."

"Sure. I need to go into town to the feed store first thing in the morning. I'll text you when I'm headed out. If she's up and dressed, I'll come pick her up."

"Okay."

Catherine shoved her hands into her pockets. She didn't want to leave. "Those ribs really were great tonight. Thanks for sharing them."

"I'm sort of addicted to them. The restaurant is one of my favorites. I order takeout from there a lot when I'm home."

Home. This was one of several roadblocks keeping their attraction from moving forward. Autumn had a career and friends in

Atlanta, and Catherine lived here, away from the crowds and other triggers that called up her night terrors and plunged her back into the bloody desert.

That voice of reason had been loud when Autumn first arrived in Elijah, pointing out that Autumn was too young, stupidly tied to her constantly barking phone, and made money by feeding social media—something Catherine considered the opiate of choice by the X, Y, and Z generations. But the reasonable voice was growing faint, and a new voice was becoming louder. Maybe fresh air would clear her confused brain.

Catherine stepped out onto the porch, determined to march her ass home and maybe smoke a bowl of Miguel's dreamless sleep. Halfway down the steps, she turned back to find Autumn following so close behind that she stumbled backward down the next step.

Autumn grabbed Catherine's shoulders to steady her. They were eye to eye, nose to nose. Autumn's eyes were tarnished silver in the moonlight.

Kiss her. She's so beautiful. KISS her.

Autumn's smile was as soft as the summer night was sultry. "You have barbecue sauce on your chin." She licked her finger, then used it to gently wipe away the offending spot. Her eyes searched Catherine's, and then she moved forward and placed a chaste kiss on Catherine's cheek. "Good night, Cat."

Before she could think, before the voices could begin to argue, Catherine cupped Autumn's face in her hands and claimed the lips, the mouth that purred her name like a siren's call. This kiss was not soft. It was not chaste. It was a demanding, heated clash of lips and tongues. It was liquid flame pouring through Catherine's body. It was a drum that throbbed in her chest and rolled through her belly like a sonar wave. She could crave this more than any opioid. *Got to stop.* She pushed Autumn away.

"We can't do this." It would never work.

"You keep saying that, but—"

Catherine took another step back, too far away for Autumn to touch her. She slashed her hand through the air to stop what Autumn was about to say. "It's not going to happen again." Catherine turned one-eighty, double-timed across the yard, and plunged into the line of dark trees.

❖

Autumn stood on the steps, her fingers pressed to her lips. Her head still buzzed with the rush of blood and hormones. So much had been said in that kiss. This was so insane. She couldn't want Catherine. They were such opposites. But she did want her, naked and stretched on her bed like a big, lazy cat. Autumn shook her head in a useless attempt to clear it.

This absolutely was not going to happen. She and Gabe would be leaving in a few weeks, and Gabe wouldn't have time off from school until Thanksgiving. That's when they'd be back.

So, this thing between her and Catherine was insane. She closed her eyes and drew in a deep, very deep breath of earth and spruce. Why was she even worrying? Catherine had said it would never happen again.

CHAPTER THIRTEEN

Autumn retrieved the two gifts from her tote while Catherine gathered their dishes and put them in the sink, and then they both took their seats again across Catherine's dining table from Gabe and Angelique. The girls sat close through dinner, both glum and quiet. Gabe would be leaving in the morning with Autumn, so Catherine had cooked Gabe's favorite foods and invited Angelique to join them.

Catherine took the slim package Autumn handed her under the table and nodded for Autumn to begin. She'd rehearsed what to say, but when she looked into Gabe's eyes, she simply spoke from her heart.

"I was only six years old when my parents began sending me to Grandma Swan's every summer. Dad left me here that first summer, and I was scared and homesick before he'd even gotten back in the truck to leave. I couldn't imagine spending months away from Mama and Daddy. I was sitting on the porch steps crying after he drove away, when Becki came out and sat beside me. She wrapped her arm around my shoulders and told me that we were going to be best friends, because she really needed one."

Autumn's throat tightened with emotion she hadn't anticipated the memory would bring to the surface. She smiled and swallowed hard, then forged ahead when Catherine's warm hand rested on her thigh. "And she was right. We loved Grandma Swan. Her house was our safe haven from our less-than-ideal parents. But as sweet as Grandma was, there are times when you need a best friend your own age to tell your deepest secrets." She reached under the table and gave Catherine's hand a squeeze in a silent plea.

"This year has been so very hard for all of us, but especially for Gabe." Catherine looked to Angelique. "Autumn and I love Gabe and will always do our best to be her safe haven. But your friendship this summer has been her greatest support."

Angelique blushed and glanced shyly at Gabe, who slid her chair even closer so that their shoulders touched. Gabe and Angelique were likely too young to understand what they felt for each other, but the obvious crush going on between them made Autumn's heart swell.

"Cat and I talked it over. Gabe's going to start at a new school and will experience a lot of new things while living in the city during the school year." She slid the slim box across the table to Angelique. "We checked with your mom first to make sure it was okay, but we want you to have this."

"Thank you," Angelique said, her voice soft as she took the gift.

"Go ahead and open it," Autumn said.

As Angelique began to carefully unwrap her gift, Catherine pushed the second box over to Gabe. "This one's for you."

Angelique's eyes widened, and her hand flew to her mouth. "Oh my god. It's an iPhone."

Gabe snatched her box up and tore at the paper. "No way!"

Wow. This was the cool part of parenting. Autumn grinned at Catherine, who returned the smile before schooling her face into a stern-parent expression.

"Before you get too excited, you need to hear the rules," Catherine said.

Gabe had just turned twelve, but she demonstrated a perfect teen eye roll at the mention of rules. Autumn decided to let it pass because Angelique's elbow jab into Gabe's ribs was better than a scolding. Besides, the eye roll came with a teasing grin rather than a sullen attitude.

"Gabe's trust will pay the phone bill. You have unlimited

texting and data. Until you are eighteen, your supervising adult will make random checks. We don't want to invade your privacy, but we wouldn't be responsible guardians if we didn't make sure you haven't downloaded films, music, or videos inappropriate for your age. The phones are preprogrammed with parental controls, but I also know Gabe could probably hack those controls." Catherine pointed at Gabe. "Just remember, I know somebody who can tell if you've done that."

"I realize you do," Gabe said, her expression serious now. "Do we get to negotiate if a video is," Gabe made an air-quotes gesture, "appropriate for our age?"

Catherine looked to Autumn for an answer.

Autumn paused to think this question over. "Only in advance. No negotiation after the fact," she said.

"Also, on school nights, you will give up your phones at eleven o'clock to your supervising adult and get them back the next morning," Catherine added. "We don't want you guys awake all night talking on the phone when you have to get up early for school the next day. During the weekends, you can talk and text as much as you want. So, before I give you guys the code to unlock your phones, do you agree to these rules?"

"Yes!" Angelique said, smiling. She jumped up and ran around the table to hug both Autumn and Catherine. "Thank you so much. This is the best gift ever."

Gabe ducked her head in a rare display of shyness. "Yeah. You guys rock."

Autumn's phone barked, and she opened a text from Jay, asking when to expect her and Gabe tomorrow. She began typing a reply.

"Oh, yeah. One more rule," Catherine said. "This one is mine—no phones at the table. Tonight can be an exception since you just got them, but I'm not sitting down to eat with a bunch of people staring at their phones and texting the entire time."

What? Autumn frowned as she typed a quick reply to Jay, then looked up and stuck her tongue out at Catherine. This was going to suck. She needed to be connected. Catherine raised a challenging eyebrow and stared pointedly at Autumn's phone.

"Fine," Autumn said, putting it away.

"Thank you. Now, who wants pie?"

Catherine draped a folded quilt over the porch railing. It would be her last night with Gabe for several months, and they'd planned to stay up late to see a meteor shower predicted to show up around midnight. She was studying the sky when Gabe stepped out onto the porch.

"Hey," Catherine said. "Ready to do some stargazing?"

Gabe shuffled her feet and stuffed her hands into the pocket of her jeans. "Um, I wanted to ask something."

Catherine stood and rested her hip on the porch's railing. "Sure. What's up?"

More feet-shuffling.

"Come on, Gabe," Catherine said, keeping her voice soft. "You know you can ask me anything, don't you?"

"I…well, if it's not okay, will you promise to be honest and say so?"

Catherine cocked her head. "I promise," she said, hoping she wouldn't regret it. What was this about?

"Maria is on the way to pick up Angel. She said that if I wanted to spend the night with them, she'd make sure I got back here before Autumn wanted to leave." Gabe's words came out in a rush, and then she stopped and held Catherine's gaze. "But I already said I'd look for the meteor shower with you. And I still want to…but I want to go with Angel, too."

Catherine was relieved this wasn't something serious, like Gabe announcing that she just couldn't go with Autumn. But she was a little disappointed, too. Her feelings must have shown on her face.

"Never mind. Forget I asked. It's no big deal."

Catherine grabbed Gabe's arm as she started to go back into the house. "Hold up now." She draped her arm across Gabe's shoulders and guided her down the steps and into the yard. Then she pointed to the sky. "See that really bright star?"

"Is that the North Star?"

"I think so." They gazed at it for a few seconds. "The world's not as big as you've imagined it. You'll be able to see that same star in Atlanta. So, if you get homesick while you're there, I want you to look at the star and know Angel, Elvis, and I are looking up at the same one."

Gabe gave Catherine a sideways glance. "Isn't that some sappy song from a kids' movie?"

Catherine laughed. "I don't know, but I'm sure you can google it."

"And I would want to because…?"

Catherine grasped Gabe's nape and gave her a playful shake. "Because if you find it and play it for Angel, she'll think it's very sweet."

"Oh." Gabe looked up at the star again. "I hadn't thought of that." She turned back to Catherine. "So you think she'd like it?"

"Hey, I might be old, but I can still teach you a few things about, uh, being a good friend." Whew. She'd barely caught herself. Gabe was so young. She couldn't possibly already know she liked girls, could she? Catherine's brain was frantically reviewing data—what she said, what Gabe said, how Gabe and Angelique interacted—so she was knocked back a step when Gabe slammed into her with the biggest bear hug she'd ever experienced.

"I love you, Cat." Gabe's voice cracked with emotion.

Catherine returned the hug, holding on for a long minute, then surprising herself by planting a kiss on Gabe's soft curls. "I love you, too." Headlights turned from the highway onto Catherine's long driveway. Maria had arrived to pick up Angelique. "Now go grab some things so you can stay up all night talking with Angel."

"You sure?" Gabe still looked uncertain.

"Positive. You will always have a home here, Gabe…on both these farms. Meteor showers aren't that rare, and maybe I can talk Autumn into watching this one with me." She ruffled Gabe's curls.

"Besides, don't you two need to get your phones set up and test the video calling?"

The suggestion lit Gabe's face like fireworks. "Yes. I forgot." She started for the steps, then turned and body-slammed Catherine with another hug, but this one quick before she stepped back. "Thanks for the phones. They'll help a lot."

"You're welcome. Actually, it was Autumn's idea, and she talked me into it. I was going to give you a bunch of gift certificates to Starbucks. Now go get your stuff so you don't keep Maria waiting."

Gabe didn't have to be told twice. She bounded up the steps and hurtled into the house yelling for Angel. Elvis, who had been watching them from the porch, yipped at Gabe's excitement and followed her inside, narrowly escaping a tail-caught-in-the-door incident. Catherine flinched when the screen door slammed shut behind Gabe and Elvis. "But don't slam the door," she muttered to herself. She eyed the door. "Maybe that's what happened to the other half of his tail."

❖

"Really. I've never seen a meteor shower." Autumn had so much to do to prepare for their trip tomorrow. She was absolutely anal about organization—making lists, packing and repacking. But when she saw the disappointment on Catherine's face that she'd hidden until Gabe had left, her to-do list didn't seem all that important. "When I was a kid, I was too worried about my parents getting busted for drugs and finding something in the house to eat when they forgot to feed me."

"But you were here every summer," Catherine said. She stood with her arms crossed, frowning down at the telescope case.

"Grandma didn't know about things like that because she went to bed with the chickens. And Becki, well, the only time she was interested in the stars was when she was mooning over the boy of the week. She never bothered with the science aspect of it."

Catherine still seemed unconvinced.

Autumn laid her hand on Catherine's arm. "Please?"

She knew why Catherine was hesitant. They'd spent the past weeks making sure they were never alone together for more than a few minutes. But avoiding their attraction had only ramped it up for Autumn. She was fascinated by the woman she'd first dismissed as nothing more than the stereotypical butch lesbian, because she'd discovered that Catherine Daye was so much more.

She'd seen Catherine wrestle a calf to the ground to free it from some wire and quiet a huge, skittish draft horse that dragged her halfway across the pasture. Autumn had been terrified, but Catherine was unruffled. She emitted a calm, solid energy that everyone around her drew upon. She'd witnessed Catherine wield an ax with uncanny precision—biceps bulging with the exertion— and then gently cradle a small seedling in her calloused hands to plant it in the dark, rich soil.

Catherine moved with the smooth grace of a dancer, and, oh boy, Autumn did love to watch her. Especially from behind. She dreamed about her hands on that ass. A lot. Wet dreams that left her so throbbing, she had to take matters into her own hand before she could sleep again.

And she'd caught Catherine watching her with the same hunger. Only her hunger had an ominous edge Autumn hadn't been able to figure out. Then other times, a resigned sadness that made Autumn feel fiercely protective replaced that hard edge.

Most important, when she looked deep into Catherine's mahogany eyes, Autumn saw deep intelligence and strength of character. She saw a woman who took responsibility for everyone around her—for her neighbor's kid, for hurt and abandoned animals people brought to her, and for every disabled, orphaned, widowed, and poor person who might need wood for their fireplace, a chicken coop repaired, or a vegetable garden planted to feed their families.

Autumn met and held Catherine's dark gaze now, and so much more than words passed between them. "Please, Cat."

Those simple words were armed and nuclear. What did Catherine say the military code was for nuclear bombs? Radiant angel. Appropriate. Because this radiant angel between them was going to either take them to heaven or straight to hell.

Catherine nodded, picking up the hard-shell case that held her telescope and the quilt, and leading her to a door between her bedroom and Gabe's. Autumn had guessed it to be a half bath, or a storage closet. She was wrong. When Catherine opened the door, a hidden staircase was revealed. The stairs were narrow and steep, lit only by pencil-thin luminous tubes attached to each stair. Still, she plunged into the gloom, focusing on the sexy ass barely a foot from her face to fight her claustrophobia as they ascended.

They emerged onto a ten-by-ten platform notched into the steeply slanted roof. It was like a covered porch until Catherine pushed a large button on the wall. The section of enameled tin over them retracted to reveal millions of stars.

"Wow." Autumn knew her mouth was hanging open, but she was so stunned she couldn't close it. No city lights were nearby to fade the blue-ink sky, so she felt as if she were standing among the stars. "Oh, Cat," she breathed. "This is amazing." When she walked to the rail-less edge, she reached back for Catherine's hand to anchor her.

Catherine stepped close behind Autumn and rested her hands along Autumn's hips. "I've got you." Her voice was a low burr in Autumn's ear, her breath warm on Autumn's neck. Autumn took Catherine's hands and guided them to embrace rather than steady her as she pressed her back into Catherine's front. They were a perfect fit.

"Autumn." Her name on Catherine's lips was a halfhearted plea for reprieve, but it wasn't in her power to grant it. They were both tangled in this inevitable net drawing them together.

"A night, Catherine. No one here but us. Let us have at least a night."

Catherine knew it could never be "just a night" for her. She would relive it forever in her dreams, in her thoughts. Still, she was powerless to refuse.

She turned Autumn in her arms. Their kiss was slow and gentle, then sensual, and finally hungry. She had spread out the thick quilt while Autumn was stargazing and now guided her onto it.

"I dream about you almost every night," Catherine confessed before delving into Autumn's warm mouth. Their tongues danced and wrestled, lips caressed, teeth nipped. She stroked down Autumn's side, then slipped her hand under Autumn's cropped shirt. Autumn wasn't wearing a bra, and Catherine moaned into their kiss as Autumn's nipple, hard and hot, scraped against her palm.

"Off, clothes, off," Autumn demanded. "I need to feel your skin."

Catherine rolled onto her back and shucked off her jeans. Her thighs were soaked with her arousal. When she reached for the hem of her T-shirt, Autumn's hands on Catherine's back and the warm breath in her ear stopped her.

"Let me," Autumn said, her voice little more than a whisper. "I love how hard and lean you are." Autumn's hands were under her shirt, massaging and stroking Catherine's back. "Your muscles ripple when you move, like a sleek cat." Kisses along her neck distracted her enough that she missed the warm hands moving along her rib cage and up to cup her breasts. "And I love that your skin is so soft and smooth." The simultaneous hard pinch to Catherine's nipples made her hips buck upward.

"Holy mother." She clinched her jaw, trying to hold back, to not pop off like a teenager.

A low chuckle, then Autumn tugging at her shoulders. "Flip over, Cat."

Autumn had straddled Catherine from behind, so when Catherine turned over, she was between her legs. Autumn spread her thighs wide, pulled Catherine to her. They were both so wet that they slicked together. Catherine trembled with the effort to hold back, and when Autumn raised her knees and dug her heels into Catherine's ass, urging her thrusts faster and harder, she lost it. Autumn's cry rang out over Catherine's growl of release. The muscles of her abdomen drew taut, and her vision flashed white. Her hips bucked through the waves of her orgasm, but it wasn't enough. Catherine pulled back enough to slide one, then two long fingers into Autumn to stroke the rough spot inside as she thrust against the back of her own hand.

"Oh God, oh God. Like that. Yes." Autumn arched up, wrapping her legs around Catherine's waist. "Another. One more."

Catherine pulled back to shove a third finger into Autumn. She drove hard, and her clit stiffened again against the back of her hand. Autumn's eyes widened, and she let out a scream as she clamped down on Catherine's fingers. Catherine pumped into her until Autumn grabbed her wrist and let her legs drop to the quilt.

"Enough. I think you fried all my brain circuits."

Catherine withdrew her fingers slowly, then rolled onto her back. Autumn cuddled against her side, resting her head on Catherine's shoulder. Catherine idly stroked her fingertips along Autumn's hip while Autumn used her fingers to trace random patterns on Catherine's belly.

"Cat?"

"Yeah?"

"Are you purring?"

Her low chuckle rumbled up through her chest. "I don't think so."

"Then we need to change that."

Before Catherine could respond, Autumn was sliding down her body and pushing Catherine's legs apart. "May I taste you?"

"Christ, yes." Catherine bent one knee to give Autumn better access.

Autumn's tongue was hot and skilled. She lapped at Catherine's thighs before moving to her sex. Catherine rested her left hand on Autumn's head, her hand trembling when Autumn found that sweet spot on her clit too sensitive to touch, but too pleasurable to abandon. Catherine gasped, tension gathering in her belly. And when Autumn raked her teeth across her clit and sucked hard, Catherine gave it up with a roar. Her next comprehension was Autumn crawling up her body, dropping kisses across her belly, on both of her nipples, and, finally, sucking at Catherine's pulse point.

Catherine shivered through an aftershock. "That was...that

was…I don't have words for it. Amazing, award-winning, a definite do-it-again…" She realized her mistake. Autumn had asked for only a night.

They were quiet for few seconds. "We've got time, Cat. The rest of the night. We can do anything you want," Autumn said, brushing back the hair from Catherine's face. "But either I felt a drop of rain or some bird just urinated on me."

At that moment, a deluge was soaking them. Catherine slapped the button to return the roof, and they ran for the stairs.

CHAPTER FOURTEEN

Autumn rubbed the spot on her forehead that she was sure had a spike sticking out of it. "No, really, Cat. The guidance counselor said they have a conference room set up for video chat especially for parent-teacher meetings."

They both were relieved when Gabe made two friends the first week she was in her new school. They weren't surprised that one was a baby butch like Gabe. But Autumn was pretty sure the other kid was a trans girl. Catherine was surprised, but Autumn only shook her head. "Don't you ever watch television?"

"I watch the weather news every day."

"Do you even have a Facebook page?"

"Why would I need one?"

"That's how you keep up with friends and family."

Even several hundred miles away and video-chatting on her cell phone, she could see Catherine's expression turn stony. "I don't have any family that I care to keep track of."

Autumn started to ask about friends Catherine had in the service but caught herself. That could trigger her nightmares again. Instead, she raised her eyebrow. "What about me and Gabe? I like to think the three of us are a weird little family."

Catherine's smile returned, and she slapped her forehead. "I wondered why you people are calling me all the time. That would explain it."

Autumn laughed. "Hey, do I need to phone Janet, our social worker, and get a copy of the legal paperwork to prove it?" They'd had only that one night, and they hadn't talked about it since. But something had changed between them. She'd finally gotten Catherine to download a video chat app on her phone…so she could talk to Gabe, of course. So what if she and Catherine called and chatted on the app for at least a few minutes almost every day under the pretense of keeping Catherine informed about Gabe? She was delighted to find out that Catherine actually had a snarky side when she let her guard down.

Catherine smiled. "Nah. Having a weird family is sort of nice." Her smile faded, and she glanced nervously off-camera. "I mean, it's never boring."

Autumn's heart soared at the small, unintended confession. Then, just as quickly, it dropped. They'd never be a real family. She'd done some research on PTSD, and it wasn't like the flu. Some soldiers or survivors of violence or tragedy were never able to break free of it completely. The city wasn't good for Catherine now, and Autumn didn't hold out hope that it ever would be.

"You're right. Anyway, I've got to get back to work. I'll go to the school, and we'll dial you into the conversation. I'll send you an Evite so all you'll have to do is click on *yes*. It'll send you reminders, and you'll click on the calendar item to pull up the Evite, then click on 'log into meeting.'"

"I'll write it on my kitchen calendar, too," Catherine said.

Autumn shook her head and heaved an intentionally audible sigh. "Of course. Write it on your kitchen calendar." The local feed-and-seed store printed cheap calendars that almost every farmer had tacked up in their kitchen. Each month hung under a farm-scene-of-the-month photo contained small nuggets of agriculture news, such as information about a new breed of livestock or a reminder that it was the month to winterize the hayfields by spreading lime to encourage the roots of the grass to grow. Catherine, of course, lived by it, but Autumn knew she had mentioned it as a tease because of Autumn's frustration with her avoidance of new technology. "Oh, and one last thing—promise me you won't go all ballistic on the teacher if she says anything negative about Gabe." Autumn wanted to laugh at Catherine's instantly defensive facial expression.

"Why? Have they been saying things about Gabe, making her feel different, and you haven't told me about it? Because if they've been letting someone bully her, I'll come beat the little turd's butt myself."

"Calm down. You know Gabe's not perfect, but I haven't been keeping anything from you. You know everything I know about Gabe."

"Okay."

Neither of them wanted to say good-bye, but they both had work waiting for them.

"The teacher meeting isn't until Thursday. I'll call tomorrow night to tell you all about the new people I just hired."

That brought a smile from Catherine. "Sounds good. I won't keep you any longer. You guys be careful."

"Always," Autumn said, holding in the three words that had been trying to pop out every time they reached the end of a call. She was so afraid that a text or call on an office line would distract her and she'd slip up. If she did say the three words, she was sure Catherine would withdraw and their "one night" would be exactly that.

❖

"No, Jay. I'm not going out with your cousin's friend."

Jay threw his hands up in a frustrated gesture. "Why not? You aren't dating anyone else, and having a kid doesn't mean you can't. Gabe's practically old enough to date herself."

"That's exactly what I'm doing."

Jay looked behind him to make sure she wasn't talking to someone else. "Have you gone totally cray-cray? Too much helium leak out of your balloon?"

"No. I work all day, try to spend a little time with Gabe, and then it's bedtime because I have to be up early to get Gabe off to school."

"You forgot about the hour you spend every night video-chatting with Catherine. She's why you refuse to date."

"She is not."

"Prove it. Go out with this girl just once to prove Catherine isn't the reason you quit even trying."

"It's absolutely ridiculous, but okay. Just once, then you don't get to EVER set me up on a date again. Deal?"

"I'll take that deal, because I know what you're afraid to admit. You're in love with the farmer."

"Stop calling her that, or I'll tell her, and she'll come kick your butt."

Jay shook his head, then wrapped her in a brief hug. "You guys need to stop dancing around the inevitable and instead spend your time figuring out how to make it work."

Autumn glanced at her phone. "Don't you have an appointment with the baseball-card-store client?"

"Shit. I need to get going." He grabbed the client's file and his suit jacket. "We're not done with our talk. We'll finish it later." He waved and ran out the door.

"Yes, we are," she said to the door he let slam. She had absolutely no interest in dating right now. That didn't mean she was going steady with Catherine or anything. They'd simply had "a night." Weeks later, her body still sang at the memory. It might never happen again, but, holy mother, she wouldn't turn it down.

❖

"I could kill Jay for getting me into this."

"Have you told Gabe yet?" Rachel gave Autumn a sympathetic look.

"No. Expect an explosion, then sulking."

Their three months in Atlanta had gone pretty well. Gabe had friends and liked the challenging courses at her new school. But she hadn't noticed the day of the date she'd agreed to after backing out twice because of work conflicts. She couldn't cancel on the woman for a third time, and her blind date had been smart this go-round. They were slated to attend a party filled with potential business clients, and her date had promised to introduce her around. It was a marketing bonanza. No way could she miss it, unless Rachel could fill in for her. And she couldn't. Rachel and her wife, Sam, were flying back to their hometown in a few hours for Thanksgiving, and she'd stopped by Autumn and Gabe's apartment to drop off some contracts that needed Autumn's signature.

"Do these contracts meet or exceed your expectations?"

"You sound like a management survey, but yes. I vetted them personally."

Two of the contracts were for the new associates they were hiring. Jay couldn't do it all by himself, and the client list was still growing. She began to sign the contracts on the lines Rachel kept pointing out.

"So, when are you going to tell her? This is Monday, and you guys were supposed to leave day after tomorrow."

Autumn sighed. "Today, as soon as she gets home."

Autumn and Gabe, however, were supposed to leave Wednesday morning for Elijah. Catherine and a few friends always hosted a big dinner for holiday orphans—people who didn't have family to visit or couldn't get the time off work to travel home to family—and anyone who couldn't afford turkey and all the side dishes. Gabe had talked about helping at the dinner and seeing Angelique in person rather than on a computer screen. She thought about putting Gabe on a bus or train on Wednesday, but she and Catherine both thought Gabe was too young to travel on her own. Catherine said she understood, but Autumn could hear the disappointment in her voice and read it in her expression. The more she got to know Catherine, the easier she was to read.

Barking drew her from her worried musings, and despite the spoiled plans, Autumn smiled when she saw Catherine's emoji pop up on caller ID. She tapped the invite and Catherine appeared. She looked fresh from the shower and still a little damp, so her hair hadn't been pulled into a ponytail yet. Delicious. "Hey, you."

"Hey, I've got good news—as good as it can be."

Autumn was aware that her smile was stretching her face,

but she couldn't stop it. She and Gabe would drive to Elijah on Thursday, but they'd get there too late for the big dinner. "You've rescheduled the big dinner for Friday so we can come?"

"I wish," Catherine said, her words ringing with disappointment. "But Roscoe Johnston owes me a couple of favors, and he's going to solve everything."

"Do I need to ask what kind of favors were traded?"

Catherine nearly spat the tea she was drinking onto her phone. Then she laughed, a big belly laugh, and wiped her eyes with her shirttail. "You don't need to worry about that. Roscoe is married to a big Amazon of a woman, and they have six beautiful children."

"And how is Roscoe going—"

Autumn couldn't hear the rest because Gabe came barreling in the front door of their apartment, then ran through the living room and into her bedroom, where she slammed that door shut.

"What the hell?" Catherine asked. "What was all that racket?"

"It's Gabe. She looks upset. Let me call you right back, okay?"

"Sure. But don't leave me hanging. I want to know what's going on, and you need this information before morning."

"I promise."

Autumn quickly signed the last of the contracts and handed them over to Rachel.

Rachel nodded toward the bedrooms. "Good luck with that. She looks pretty riled up."

"She'll be fine, I'm sure." Autumn thought back over the past couple of days. "She's been brooding about something all weekend."

"Well, I'll see you in about a week." Rachel gave Autumn a reassuring pat on the shoulder. "Don't worry so much. Teen years are nothing but drama. Whatever's bothering her is likely something petty she'll forget by tomorrow. Trust me. I practically raised my younger sister through her teen years."

"Thanks, Rach." Autumn was truly grateful for the invaluable help with AA Swan. She didn't think they would have grown nearly this fast if she didn't have Rachel running the business side.

"No problem. Go check on Gabe. I'll let myself out."

"She probably won't come out unless I do," Autumn said.

❖

Autumn knocked quietly on the door to Gabe's room.

"Go away. Nobody's in here."

Autumn thought she detected some tears in Gabe's voice and turned the doorknob. "I'm coming in, Gabe. I need to know what's wrong." When she got no answer, she forged ahead. She was stunned by the clutter. "Holy crap! You need to clean this up, young lady."

Gabe's only answer was a small sob. Gabe was curled into a fetal position, a pillow pressed against her belly.

Autumn rushed to the bed. "Oh my god. What's wrong? Do we need to go to the hospital?"

Gabe shook her head. Her shoulders jerked with every swallowed sob, and her face was streaked with tears.

"Did somebody hurt you?"

Again, Gabe shook her head. This time, though, she mumbled something unintelligible.

Autumn stroked Gabe's soft curls and tried to channel Catherine's calm. "Take a deep breath and say that again. I couldn't understand you."

Gabe moaned. "I'm going to die. It hurts." She sucked in a deep breath and wailed. "I want my mom." She began to cry in loud, sloppy sobs.

Autumn froze. What should she do? Was Gabe having a breakdown? She stroked Gabe's back and found the muscles hard with tension. "Okay. We need to get you to a doctor. I'll call mine and tell them we're coming."

"No-o-o."

Autumn was so startled by Gabe's hysterical shriek, she nearly fell from her perch on the edge of Gabe's bed. She wished Rachel hadn't left. Even more, she wished Catherine were here. Cat. Call Cat. "Gabe, honey, I'm going to call Catherine. Do you think you could tell her what's wrong?"

Gabe squeezed her eyes tightly shut for a few seconds, but her sobs quieted to simple crying, and she nodded several times.

"Okay. Is your iPad in your backpack? Should I call her on that so you can see her better?"

Gabe nodded.

Autumn opened the backpack that Gabe had dropped by the bed and pulled out the iPad tablet Gabe used for school. The second it booted up, she accessed the video app and tapped on Catherine's contact icon before handing the tablet to Gabe. Autumn started to rezip the backpack when she spotted the plastic grocery bag. They didn't have plastic bags in their apartment because of their bad effect on the environment. Had somebody given Gabe something?

"Hey, kiddo. What's up?" Catherine's soothing alto came from the tablet at the moment Autumn drew the bag from the backpack and realized that it held Gabe's jeans and—Gabe's wail filled the room—bloody underwear.

"I started my period, and I want to come home."

Good Lord. That was what all this drama was about? Hormones had turned her strong, rational, and sometimes stoic Gabriella into a complete drama queen. She wanted to laugh as hysterically as Gabe had sobbed. She was so relieved. At the same time, she was a bit hurt that Gabe couldn't talk to her about this. She gave herself a mental shake. This wasn't about her.

"Calm down," Catherine said. "Where's Autumn?"

"Sitting right here."

"Can you sit up so I can talk to both of you?"

"I think so."

Autumn took the tablet Gabe handed over, then held out her arm in invitation. To her relief, Gabe readily accepted and snuggled against Autumn's side.

Catherine smiled at them from the tablet's screen. "Hey, again. You guys ready?"

Gabe shivered. Autumn wasn't sure if she was cold or if the shudder was just the aftermath of Gabe's tears, but she grabbed the fleece throw at the foot of the bed and draped it over Gabe's slender shoulders before settling back into their snuggle. "Okay, we're ready," she said to Catherine.

"Gabe, Autumn was going to tell you when you got home from

school today, but she has an important work thing she has to go to Wednesday evening."

"No! We'll miss Thanksgiving." Gabe tried to yank away, but Autumn held her tight. "It's not work. Jay says she has a date." Her petulant tone was turning angry. "I'm not going to miss Thanksgiving so she can go on a date."

Crap. Jay and his big mouth. "It's not a date. I wouldn't mess up our plans for that." Autumn was frantic for Catherine to believe this. She tightened her hold on Gabe and gave her a little shake. "Stop. It's not a date. Let's hear what Catherine has to tell us." Gabe stopped trying to free herself from Autumn's hold but wouldn't look at her or Catherine. "Go ahead, Cat."

"Gabe, you remember Roscoe?"

Gabe looked up, her sulk forgotten. "The Roscoe who flies planes?"

Catherine nodded. "He flies charters out of the small private airfield just outside Elijah," she said to Autumn. "Anyway, he owes me a few favors, so we worked a deal for him to pick up Gabe at Fulton County's Charlie Brown airfield not too far from you and fly her home tomorrow morning. Then Autumn can drive up on Thursday. How's that?"

Gabe sniffed and wiped her nose on the fleece throw. "I'll get to fly in an airplane?"

"Yep. Roscoe was a navy pilot until he busted his eardrum and couldn't fly those supersonic jets any more. He's a great pilot. You'll be safer with him in the sky than you would be on the roads this weekend."

Gabe brightened. "I'm so sprung," she said, then grimaced and clutched her stomach.

Catherine's brow furrowed, so Autumn translated. "She's excited about flying. I'm familiar with Charlie Brown Field. What time does she need to be there?"

"He'll meet you in the waiting area around eight in the morning."

"I'll have her there."

"Great. And you can take care of...the other crisis?"

"A quick walk to the drugstore, and I'll have her all fixed up now that I know the problem."

"See you guys soon, then."

"Wait," Gabe said. "Is Elvis there?"

Elvis's big head appeared in place of Catherine's.

"Hey, Elvis." Gabe's eyes filled with tears again. "I miss you, boy." She giggled, though, when his big pink tongue swiped across the screen.

"Yuck," Catherine said, reappearing on the screen. "See you tomorrow, Gabe."

"Bye." Autumn got a little wave in response before the screen went black. Damn. They needed to talk, but first things first. "You need to soak in a warm bath while I run to the drugstore, then put on those baggy sweatpants you love and a long-sleeve T-shirt. But let me get you a couple of pain pills first. Then I'll go forage for menstruating essentials."

"The nurse at school gave me a couple of, uh, pads."

"I'll pick up more, but you also need chocolate, cola, and soup."

"Okay." Gabe clutched her pillow to her stomach.

Autumn grabbed her phone as she headed to her bathroom for a couple of pain-relief tablets and typed a quick text.

It's not a date.

CHAPTER FIFTEEN

Autumn stood at the entrance to Becki's barn-slash-studio. Four folding tables were pushed together in the middle of the barn to form a banquet table and several more placed against the wall and laden with warming trays filled with the fixings of a traditional Thanksgiving feast.

Her escort had been a very attractive, successful woman—just the type she usually dated—and the party was loaded with people she needed to meet. But her heart was in Elijah.

The men in expensive suits and women in designer dresses seemed so needlessly extravagant in contrast to Catherine's friends who worked in less glamorous jobs for less money. These people didn't have to worry about heat during the winter or grocery bills. They wouldn't be financially devastated by an emergency hospital stay or a major car repair. When she surveyed the room, she realized those people just didn't seem all that important now. After a few hours, she'd faked a migraine and told her not-a-date to stay, because she obviously was having a great time. Then Autumn took a taxi home, threw her stuff into the car, and steered toward Elijah.

She'd had to stop twice for naps and was tired and stiff from the ride. But she was here, and this farm, this community of people felt more like home than her Decatur apartment.

"Aut, you're here." Gabe looked much better, having made it past that first day of menstrual cramps. Her smile was radiant as she crossed the room, tugging Angelique along with her. Elvis was at their heels and yipped a greeting when he spotted Autumn.

Autumn opened her arms and hugged each of the girls, then bent to receive a lick on her cheek from Elvis. "Where's Catherine?"

"She's out back where they're frying turkeys. You got here just in time. They're almost ready to eat."

"She'll be so surprised to see you," Angelique said. "Go ahead. We'll get them to put an extra place setting next to ours."

"Thank you, Angel. That's so sweet."

"We'll take care of everything," Gabe said, puffing her chest out. "Cat's been a little grumpy. Maybe you being here will put her in a better mood."

A playful shove from Gabe started Autumn walking toward the opening at the other end of the barn, but she was stopped repeatedly by Maria, Ed, Gaylord, Jody, and Jody's wife for hugs and greetings. When she finally made it outside where several turkey fryers were gathered, Catherine and two men were extracting the last of the turkeys to take inside for carving. She waited until they were done and one of the men hurried the turkey inside, while the other shut down the fryer.

"Cat," she called out.

Catherine turned, her eyes searching for who was summoning her. When Autumn gave a little wave, Catherine spotted her, and her face transformed into a huge, beautiful smile. Then the welcome in her eyes dimmed a bit, and the dazzling smile dropped a few kilowatts before freezing in place. She'd expected as much. Catherine hadn't answered her text Monday night, and she hadn't heard from her at all Tuesday or yesterday. "It was not a date. It was work." She wasn't going to let this misunderstanding continue. "I made that clear when she picked me up and gave her the option to take someone else to the event. Then we went to the event, she graciously introduced me around to some people I needed to meet, and I took a taxi home after a few hours and drove all night to get here in time."

"Autumn, you can date anyone you want. We're friends. We had one night. I don't have any claim on you."

Someone rang a dinner bell inside, and the few folks who were smoking and talking by a couple of burn barrels extinguished their smokes and headed inside.

"They're ready to eat," Catherine said, moving to follow the smokers.

Autumn grabbed her hand and tugged her back. "Do you want one?"

Catherine frowned. "One what?"

"Would you want to have a claim, or was one night all you wanted, all you still want?"

"Autumn—" Catherine glanced at the barn, where Ed was waving for them to come inside.

Autumn stepped close and reached up to curl her hand around Catherine's neck. She tugged her down and kissed her quickly, but with purpose. "We don't have time now, but we're going to talk about this later." She held Catherine's gaze, hoping to feed her some of the certainty she was beginning to feel about their future. "Because I want more than a night with you."

❖

The leaves gone from the trees, the full moon illuminated the path through the woods between the farms, and Catherine could easily see Autumn trotting in her direction.

Catherine had volunteered to help some of their elderly or infirm guests back home after the dinner, while Autumn had stayed to help with the final cleanup. She'd needed time to think. Her brain was still spinning with Autumn's surprise appearance and declaration. *I want more than a night with you.*

Dinner had been exhilarating and excruciating. Autumn had been seated between her and Gabe, and the conversation flowed easily among and around them. Autumn seemed to move seamlessly between her city friends and the Elijah community. Catherine could easily envision her, Autumn, and Gabe living here like a real family. Except Autumn's work was in the city, and Catherine had little hope she could survive, much less ever be happy there.

Even if they could overcome that distance, Autumn was beautiful and accomplished. Her future seemed to hold limitless possibilities. Catherine was a farmer with calloused hands and plain features. Her jaw was too square, her brown hair too straight, and her eyes an unremarkable brown. Just an ordinary woman of average talent living an unremarkable existence because her future was limited by her past. She was damaged goods.

Still, they'd have to face this situation at some point. Avoiding Autumn wasn't an option since they shared Gabe. She took out her phone.

Coffee?

Do you really need to ask? On my way.

Now Catherine stood on the porch, her emotions shifting between unease and anticipation as Autumn grew closer, her smile already showing in the semi-light. She stopped a few feet from Catherine, uncertainty etched in her expression. Autumn was beautiful anytime, but she was radiant in the soft moonlight.

"Hey," Autumn said, her breath sending little puffs of white into the chill night air.

Hell. They could talk later. Catherine held out her arms, and Autumn launched into them, nearly knocking them both to the ground. Their mouths met, and their tongues dueled until they were out of breath and already tugging at clothing in their eagerness to share skin.

"Inside," Autumn ordered her. "Inside the house, inside the bedroom, and inside me."

Catherine shuddered at the image, then scooped Autumn up and bounded into the house. She was good at following orders.

They made love for hours before entwining their bodies and falling fast asleep. And when Catherine woke with the faint light of dawn, she was wet and ready again—probably because Autumn was already awake and tracing an erotic message across Catherine's abdomen and breasts.

"Remember the wet dream you told me about after we made love our first time together?"

Catherine's breath quickened. "Yeah." She hardly recognized

her own hoarse whisper. She did remember. She had remembered over and over during the past months.

Autumn rose and straddled Catherine's thighs. She slid her fingers between Catherine's legs, along her sex, lighting a fire in Catherine's belly. Then she held the fingers up as glistening proof of Catherine's readiness.

"I brought a little present with me," she said, hovering over Catherine to reach for the other side of the bed and the gift she'd hidden there.

Catherine sucked in a sharp breath when Autumn held up a double-headed dildo. Holy crap. Words eluded her, so she nodded her consent. Autumn smiled, her eyes bright as they held Catherine's while Autumn's fingers found her entrance. Catherine moaned as the smaller end filled her and the curve of the prosthetic fit against her stiff clit. Then her sex tightened when Autumn fisted the larger end and pumped several times, and her eyes almost rolled back in her head when she bent to roll her tongue around it before taking it into her mouth and pumping two, three more times. A telltale tingle of pleasure began to gather in her belly.

"Not going to last," Catherine groaned.

Autumn rose over her and guided the thick end into herself. "Oh, God, Cat. It feels so good, so tight inside me." Catherine grasped Autumn's slim hips and guided, paced her thrusts. Back and forth, in and out, up and down. Back and forth.

Catherine's belly began to tighten again, the tingle gathered, and she quickened the pace. Back, forth. Up, down. She felt her clit swell with each slide, then the crush of the dildo on her clit. It built until she could wait no longer. She grabbed and held Autumn's hips to stop the up and down in favor of back and forth, in and out, in and out, in and out. Then she was yelling, and her belly was exploding and firing synapses of pleasure in every part of her.

Just as pleasure had filled her body, Catherine's libido was filled with a mission. She hugged Autumn to her and rolled. She pumped into Autumn, fast and hard. Autumn grabbed for a hold on the sheets while Catherine rode her.

"Oh, God, Cat. Don't stop. Don't stop."

Urged on by Autumn's plea and the heels digging into her thighs, Catherine pushed Autumn's knees up and pumped deeper, harder, faster still. Amazingly, the sight of Autumn with her knees to her chest, the fat cock pumping in and out to a chorus of grunts and whispers primed, fueled Catherine's desire anew. Autumn's hands fluttered along Catherine's arms, then grasped her shoulders.

"Yes, yes, yes," Autumn screamed at the ceiling, throwing Catherine over the edge again.

Once Catherine slowed, then collapsed, they lay panting in the aftermath.

"Oh, yeah." Autumn whispered. "We'll have to do this again… not right now…but soon. I'm not sure I'll even be able to walk right today."

Catherine chuckled. She'd never, well, she'd only dreamed of the passion, the pleasure that came with their abandon. "Has my vote, too," she whispered in Autumn's ear before pulling out slowly, then divesting herself as well.

Autumn glanced at the clock, then popped up. "Shit. We have to get out of this bed. The girls are probably awake. I have to get back to my place." She ran around gathering her cast-off clothes, then disappeared into Catherine's bathroom and shouted over the sounds of the toilet flushing, then water running in the sink. "Angel's sister stayed the night with them. I think the little stinkers are on to us and conspired to set us up for a night to ourselves."

Catherine smiled and shook her head as she rose more slowly, pulling on her jeans when she found them. She wanted to bask in the morning afterglow, but having a kid around didn't always allow that. Still, she enjoyed the feeling.

She picked up her shirt, then closed her eyes. They needed to talk about this. About them. About whether they had a future. And she had to be honest about some other things with Autumn, even if her revelations sent her running far away. "Isn't this your underwear?" She held up the pink panties she'd found from the "wing" of her wing-backed reading chair. She realized Autumn had gone silent, and she turned slowly to face the bathroom door.

Autumn's face was a tornado of emotions—sadness, anger,

pain, stoniness—changing so fast that Catherine's happy glow froze in her chest. She held up the prescription bottle that was capped with a dropper. "What is this?" Her question was flat and devoid of emotion.

Catherine's mind raced for how to explain, and then she simply answered. "It's a legal prescription for when I have a bad episode of PTSD."

Autumn's glare stabbed into Catherine. "It's cannabis, and it's not legal in this state and most of the country. You keep this around where Gabe can see it?"

"She knows it's a prescription drug and not for casual use. Having it in my bathroom is no different than Becki having an opioid prescription in her medicine cabinet, except that opioids are a hundred times stronger and more addictive."

"Don't lecture me about weed. I grew up with parents who did nothing but farm and smoke it." She tossed the bottle onto the bed. "They grew it even though they knew if they got busted and sent to jail, I'd end up in foster care. They were so busy smoking their harvest, they couldn't hold real jobs." Her volume rose with each word. "So I had to wear thrift-shop clothes to school and take the bus to the food bank for poor people to put some groceries on the table. They cared more about their marijuana habit than they did me." Tears ran down her cheeks. "The distance, our age, and our differences didn't matter to me. But this does." She pushed past Catherine and yanked open the bedroom door they'd closed in case Gabe popped over before they were awake.

"Wait. We need to talk about this."

Autumn paused but didn't turn around. "I have absolutely nothing to say to you. I'm going back to Decatur as soon as I can load the car, and I'm taking Gabe with me. I'll be in touch with Gaylord to file for full custody. She's my blood kin, not yours. And if you fight me on this, I'll tell them why she can't live with you."

The front door slammed shut behind her, and so did Catherine's shattered heart.

CHAPTER SIXTEEN

Gabe's two friends shot nervous glances at Autumn as they followed Gabe through the living room on their way to her bedroom. Autumn sighed. Tomorrow was the first day of Christmas break, and Gabe was still giving her the silent treatment after she'd terminated their Thanksgiving holiday prematurely. She half expected Gabe to be gone one morning, having found a way back to Elijah and Catherine. She knew that Gabe talked almost daily with Catherine because Gabe made no effort to hide their conversations.

The past three weeks had been worse than rough.

Sheriff Cofy had called and tried to talk to Autumn. He knew about Catherine's prescription. No, she wasn't going to jail for having it if he had anything to do with it.

Catherine had called and texted repeatedly for more than a week, pleading for Autumn to talk with her. Then she stopped, and the silence grew more deafening with each day.

The only time Gabe said more than yes or no to her questions was when they had repeated shouting matches about Catherine. Gabe had screamed, cried, and, the last time, told Autumn in a deadly quiet voice that she hated her.

As if that wasn't enough, she tortured herself over whether she was doing the right thing. She had contacted Gaylord like she'd threatened. She'd also spent hours reading studies on the use of cannabis to treat PTSD. She worried that she was piling her childhood baggage onto Gabe.

The situation was tearing her apart. She'd snapped at Jay so much, he was avoiding her and going to Rachel for everything. Rachel was great. She listened to the whole story, then shrugged. "I don't think anyone but you can decide what to do. But you should talk to Catherine. You never gave her a chance to tell her side of this story. Then listen to your heart, not your head. It always knows best."

Rachel and Sam were throwing a Christmas party tonight. She was invited, of course, as were Jay and Evan. When she tried to use Gabe as an excuse to not go, Rachel gave her a pointed stare. "Gabe is invited, too. Several people are bringing their kids."

She wasn't sure Gabe would go anywhere with her, and the last place she felt like being was at a holiday party. This was going to be the worst Christmas ever.

She scowled when a knock at the door pulled her from her pity party. She missed her old apartment that had a doorman and a keyed elevator that let only residents with a key fob past the lobby. It was probably another of Gabe's friends, but she checked the peephole anyway. She yanked the door open when she recognized the man standing there.

"What are you doing here?"

"Is that any way to talk to your father?"

Autumn stared at him. He looked old. His hair had turned completely white, and he was thinner than she'd ever seen him, but fairly fit for a man in his late sixties. Why was he here? The next thought hit her hard. "Mama?"

"She's at home. She's not sick or anything, just very upset right now. But I'd rather not talk about this from the hallway. Can I come in?"

Autumn hesitated. More than one therapist had told her that she'd never resolve her childhood baggage unless she discussed her feelings with her parents. Maybe she should before she fucked up any more lives. She stepped back and motioned for him to come in.

His eyes roamed over every inch of the living area, taking it all in. "You've done well for yourself, Princess."

She flinched at his pet name for her. She felt more like a troll. "If you and Mama need money—"

He gave her a sharp look. "We're more than comfortable financially. That's not why I'm here."

"I'm going to have a drink. Do you want something?" She went into the kitchen, and he followed but stopped on the other side of the granite-topped island.

"A glass of water would be welcomed."

She poured him a glass of bottled water, then pulled her favorite blended whiskey and a glass from the cabinet for herself and carried it to the dining table and sat. "So, sit down and tell me why you're here. It's been, what, eight years? No, there was Grandma Swan's funeral. That was my chance to reconnect with Becki, but you and your brother managed to get into an argument that messed up that family reunion."

"Go ahead and say it all. Every little thing you've been carrying around since you were a headstrong kid. I probably deserve a lot of it and should have shown up a long time ago to let you get it all off your chest. Your mama and I know you had it rough, and we should have been able to do better by you. But there's another side of the story."

Autumn was about to lay into him, but Gabe's door opened, and the kids headed for the front door.

"We're going to get some pizza," Gabe said without looking their way.

"If Becki heard you talking to an adult with that attitude, she'd have a switch after you in a skinny minute."

Gabe whirled, her face lighting up with her first smile since they'd returned to Decatur. "Uncle Peter!" She flung herself at him, and he caught her with a big hug.

"Hey, Tadpole. I'm sorry I missed your mama's memorial." He glanced at Autumn. "We just thought it might go better if we weren't there."

Autumn was stunned. Gabe knew her father? Why didn't she know about this?

"I want to go home, Uncle Peter. Take me back to Catherine and Elvis, or take me home with you."

He looked at her friends, who stood frozen by the door. "If you guys don't mind, I need to visit with Gabe a bit." He set his glass of water on the table and fished a couple of bills from his wallet. "You guys go have some pizza on me."

The girl, Julie, grabbed the money. "Thanks."

He cocked his head. "Does that place deliver?" When both kids nodded, he fished two more twenties from his wallet and handed them over. "Can you ask them to send a large sausage and pepperoni to this address? Y'all can keep the change."

"Sure," Julie said. "We can do that."

"Great. It was nice meeting some of Gabe's friends."

"Nice meeting you, sir," the boy said.

"Nice to meet you," Julie echoed before they darted out the door with big smiles and clutching the pizza money.

He turned to Gabe. "Get you something to drink, and then I want you to sit down with us."

Gabe's face clouded with a scowl, but he put a hand up.

"Don't give me that look. I've seen it too often from Princess here, so I've built up an immunity. Just get your drink and sit down, Gabriella. Both of you need to hear what I've got to say. But you need to have a little patience because I'll have to start from the beginning for it all to make sense."

Autumn had been silent long enough. *After all these years, he just strolls in, hands out pizza money to Gabe's friends, and thinks he can order me and Gabe around in my own house?* "How about we start with why you kept in touch with Becki, but not your own daughter?"

"My daughter wouldn't talk to me or her mother. But we've been around. You just didn't know it."

"Right. Where were you when I was struggling through college and starting up my business?"

"I'll answer that one question, but then you have to let me tell it the way I need to." He took a long drink of his water while Gabe sat at the end of the table, between him and Autumn. "The scholarship you received your sophomore year, and every year after that your tuition, books, and meal plan?"

"The Addison Ridge scholarship."

"Yes. Your mama and me set up and endowed that scholarship at Emory."

Autumn snorted. "Yeah. Right. You guys were living in that little shack outside town, growing pot and smoking your days away when I graduated high school early and left."

"You left in the middle of the night, and it took a while for us to find where you were." He waved a dismissive hand. "But I'm getting ahead of myself."

The doorbell rang, and he paused while Autumn went to the door to get the pizza and Gabe got plates and napkins for them. When they settled again, he started over.

"We never told you because any mention of it still throws your mama into a depression, but we had a son before you came along."

Autumn stopped chewing and swallowed. "I have a brother?"

"Had," Peter said. "He died when he was still a baby. Your mother was already pregnant with you. I still think her having all those pregnancy hormones in her body when we lost him is what caused her to take it so hard and never get over it." He took a bite of pizza and stared down at the table while he chewed. His eyes were watery when he looked up. "Actually, I don't think any parent gets over the loss of a child, but most of us find a way to live with it. Your mother still struggles even after all these years."

He put his pizza slice down. "Here's the whole story. Addison Ridge Swan was born three years before you. We both blame our drug use in our teens for him being born with a rare disease that causes constant seizures. The doctors said it was genetic, but we still feel responsible. He was a beautiful baby."

Peter dug his wallet out again and extracted a faded photo that he slid across the table for her to see. The two-year-old in the picture was nearly identical to her at the same age.

"During the three years he lived, his medical bills were huge. We didn't mean for your mama to get pregnant when she did. We both believe every woman should make her own choice, but ours was to take responsibility. When Ridge was born, his illness took all our time and money. We were nearly at the end of our rope when your grandpa on your mother's side died and left her some mountain land. He'd moonshined up in those hills, but we grew cannabis.

"It wasn't legal, but it was hard to hold jobs when you had to constantly be with your baby at the hospital. That shack we lived in was close to the land. We wouldn't risk living on it because of you. If the feds saw the plants from the sky, they could cut it down but couldn't charge us with anything unless they caught us on the property with the plants. That's why we didn't live there, and why we sent you to stay with my mama every summer when we had to harvest. It was a risky time of year, and if we did get caught, you'd be safe with Mama instead of social services putting you in with a bunch of juvenile delinquents until she could wade through all the paperwork."

Gabe took the photo Autumn put back down on the table and scrutinized it. "He looks like the pictures Mama had of her brother."

"They were cousins," Peter said, patting Gabe's arm. "Anyway, our biggest mistake was the one we made after our little princess was born. Mary was so depressed over Ridge's death that I had to step up and take care of you. Doctors told us later that not forcing her to bond with you right after you were born damaged her relationship with you from the get-go."

"So that was your big mistake?" Autumn was still skeptical.

"No. Some research was finally being done on medicinal uses for cannabis. Before it was illegal, it was the poor man's medicine because you could grow your own instead of going to the drugstore. Your mama had become obsessed with finding some cure for Ridge's disease, and when she read in *The New York Times* that some doctors were finding cannabis might help other kids with the same disease, she wrote to the doctors. You were two years old. To shorten the story, we began to raise a certain type of cannabis for those researchers, and we also donated every penny we didn't absolutely need to their cause. Every time I tried to keep more for us and you, your mama would sink into a deep depression. You probably don't remember the times when she was in the hospital for months after trying to take her own life."

"Mama tried to commit suicide?"

"Three times. You were Gabe's age the last time. But it was in the late spring, and she was out of the hospital by the time you came back to start the school year." His eyes began to fill with tears again. "Giving more of ourselves to our dead son than our living daughter was our biggest mistake. I knew it was wrong, but you were so strong, and your mama was so fragile." He straightened his shoulders and held her gaze. "I should have stood up for you, but I didn't. I'm not making excuses or asking to be forgiven. That's something I have to live with."

Autumn didn't think she could forgive him. "So why are you telling me all this now?"

"Because if you throw Catherine away and drive a wedge between her and Gabe, you're the one who'll suffer the most."

Autumn pushed her chair back and went to the window at the other end of the small dining area, turning her back to him. She didn't want him or Gabe to see her struggling against new tears. When her throat loosened, she spoke without turning around. "Are you Catherine's supplier? Is that how you know her?"

"Not exactly, but that's the other part of the story." He sipped the water, then put a couple of pizza slices on his plate and slid it out of Gabe's reach. "Just so you don't eat it all before I'm done. I swear you're growing like a weed."

"I was going to save you some," Gabe said around the big bite she had in her mouth.

He smiled, then turned back to Autumn. "Catherine bought the property next to Mama after the army gave her her walking papers. She was still in pretty bad shape. Her last tour in Afghanistan ended very badly, but that's not my story to tell. Their doctors healed her physical injuries, then honorably discharged her when they couldn't fix her mental wounds as easily. She came to the farm to hide out, but you know Becki. She wouldn't let such a young woman turn into a hermit. Still, Catherine was losing her battle with PTSD when Becki read somewhere that they were experimenting with medical cannabis to treat PTSD and depression. So, she got in touch with me and introduced us. We began to haul in a pretty good income right when you left home because the kind of cannabis we grew showed the most potential for medical uses. That's how I set up the scholarship once we tracked you down."

"Cat started growing cannabis for you?" Gabe asked.

"No, honey. I suspect she has a few plants tucked away somewhere on her three hundred acres, but I never asked. The medicinal cannabis saved her. Becki's death seems to have triggered her flashbacks again, but they've been rare for several years. She's seeing her therapist again to get back to that point, and he's unofficially endorsed her cannabis prescription.

"Anyway, because of Catherine's concern for lots of other soldiers dealing with PTSD and getting addicted to opioids, she put together a blind consortium of investors from her military and family contacts. Although Catherine won't have anything to do with them, her family is very rich and has connections all over the world. Anyway, the consortium invested in a guy who was sure Colorado was going to legalize cannabis and had plans for a big farm and laboratory to research and produce medical cannabis. She let me into the group and ante-upped for Becki, who later paid her back. She's way more than a farmer. She's a financial planner. A very good one. We've all made millions. That consortium is still pouring money into Gabe's trust every quarter."

Autumn was stunned. "The money Becki willed to me, that I've been investing in AA Swan LLC, is drug money?"

"Pharmaceutical profit. There's a difference. If you'd bothered to check, you'd know that your mama and I have lived in Colorado for a while now. We don't grow anything but the petunias in the front-yard flower bed. I work as a lobbyist for the National Hemp Growers Council. A lot of children like Ridge live in states that won't approve medical uses for cannabis. I intend to change that in as many states as possible before I head off to the afterlife."

"I need some time to digest all this," Autumn said, her head spinning.

"Listen to your heart, Princess. Your head will spend years overthinking this. Your heart already knows what's right. Catherine Daye not only found a way to survive, but she's spent her time since she got out of the army saving a lot of other people—other victims of PTSD and depression, poor folks like those in Shady Grove who needed land to grow their own food, and every stray dog and horse that gets dropped off there. She patches them up and helps them find a new home."

"I miss Elvis," Gabe said, staring down at her empty plate.

Peter reached across the table and grabbed Autumn's hand, holding tight when she tried to pull back. Then he took Gabe's in his other one. "Both of you listen to me. Autumn, if you never do it again, you need to try to see past the walls you've built. If you don't, you're going to damage more than just your life. Gabe needs you, and you need her. I want you to tell her about what you suffered as a kid. And, Gabe, I want you to listen. It'll help you understand why Autumn reacts the way she does."

Gabe scowled. "You mean why she freaked out over Cat's medicine and fucked everything up for all of us?"

"Language," Autumn and Peter said at the same time. Autumn shared a smile with him for the first time since she was very small.

"Y'all both sound like Grandma Swan," Gabe said.

"Where do you think we heard it?" Autumn said, poking Gabe's arm. Gabe smiled...a little.

Peter looked at his watch. "Well, I've got a plane to catch. An Uber's picking me up out front in about ten minutes."

Gabe jumped up and grabbed his plate of uneaten pizza. "I'll put this in a bag, and you can eat it on the way to the airport, Uncle Pete."

"Thanks, Gabe."

Autumn followed him to the door while Gabe ducked into the kitchen. Peter lowered his voice. "Catherine will fry my ass if she finds out I told you, but she's been trying to work up the nerve to come see you since you won't take her calls. The city has a lot of triggers for her, but you can bet she won't bring any of her medicine with her, just because of the way you feel about it."

"She shouldn't have that stuff around Gabe."

"Have you heard nothing I've said?" He leaned in nose to nose with her, his whisper fierce. "Your stupid blind spot about cannabis has devastated her. I'm worried. Becki's not there anymore. She's out there working both farms and spending every night alone. Ed tries to get by there every day to check on her, but that's too much time alone with her flashbacks and night terrors. Thank the stars for Elvis and Gabe. Right now, they're her only two reasons to keep living." He grabbed her hand and slapped a small breath mint tin into it. "If she does try to come here and shows up in the middle of a flashback, you see if you can find at least a shred of humanity in yourself and give her this chewable. If she hasn't shown up by New Year's Day, you can flush it."

He took the bag of pizza and the bottled water Gabe held out for him. "I'll be checking on you, Gabe. I feel like this is all my fault, but if Autumn doesn't come around and tries to cut Catherine out of your life, I will hire the best lawyers I can find to fight for what's best for you and Catherine."

Autumn was stunned. Would he really shut her out?

He met her and held her stare. "I'm sorry, Princess. Sorry for messing up your life. If I can't save you, then I'll do what I can to save Gabe—to keep you from making her as bitter as you are."

CHAPTER SEVENTEEN

Autumn sulked and drank herself into a sure hangover after her father left. His news and her feelings were too tangled to sort.

When she reached the bottom of the bottle and had nearly drowned in her pool of pity, Gabe came out of her bedroom and picked up the empty bottle. She looked at Autumn in disgust, then got a soda out of the refrigerator and went back to her room.

Autumn had never felt so low—like the carcass of an animal too slow to dodge that first car, then continually flattened into the pavement as more and more tires crushed her out of existence.

She'd never felt so lost. Her father's side of the story shed a whole new light on her childhood, Autumn had grown accustomed to the emotional baggage born from her perspective as a child. She wasn't ready to give up her anger. It'd been the force that drove her to be better, more successful than she'd perceived her parents to be. What would propel her now?

❖

Catherine's warm exhales were wispy white puffs as she broke the ice on top of the watering trough in the lower pasture. She had to take her gloves off to open the small lock on the battery housing of the trough's warmer—the device that was supposed to keep the water from freezing—and cold almost instantly numbed her fingers. "God damn it." She cursed the cold and the cow that'd sloshed mud over the solar panel so the batteries couldn't get enough light to recharge. She'd cleaned off the panel, but the batteries were depleted, and the trough would freeze again before they could recharge, so she had to change them out. "I don't know what the hell I was thinking when I bought these warmers. Just another stupid thing in a long string of stupid things I've done."

She muttered more to herself than Elvis, who was keeping the thirsty cows at bay until she could finish.

She usually liked the crisp cold of winter because it was so opposite from the hot desert. The fields lay fallow, recharging the soil's nutrients for spring, so she only had the animals to tend. That left her lots more time to read in front of the fire. She'd always liked the solitude of the season and the quiet of a snowy day. But this winter was too lonely, the days too quiet.

Today was especially bleak.

Ed Cofy had come by earlier to give her the summons. Autumn was making good on her threat to sue for full custody of Gabe, and worry gnawed at Catherine. Each nightly communication found Gabe growing more and more bitter. She begged Catherine incessantly to let her come home to the farm, but Catherine could only implore her to be patient and give Autumn time to think things through. Two nights ago, Gabe declared that if Catherine didn't want her anymore, she'd rather live in a foster home rather than stay with Autumn. Last night, for the first time since Thanksgiving, Gabe hadn't called or answered Catherine's invitation to connect via her tablet.

Shoving the batteries into place and relocking their housing, Catherine watched the underwater heating element flicker, then glow. She wished the rest of her life could be fixed so easily.

"Come on, Elvis. Let's let 'em have a drink." She headed for the gate, and the cows edged tentatively up to the trough as Elvis turned and followed her.

Catherine was so tired. Her nightmares had returned. Last night, when one young soldier turned toward her, it was Gabe's face she saw peeking from under the helmet. And when she drew back the blankets with her baton, it was Autumn, not the old lady who stared at her in terror. Elvis had been her anchor through each dream, each night. But Gabe needed him more. She might be a lost cause, but Gabe wasn't.

"Elvis, how do you feel about becoming a city dog?"

❖

Autumn squinted against the diffuse midday sun that penetrated the cloud cover and lit her bedroom. The pounding in her head and queasy stomach was a stern rebuke of her pity party the night before. She groaned and clutched her stomach when she sat up too quickly, then waited for her head and stomach to stop spinning. Shower, then coffee. It was time to face the world again, along with the problems still waiting.

After two glasses of water, aspirin for her headache, and a long shower, she ventured out into the apartment. Gabe was watching television and eating some two-week-old chips.

"Aren't those stale? I was going to throw them out," Autumn said.

Gabe stared at the television. "Nothing else to eat."

Autumn sighed. Teens were so dramatic. Surely there was something better than stale chips. "I'll make some dinner for us."

She slogged into the kitchen and began opening cabinets. They were empty of anything that could make a meal. So was the refrigerator. She closed her eyes against flashes of searching for something, anything to eat while her mother hid in her dark bedroom, sleeping for days. Then she sat down at the table and began to cry.

"I'm sorry. I'm so sorry. This is what my mother did to me. I can't do this to you. God, I'm glad Becki isn't here to see me treat you like this."

Gabe looked over at her. "What are you talking about?"

"There's nothing in the house to eat. Not even stale bread you can toast and pour catsup over."

"Yuck. That sounds nasty. I wouldn't eat that anyway." Gabe clicked the television off and got up from the couch. She walked over to the table where Autumn sat but propped against the wall on the other side, like Autumn was a wild animal that might lunge at her. "Is that what you ate when you were a kid?"

"That's all that was in the house. Sometimes not even that."

Gabe shrugged. "So why didn't you order pizza or something?"

"There was no money. When Dad went on trips, Mama would stay in her bedroom for days. I don't know how she survived. At least I got to eat at school. I used to swipe food that kids didn't eat and left on their plates, like yogurt cups or an apple. Until one of the mean girls saw me and everybody started calling me DD."

Gabe sat down across the table from her. "DD?"

"Dumpster diver."

"Man, that's harsh."

Autumn should have been embarrassed, but the more she told Gabe about her childhood, the lighter she felt.

"No wonder you weren't that happy to see Uncle Peter."

"It's hard to find out things weren't the way you remembered them. I can hardly wrap my mind around it."

"Well, Grandma Swan would say, you can't drink your problems away. They'll still be there the next morning, and you'll have to deal with them while your head's pounding and your stomach wants to come up."

"Why didn't you order some pizza instead of eating those stale chips? You know my wallet and debit card are in my purse right over there."

Gabe looked at her. "I didn't have permission. I wouldn't go through your purse, much less use your credit cards, without permission. Mama taught me better."

Autumn stared at her, but Gabe stared back with the same truthful calm she'd seen in Catherine's eyes so many times. It made her want to cry again. "Gabe, if I ever get too busy or too self-centered to keep food in this kitchen for you, I'm giving you permission to use my credit card to order takeout or visit the grocery store for whatever you need."

Gabe studied her, then nodded. "I could go for some Chinese right now."

Autumn stood and went into the kitchen to get a menu from the take-out drawer. "That actually sounds good." She spied the empty liquor bottle on the counter and dropped it into the trash chute after handing the menu to Gabe.

"Cat hardly ever drinks," Gabe said. "She has two bottles of wine, red and white, in case a friend who likes wine visits. And she has that bottle of brandy that she likes to drizzle over desserts, but she keeps that in a locked cabinet, which is where she keeps her medicine for PTSD, too. I don't know why you found a bottle on her bathroom counter. She's always careful, even though she knows I'd never touch it." She scanned the menu. "You've got a lot of liquor in that unlocked cabinet. Julie and Ricky pointed that out last week when they came by and you were still at work. They said you'd never miss just one bottle if we took it."

"They're probably right. I have no idea what all's in there. Did they take any?"

Gabe shook her head. "I thought about letting them because I was so mad at you. But I didn't because, if Cat found out, she'd be disappointed in me." Gabe looked away at first, then bravely turned back to let Autumn see the tears. "I don't want to ever disappoint her. I want to be like her."

"I miss her so much." Autumn's choked admission broke the last barrier, and she cried for the child she'd lost and for everyone she'd thrown away.

"Then you need...you need to fix this," Gabe said, sobbing along with her.

"I'll need help. I used to think I could do everything myself, but I can't. I don't want to try anymore."

❖

"Are you sure, Cat?" Roscoe zipped his leather flight jacket against the cold front pouring into the Atlanta metro area ahead of a storm front coming up from the Gulf. The two fronts were forecast to meet and create a snowstorm that would hang around for several days. "I can go with you and wait outside."

"No. I'll be fine." Catherine eyed the snow clouds gathering overhead. "Looks like this storm is rolling in faster than they thought. You don't want to get trapped down here. You've still got time to get out ahead of it. Go home to your wife and kids. Elvis will watch out for me." Elvis looked up from where he stood by her side and woofed.

"When my son gets a little older, we're going down to the shelter and get a dog just like Elvis. He's spooky smart." He looked up at the clouds, and she could see he was worried.

"You don't find dogs like Elvis. They find you." She smiled at Roscoe. "Go. Thanks for getting me this far." A cab pulled up to the hanger where Roscoe's plane was refueling. "See, there's our ride." He waved as she walked away, then headed for his plane.

She focused on her cab when the whup-whup of a helicopter approached overhead. She was not in the desert. She was relieved to see her driver was a black woman, not a Middle Eastern man. The more triggers avoided, the better.

The driver stared down at Elvis, who offered his paw. The woman broke into a smile and bent to give his paw a gentle shake. "Aren't you a handsome guy."

"I called ahead. They said there wouldn't be any problem letting him ride with me." Legally, the driver couldn't refuse service since he was wearing his official service-dog vest and Catherine had his certification papers in his pocket. But she found being polite and prepared usually stopped any confrontations before they started.

"No problem at all. Looks like he washes his hair regularly. Some of my customers don't. Then you have to worry about lice in your back seat. That's why I won't drive cabs with cloth seats. You can never get those completely clean."

Inside the cab, the music was low, but the rhythmic chant of the rap song and the whup-whup of the chopper circling overhead ate at her. They were on the interstate loop now, and the desert flashed in front of her when the whine of a motorcycle whipping past them made her duck. "Incoming," she muttered. Her chest was growing tight, and she couldn't seem to draw in a full breath. Elvis whimpered and sat up to huddle against her side. She hit the window control to lower it and let the wind rush onto her face.

"Is it too warm back there?" her driver asked. "I can turn the heat down." She pointed to a sign on the back of the seat in front of Catherine. "Better let me know if I need to pull over. It's a hundred-dollar cleanup fee if you puke in the cab."

"Yeah. It's a little warm." Catherine raised the window, but the rap chant was louder with the window closed. "Could you turn off the music or change it to blues or classical? Something instrumental and soothing?"

The woman eyed her in the review mirror but turned the music off. "You okay?"

"Sorry." Catherine massaged her temples. "Traumatic head injury when I was in the service. I don't have any prejudice against rap music, but the repetitive rhythm of some music can trigger a migraine. I know it's pretty frigid outside, but the cold helps if you can stand it."

"No problem. I guess that's why you have the handsome guy with you." She pressed the controls on her door to roll Catherine's window down for her. "I'm down with it. My brother played football in college, and he had so many concussions, he can't listen to some songs either."

"Thank you. I really appreciate it." Catherine turned her face to the icy wind and concentrated on what she'd say if Autumn would open the door. She'd talked herself out of hoping she and Autumn could ever have a future. The best she could hope for was a truce for Gabe's sake. But she was forcing herself to brave the city, because during her nightly chats, she could sense Gabe's anxiety growing as Christmas neared. Autumn had said her building allowed pets, and she was bringing Elvis for Gabe. She didn't know how she'd make it out of the city without him, but Gabe needed Elvis more than she did.

Catherine was relieved when her driver finally pulled over next to a small park surrounded by tall apartment buildings.

"I can't turn right at the corner because it's one-way, but the building you want is that second one on your left."

Snow had begun to fall, forcing Catherine to close the window for the last ten minutes of the ride, and the cab was beginning to close in on her.

"That's 68.75, plus tax." The driver tapped a few icons on her tablet. "Hold on. It's figuring the total. The city's got to get its due, you know."

Anxious to get out of the car, Catherine handed over two hundred-dollar bills and opened her door. "Just keep the change. You might need it to buy cold medicine after riding with me." She stepped out into the winter landscape, and Elvis followed. The snow was coming down in large, fluffy flakes.

The driver looked at the bills. "Hey, thanks. Merry Christmas."

"Merry Christmas."

The cab disappeared around the corner, and an eerie quiet settled around them. Catherine was used to the way snow seemed to silence the landscape. But she wasn't used to shadowy figures moving cautiously between the cars parked on an adjacent lot and sneaking between buildings. She closed her eyes. Just people trying to get inside before the snow got too bad.

The poor visibility bothered her. Neon lights from restaurants and stores on the next blocks were fuzzy behind the screen of snowfall. Blues, reds, and orange reflected and refracted, blinking like the glow of mortars hitting distant targets. Elvis pressed against her leg, and she shook her head to clear it. She started across the snow-covered lawn toward the building the cab driver had pointed out.

There were several trees in the park, and Elvis tugged her toward one to relieve himself. Then a muffled thud like an IED exploding under a Humvee and the screech of metal on metal turned her blood cold. Down the street to her left, a car was turned on its side, and a shadowy figure ran from it. Ran toward her. Where was her rifle? She clawed at her ankle. That gun was gone, too. Two vehicles skidded to a stop where the taxi had let her out. Lights flashed all around her. Elvis growled, then barked at the figures coming toward her, guns held out in front of them, pointing at her. Shouting at her. She was surrounded.

Catherine threw her backpack onto the ground and dug into it frantically. "Where is my gun?" she muttered. "Where is my gun? Where is my gun?" Her volume increased with her frustration. Elvis moved in front of her, snarling and barking, but the figures still advanced.

Their shouts mixed with Elvis's barks, and she couldn't understand what they were saying.

❖

Autumn checked the refrigerator one more time for anything that could spoil, then yelled so she could be heard in the next room. "Are you all packed?" Her question got a muffled response.

"Where are my wool socks? The blue ones?"

She glanced over at the laundry closet. The doors were wide open with a pile of laundered but not folded underwear and socks covering the top of the dryer. "Check the laundry closet."

She couldn't decide what was worse—them yelling at each other from different rooms or texting each other from different rooms. They planned to stop for breakfast as soon as they cleared the Atlanta-metro-area traffic, but Gabe would probably eat these leftovers, too, at some point during their six-hour drive.

Yesterday's teary afternoon had been a beginning for them, and tomorrow they planned to drive to Elijah in time for Christmas and hope that Catherine would forgive Autumn. None of them had chosen to be a family last spring. Becki's death had thrust it upon them. Next year, they hoped to be together because it was what they all wanted.

Gabe slid around the corner in her socks, changing direction at the last second to stop next to the pile of clothes on the dryer. "Here they are," she said, holding up blue wool hiking socks. She looked out the window. "Hey, it's snowing."

"That whole pile belongs to you. Take it to your bedroom, please, and put them away."

"You are such a neat freak," Gabe said. But her complaint held a playful tone.

Autumn bent over the deep drawer that held her plastic containers, searching for something to hold the lo mien leftover from the dinner the night before. Lo mien was good, even if it was cold. "Did you roll your eyes at me? I'm sure I heard eyes rolling," she teased back.

Gabe frowned as she peered out the window.

"Don't worry. A couple inches of snow won't stop us from leaving. I had the snow tires put on last week. What are you staring at?" She joined Gabe at the window. "Holy crap." She tried to turn Gabe away from the window. "Don't look. They might shoot that person or the dog, or both."

"That looks just like Elvis," Gabe said.

Autumn turned back to the window. It was hard to see with the snow falling. A third police officer holding a big flashlight joined the first two. When his light beam flicked across the dog, Autumn saw the service vest. She ran to her bedroom and grabbed the mint tin.

"Stay here," she yelled as she bolted for the door, praying she wouldn't be too late.

❖

Two new figures ran toward her from one of the buildings, yelling and waving their arms.

"Cat! Elvis!"

Elvis stopped barking and listened, and then he began to yip and twirl, but he didn't leave Catherine's side.

"Don't shoot, don't shoot. She doesn't have a gun."

Catherine squinted at them. She was dreaming. That happened in the desert. If you stared across that vast wasteland long enough, you started to see things in the thermal waves that seemed to rise from the sand. She was imagining Gabe and Autumn, because that was who she wanted to see more than anyone in the world.

The men shouted at the newcomers, who shouted back. Nobody was listening. Everybody was shouting. Elvis was yipping and dancing. Their shouts became barked orders, the sharp yips the twang of bullets flying past her ears.

What was she looking for? She couldn't remember. She pulled something from her pocket. Her phone. It slipped from her hand and fell to the ground.

"Damn it. Stop shouting."

Did she say that? Or was it somebody else.

She knelt in the snow…not sand.

"Hands up, hands up. Don't reach for that gun."

"Stop them. Shoot the dog. He's going after them."

Catherine searched the two inches of snow around her knees, finally closing her hand around the phone. When she raised her hand to make sure it was her phone, something slammed into her, and then everything went black.

CHAPTER EIGHTEEN

The gunshot cracked the night a split second before Autumn slammed into Catherine, taking her to the ground. Then everything stopped—people running, the shouts, the barking, the squeak of shoes on the packed snow—and the next long moment was silent except for the gunshot's echo ricocheting between the tall buildings.

"Cat. Autumn. No." Gabe's plaintive cry seemed to restart the action. The young police officer pointed his gun at Elvis when he ran over to Catherine and Autumn lying in the snow.

"Give me that weapon, you stupid rookie." The cop with the flashlight snatched it from him and ejected the chambered bullet. "You don't shoot a service dog."

"How was I supposed to know he was a service dog, Sarge?"

"Did you think that was a raincoat he's wearing?"

"I didn't get close enough to see."

The sergeant gave the young officer a shove. "Did you just hear yourself? You weren't close enough to see a fuckin' orange vest but thought it'd be okay to shoot anyway. I've been on the force for thirty years. Do you know how many times I've fired my weapon outside the gun range?"

"No, sir." Every time the rookie backed up a step, his sergeant advanced two. He was up in the rookie's face shouting.

"Zero. I have *never* fired my weapon in the line of duty, and I've worked the worst neighborhoods in Atlanta. This isn't the OK

Corral. Go sit in my squad car. You're not going back on patrol tonight."

The other officer radioed for an ambulance while the rookie got his butt chewed, then squatted next to Catherine.

Autumn ran her hands frantically over Catherine's body, inside her jacket, searching for a wound or bleeding. "If you've hurt her, I'm going to own the city before I'm done with this police department."

"Autumn."

"Ma'am, he only shot once. But the sarge saw it coming and pushed his gun up toward the sky. If he hit anything, it was some pigeon flying overhead."

"Autumn, you need to get off her," Gabe said.

But Autumn wasn't listening. "Catherine, honey, wake up." She felt Catherine's neck for a pulse. At least she thought that was where you were supposed to feel for it.

"Listen to me. You need to get off her." Gabe grabbed her arm and pulled. "She won't know where she is when she regains consciousness. Let Elvis handle it."

Elvis crowded close and licked Catherine's hand.

Gabe looked to the cop. "Sir. She was a soldier in Afghanistan. She was just having a flashback. She doesn't have a gun, but she might be confused when she wakes up."

"She'd be awake if she wasn't hurt." Autumn began to cry as she patted Catherine's face. "Cat, sweetie, please open your eyes."

"I'm telling y'all."

The ambulance driver gave his siren a blast before he drove through the intersection and pulled up next to the overturned car on the next block. Catherine's eyes popped open at the sound. She grabbed Autumn and threw her at the officer. They went down in a tangle of legs and arms, and Catherine rolled to her knees, swayed when she tried to stand, then dropped to them again. Elvis pressed close, his side against her chest while he licked her hand and cheek.

Autumn accidentally kneed the officer in the groin as she scrambled over him. She crawled the few feet to Catherine on her knees.

"Ma'am." The officer groaned but tried to stand. "You should back off. She might hurt you."

"No, she won't." Autumn kept her voice calm. "Cat, honey, it's Autumn. I've got your medicine. Dad brought it to me."

Catherine swayed and wrapped her arms around Elvis to steady herself. He licked her cheek several times, and she gave her head a shake, then groaned.

"Are you hurt, Cat? Tell me where you hurt."

She didn't answer but put her hand to the back of her head and groaned again. Her hand came away red with blood. Elvis licked at her bloody fingers.

Autumn motioned for Gabe to come over where Catherine could see her. "Talk to her, Gabe."

"Cat, it's Gabe. I tried to call you a couple of hours ago."

"Gabe?"

"Yeah." Gabe's smile was huge. "We were coming to see you tomorrow."

Autumn moved forward on her knees and took the tin from her pocket. "I've got your medicine, sweetie." She popped the tin open and peeled the wrapper from it, then crept closer. She could tell the minute Catherine's eyes began to clear.

"Autumn." It wasn't a question.

"That's me, the stupid, pain-in-the-ass city girl who loves you." Autumn cautiously took Catherine's hand in hers and placed the soft chewable in her palm. Catherine frowned down at it, and then her eyes shot back up to Autumn's. "Dad brought it, in case you needed it." She took it from Catherine's hand and placed it against her lips. "Open up, and then chew. I'm afraid your head hit a rock when I tackled you. You might have a really bad headache an hour from now."

Catherine made a face as she chewed. "Got one now. Why'd you tackle me?"

"So the cops wouldn't shoot you," Gabe said, her teeth chattering.

Catherine frowned at her. "Where's your coat?"

Gabe laughed and sidled close when Catherine held her jacket open in an invitation to share the warmth. Then she opened the other side to Autumn. The three of them and Elvis huddled together in the snow for a quiet moment.

"We're a weird family," Gabe said, and nobody disagreed.

EPILOGUE

Catherine stomped the snow from her boots and then stepped inside her kitchen. Their kitchen. She'd fed and watered the few animals currently living on the farm and put some extra bedding down for the goats. The heat lamp was on in the chicken house. Now it was her turn to thaw out.

Gabe looked up from her laptop and the papers spread around her. "You better take your boots off before you track across the floor and she sees it," she whispered.

"Take those boots off at the door. I don't want to see muddy tracks across my kitchen."

They both looked toward the living room, the source of the disembodied voice, then shared a smile.

Catherine toed off her barn boots and took a pair of soft Ugg boots Autumn had given her for Christmas from the shelves of shoes by the door. "I feel kind of silly in these, but they sure are comfortable."

Gabe stretched one long leg up above the table to show she was wearing an identical pair. "I love mine. Angel wants a pair, and her birthday's coming up soon."

Catherine padded to the coffee machine and punched the appropriate buttons to brew two espressos. "You'll have to check with the boss." She gestured toward the living room. "She keeps tabs on your allowance."

"Okay."

"You going to be much longer there?"

"Nope. Just two more math problems. I've got to finish *Great Expectations* for English lit, but I'll take that to bed with me tonight. I don't have much more to read."

"Okay. We were going to watch a movie, but we'll wait till you're done to start it." She carried the coffees into the living room and sat next to Autumn while she finished a video call with Rachel.

"That works for me." She accepted the coffee Catherine offered and tipped her nose with a quick kiss.

Catherine waved at the webcam. "Hi, Rachel."

"Hi. Autumn and I were hammering out the details of our new partnership."

"As long as she gets to spend most of her time in the country, I'll be happy," Catherine said.

Rachel smiled. "I don't think that'll be a problem."

"Okay," Autumn said. "Have your people call my people to figure out the fine print."

Rachel laughed. "Uh, your people are my people."

Autumn gave her a cheeky smile. "Then this should be simple. Talk to you Monday." She turned to Catherine for a longer, deeper thank-you for the coffee. "So, it's Friday night. What are we planning?"

"Well, Gabe has a flying lesson in the morning with Roscoe, and then she's going to Angelique's for a sleepover." Catherine moved in for another kiss. "So, tonight is family night. Gabe's finishing up her schoolwork, and we'll watch a movie together. It's Gabe's turn to pick, so no telling what we'll have to see."

"That sounds perfect."

Catherine chewed her lip.

"What's wrong?"

She shook her head. "I just worry that you'll get bored with this life. And maybe with me. You'd tell me if you do, right? We don't live extravagantly, but we're a long way from poor. We can travel. If you want a bigger house, we can build one."

Autumn's fingers pressed against her lips.

"Cat, I grew up wishing for a normal life, like on the old television shows. You know. Where the family sits down to dinner and talks about their day, then watches a few hours of television or plays video games together."

"I don't think they had video games."

"Okay, board games like Monopoly, or card games like bridge or gin rummy."

"Then what happens?"

"Then the parents tuck the kid into bed and go to their bedroom and have wild monkey sex."

Catherine nuzzled Autumn's neck and nipped at her earlobe, smiling at the hitch in Autumn's breath. "It sounds very ordinary to me."

Autumn cupped Catherine's face and held her gaze. "I love you, and I don't need thrills and awards to make me happy. We have good friends, we're financially secure, and our kid has a trust fund, thanks to you. If other people think our lives are too ordinary, then screw them. I happen to think ordinary is perfect."

About the Author

D. Jackson Leigh grew up barefoot and happy, swimming in farm ponds and riding rude ponies in rural south Georgia. She is a career journalist but has found her real passion in writing sultry lesbian romances laced with her trademark Southern humor and affection for horses.

She has published twelve novels and one collection of short stories with Bold Strokes Books, winning a 2010 Alice B. Lavender Award for Noteworthy Accomplishment, and three Golden Crown Literary Society awards in paranormal, romance, and fantasy categories. She also was a finalist for four additional GCLS awards and a finalist in the romance category of the 2014 Lambda Literary Awards.

Friend her at facebook.com/d.jackson.leigh and on Twitter @ djacksonleigh, or learn more about her at www.djacksonleigh.com.

Books Available From Bold Strokes Books

Emily's Art and Soul by Joy Argento. When Emily meets Andi Marino she thinks she's found a new best friend, but Emily doesn't know that Andi is fast falling in love with her. Caught up in exploring her sexuality, will Emily see the only woman she needs is right in front of her? (978-1-163555-355-0)

Escape to Pleasure: Lesbian Travel Erotica, edited by Sandy Lowe and Victoria Villaseñor. Join these award-winning authors as they explore the sensual side of erotic lesbian travel. (978-1-163555-339-0)

Music City Dreamers by Robyn Nyx. Music can bring lovers together. In Music City, it can tear them apart. (978-1-163555-207-2)

Ordinary is Perfect by D. Jackson Leigh. Atlanta marketing superstar Autumn Swan's life derails when she inherits a country home, a child, and a very interesting neighbor. (978-1-163555-280-5)

Royal Court by Jenny Frame. When royal dresser Holly Weaver's passionate personality begins to melt Royal Marine Captain Quincy's icy heart, will Holly be ready for what she exposes beneath? (978-1-163555-290-4)

Strings Attached by Holly Stratimore. Success. Rock star Nikki Razer always gets what she wants, but when she falls for Drew McNally, a music teacher who won't date celebrities, can she convince Drew she's worth the risk (978-1-163555-347-5)

The Ashford Place by Jean Copeland. When Isabelle Ashford inherits an old house in small-town Connecticut, family secrets, a shocking discovery, and an unexpected romance complicate her plan for a fast profit and a temporary stay. (978-1-163555-316-1)

Treason by Gun Brooke. Zoem Malderyn's existence is a deadly threat to everyone on Gemocon, and Commander Neenja KahSandra must find a way to save the woman she loves from having to make the ultimate sacrifice. (978-1-163555-244-7)

A Wish Upon a Star by Jeannie Levig. Erica Cooper has learned to depend on only herself, but when her new neighbor, Leslie Raymond, befriends Erica's special needs daughter, the walls protecting Erica's heart threaten to crumble. (978-1-163555-274-4)

Answering the Call by Ali Vali. Detective Sept Savoie returns to the streets of New Orleans, as do the dead bodies from ritualistic killings, and she does everything in her power to bring their killers to justice while trying to keep her partner, Keegan Blanchard, safe. (978-1-163555-050-4)

Friends Without Benefits by Dena Blake. When Dex Putman gets the woman she thought she always wanted, she soon wonders if it's really love after all. (978-1-163555-349-9)

Invalid Evidence by Stevie Mikayne. Private Investigator Jil Kidd is called away to investigate a possible killer whale, just when her partner Jess needs her most. (978-1-163555-307-9)

Pursuit of Happiness by Carsen Taite. When attorney Stevie Palmer's client reveals a scandal that could derail Senator Meredith Mitchell's presidential bid, their chance at love may be collateral damage. (978-1-163555-044-3)

Seascape by Karis Walsh. Marine biologist Tess Hansen returns to Washington's isolated northern coast, where she struggles to adjust to small-town living while courting an endowment from Brittany James for her orca research center. (978-1-163555-079-5)

Second In Command by VK Powell. Jazz Perry's life is disrupted and her career jeopardized when she becomes personally involved with the case of an abandoned child and the child's competent but strict social worker, Emory Blake. (978-1-163555-185-3)

Taking Chances by Erin McKenzie. When Valerie Cruz and Paige Wellington clash over what's in the best interest of the children in Valerie's care, the children may be the ones who teach them it's worth taking chances for love. (978-1-163555-209-6)